# The Stars We Wrecked?

dpInk: DonnaInk Publications, L.L.C.

United States of America

# The Stars We Wrecked?

A novel by

# Milan Kalis

dpInk: Donnalnk Publications, L.L.C.
129 Daisy Hill Road, Carthage, North Carolina 28327
Visit our website at www.donnaink.com

Translator: Anna Jurisova; Editorial Team: dpInk: Donnalnk Publications, L.L.C.; Cover: Petra Nemethova; Layout and Design, Ms. Dana Queen of ZenCon Art of Zen Consultancy, Ms. Dana Queen.

First Paperback Edition: December 2015. First Electronic Edition: December 2015.

*Library of Congress Cataloging in Publication Data*

Milan Kalis, 2015 -
   The Stars We Wrecked / Kalis, Milan - 1st Ed.

ISBN: 978-1939425874

   222 p.cm.

**Summary**: Fictional account of the underbelly of the world of music, where politics and personalities warp time and space relative to the talent craved by millions. Using Elvis Presley as an example, Peter – a field agent on a mission to foster sociologically aesthetic musicians – approaches the King to gain his trust. The goal: elevate the minds of listeners. This is a conceptual narrative where the sociological paradigm of entertainment and fame and its resultant fan-pop enter the political and clandestine operations machine. Who will win?" ~ Summary provided by the Publisher.

[1. Literature - Fiction, 2. Fiction - Drama, 3. Fantasy - Music, 4. Music – Infamous, 5. Fiction – Elvis Presley, 6. –Fiction - Clandestine, 7. Fiction - Mysteries, 9. Fiction – 1960's, 10. Literature – United States, 11. Literature - Slovakia, 12. Literature – Men's.]

I. Title. II. Title: The Stars We Wrecked
Dewey Classification: 398-398.8
10   9   8   7   6   5   4   3   2   1

2014949745

*Printed in the United States of America*

# Contents

# The Stars We Wrecked?

# Epigraph

*"...the image is one thing and the human being is another...it's very hard to live up to an image."*

~Elvis Presley.

# Prologue

In his will, Arnold Lane asked me to print this text and to distribute it to selected people whose names are stated in his will. Simultaneously, he wished not to have the text changed, "I lived all my life as a mental amateur, so let it be felt at least once."

In the production of, "The Stars We Wrecked," I'm fulfilling Arnold's wish and I have to admit . . . if his work were developmentally edited - it would provide a much more cultured experience because Arnold forces ideas on readers, which, I feel, is a professional disease.

Judging from the constant repetition and moralizing, it can be inferred it took Mr. Lane quite some time to write this title. It appears he had no time to revise his writing. As far as I am aware – the final chapters were written by him as he lay dying.

As you have decided to read Arnold's work, use a bulldogged relentlessness and use patience because, like you, I needed it myself. "The Stars We Wrecked" serves as an imitation of life and presents writings from 1968.

This title may drive readers toward a threshold of embattlement between because there could be greater anticipation referencing new scenes while obscurity leaves one feeling confused and in the end, as readers, we are left to face every Arnold Lane in our midst. But "The Stars We Wrecked" isn't about what was just read; it is about what keeps readers reading.

Readers may ask, "What was my personal impression after I finished reading *The Stars We Wrecked*?" My answer is . . . somewhere between the kitschiest soap opera and an intimate confession of a CIA agent with no literary talent. Perhaps, I would have never read it through without the respect I hold for Mr. Arnold Lane; however, perhaps I would because, after all, this book is about what keeps a reader reading and the underbelly of Elvis Presley's profession aligned to international intrigue and entertainment's place in its history.

Arnold's friend.

# I

# The Stars We Wrecked?

By way of introduction . . .

I did not want to write this book, but over time it became necessary.

Between 1962 and 1969, I worked for the CIA as an expert on "artists." To be more exact, I took care of several pop stars. Dylan, Elvis, the Beatles, standalone Lennon, the Rolling Stones, Led Zeppelin and a few others served as the meaning of my life. I was to shape them, lead them and make certain they would not interfere with the thinking of the world's growing youth.

I'm not going to pass judgment, I'll leave that to you. My desire is to share this work and my memories, even though . . . I won't be able to avoid some level of subjectivity. After all, this is not a confidential report.

I believe, while reading, you'll note who I felt really close to and who I did not.

Arnold Lane

# 2
# Elvis in His Heyday - Memphis

## How We Met (1968-1969) . . .

Elvis wasn't my first pop artist assignment. However, the scope and depth required for penetration into the clan and mobsters surrounding America's golden boy made Elvis one of my easiest assignments.

I was assigned to the Elvis detail by J. on 15 May 1968. At that time, speculations emerged regarding Elvis coming back to life. His previous period, 1961 through 1967, was not artistically successful. That is with the exception of, *How Great Thou Art (1967)*, a collection of gospels the music scene moved toward during Elvis' seeming respite in performances.

Like any other operation I was involved in, my budget showed no limitation whatsoever. My team was comprised of only two people. There was me, the boss; and M . . . a provider of all things necessary to perform requirements.

M. was born in California; officially that was all I knew about him. All other information and reports was unrepresented – I was on a need to know basis and basically didn't need to know. M. was my boss and that was it. M. approved my conclusions, signed my reports and collected my receipts.

Once assigned, I was provided one month to study all materials referencing Elvis. The operation was scheduled to start June of 1968. In my recollection of the historical archive, a share of the information was well-known and doesn't warrant repetition; however, other things, are not known and I found that share of my research information quite interesting.

Elvis wasn't considered a genius. He was easy to work with as an entertainer. Albeit Elvis loved women, it was suggested his sexual bravado was not as exceptional as his voice but women swooned over him regardless.

Elvis had a basic education and he wasn't like "other" entertainers of his era, some mentioned herein, he didn't seem to have the inspiration to work on himself to develop his intellect.

Elvis enjoyed drinking alcohol. He demonstrated weakness for substances that blunted his senses but many musicians seem to have this same predilection.

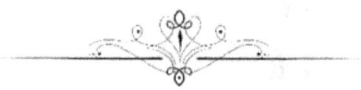

At the beginning of 1968, I received information regarding Elvis and his being dissatisfied with his career. It appeared, he wanted to start from scratch while he was approaching an equivalent stardom to that of the Beatles or Beach Boys (in particular the album *Pet Sounds*). I knew my assignment was forthcoming at that time . . .

Elvis' disinterest opened two lines of thought for me. Either he would begin writing on his own (even though he never showed any ability of this kind) . . . or he'd use songs with topics differing from other writers.

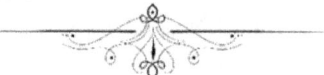

It was thought by my leadership Elvis' new album may serve as a threat and attack American society prior to this time he was known as America's patriotic musician having served in the United States Military.

I requested transcripts of all phone calls made by Elvis in 1967 and received this transcript (select passages) of calls between Elvis and his wife from 8 December 1967 . . .

*Honey,*

*I owe this letter to everyone and write out of conviction. I will not use any vulgar language here. I know the world wants me to be powerful and in control. I'm gonna write a real hearty folk song about it. Some kind of . . . confessional . . . like only a Judas could make, ha-ha.*

*Love Elvis*

*Elvis,*

*I just wanted to tell you . . . . . . but you . . . . . . I guess you've already sung big stories about great love. I'm sorry, I . . . you . . . know very well*

**Milan Kalis**

*what Parker thinks about this kind of stuff, don't you?! (That was Colonel Parker . . . Elvis' manager.)*

*Love you . . .*

*Honey,*

*I don't care what people say. It's in me and that's that.*

*Love Elvis.*

Based on Elvis' discontent in these and other statements, it appeared Elvis was becoming disenchanted with his role and perhaps even his country. Any such reality could be a potential threat to national security "if" Elvis became disenfranchised with America's expectations of him as a world leader in the entertainment industry.

**Field Notes Entry 101 - Arnold Lane**: "Elvis will have to be worked on, even though it seems he doesn't need it – there is a potential for issues."

Having assessed Elvis' recordings up until 1968, I wrote the following:

**Field Notes Entry 102 – Arnold Lane**: The only thing worth anything is Elvis' first album (*Elvis Presley*, 1956) and *How Great Thou Art* (1967, winner of a Grammy Award).

Today, from a business perspective I see this notation differently because I now own a few shares in a large recording company. But even then, I knew Elvis' additional recordings were "just good business."

# 3

# The Plan

The plan was simple, we used the oldest known system to influence an artist. We had one of our colleagues infiltrate among his groupies. We considered P.T. for the job. The work could have been accomplished by anyone of the following people: Billy Smith, Mill Morris, Lamar Fike, Jerry Schilling, Chief of Memphis Police Roy Nixon, Charlie Hodbe, Sonny West, George Klein, Martin Lacker or Red West . . . but we determined P.T. was most likely the best candidate for the job. P.T. had been one of the Elvis paid mobsters since 1962.

The company contacted him in 1964 in November. This is when the Beatles demonstrated pop stars played a greater role in the life of adolescents and that they seriously affected young people's worldview.

To keep P.T. on our books, we provided a salary much greater than Elvis paid him. P.T. worked his way up to become a very trustworthy person in Elvis' clan, so much so, he was tasked with finding bodyguards and a place for me among Elvis' crew. My role was to become one of those who took care of Elvis in the day-to-day activities of life.

P.T. was intended to pretend he knew me. He reported I had graduated from the University of Illinois just a year prior.

He recommended me, saying I came from a blue-collar worker's family (this was important to Elvis) and that I aspired to work for Elvis because I thought he was a genius.

Basically, P.T. sold me to Elvis and vouched for my capabilities.

And, he did just that. For his efforts, P.T. was provided a bonus.

I started my job in Elvis' bodyguard detail the second week of June. I was posted among Elvis' "psychological" bodyguards and P.T. was my boss.

Of course, he was a boss on a shred of paper . . . not in real life.

# 4
# Off to Graceland!

I arrived in an old Buick.

P.T. waited for me at the entrance.

I got out of the car and shook his hand. I knew that all we were doing was being recorded on omnipresent cameras.

Elvis, like most celebrities, was beginning to suffer from paranoia. He set up his own secret service team, comprised of all of the people who worked for him on security details. The team operated in a very elaborate manner; every "section chief" who basically waited on Elvis hand and foot, was Elvis' principal informer. No matter whether it was a cook or a cleaning woman . . . everyone was an informer. The more surprising news they delivered to Elvis, the better.

Elvis was held captive by the lies and fabrications provided by the people around him. There was no way he could escape them.

Personally, I believe, anyone who reaches a certain level of fame and becomes an icon has no real investment in the lives of average people any longer. A person like this is then simply used for the masses.

What's important is whether the celebrity knows about it or not. And Elvis didn't know or that is what everyone believed. The fact Elvis wasn't in the know was clearly referred to in the file I was given to study. However, a file can never replace reality, even though the investigative service I was a part of was rarely wrong. Granted, I was to make certain facts were accurate – even though I was convinced we were faultless in our findings.

P.T. wore a white T-shirt and blue jeans. His black sunglasses were too big for his round face. P.T. had a stout figure and somehow resembled Elvis towards the end of his life. But this was just the first impression, because after all, P.T. was just an insignificant informer.

Upon my arrival at the residence . . . P.T. told me where to park my car. It was 6 p.m. and the sun was nowhere near to start setting.

P.T. shared with me the King didn't like it when someone used foul language. Apparently, the King had morals.

I knew Elvis liked using foreign words. I also knew Elvis liked showing he was superior at times, usually to people with better education. I have to admit, I was personally looking forward to meeting him. We usually look forward to meeting people who are important and I was no exception. And, of course, I knew how important or talented people are worked on, how the system processes them to get what it needs, once an individual is found to be "exceptional."

You know how it is: *a role model is a role model.*

This was the first time in my life I felt I was getting something I'd always desired. Some folks want to be famous, while others want to contribute to running and developing society. I wanted a taste of fame, fortune and everything that goes with it.

I spotted him . . . The King. And, I remembered the last sentences from the 1955 assessment I'd been presented with for this assignment: . . . *His abilities are not above average. In fact, they were more the other way around. However, with the types of people he is surrounded with he is proving changes in thinking can occur as rapidly as technological changes do . . . in fact, he is learning and adapting very quickly.*

Who could have known then one of the Company's assignments would be to take care of a man he wasn't an educational genius . . . rather an entertainment genius? Who would have fathomed the secrets of people and their thinking are controlled and shaped? You may wonder why I'm saying this now, but some these things were managed by some people. And, they are mentioned throughout the narrative of this story.

As an icon, in the 50's and the 60's Elvis was used to prove an ordinary boy can have a chance. As it transpired, a long time before he became famous, Elvis has dreamt of being famous.

When I was introduced, we shook hands. He smiled.

I noticed his teeth were a bit yellow.

In any case, my initial thought was, he was not as attractive as he looked in his pictures; even though he looked like Shiva from a fairy tale he created for himself. At the time, I thought, it is funny how most important people look better in photos than in reality. I now believe it's the first sign. *The first sign of charisma.*

It seems to me, people who are aware of their personal charisma cannot only sell it to their world but also the illusion to the entire world that their world has something in common with your world. You had that feeling with Elvis. He was monolithic.

Elvis had a charisma and he sold his world to the world. He wasn't essentially sure about his charisma as far as I could tell. To me, Elvis just wanted something, really wanted it, and was lucky or skilled enough to achieve it. Lucky is not the outcome of this story but it is true Elvis achieved what he wanted.

In taking his hand and shaking the first time, I found his handshake wasn't too strong. His palm was wet. I thought deep inside this man was not confident about himself.

Regardless of his photographs and celluloids, in person Elvis' charisma was one where *you felt it* . . . but you weren't afraid of.

Yes, Elvis appeared to be a man who could sing songs with other people's lyrics and never his own. His eyes were tired. His brow . . . his brow showed he was significant . . . it said he knew he was significant and he thought it was important he believed in it. Of course, I had a momentary streak of recognition, *So this is him, one of the only men to make the CIA raise its budget!*

This is something an agent or intelligence officer is to avoid on assignment to a celebrity. The recognition only lasted a moment – it was a momentary lapse in professional judgment. In any job, most of all when working with private individuals, there is a need to be self-confident. So it goes . . . in this world . . . I needed to remain confident.

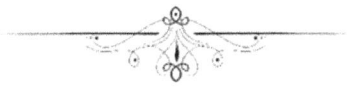

"Hey, I hear you studied philosophy. What kind of philosophy?" Elvis was relaxed. He was at home. He knew P.T. and glanced at him a few times while speaking. Still, there was something about him that didn't seem right. Perhaps it was too early to be sure but at that moment I knew we were not going to be friends.

I attempted to give the impression of someone much more scared than I would be if I were acting normally but I knew the role I was playing. Right after we shook hands I knew this was going to be just a game on my part. No chance to open up, like with Lennon. I thought to myself, *I'll do what I'm supposed to do, I'll take care of what I'm supposed to take care of.*

"What kind of philosophy? "Well, philosophy . . ." I smiled and looked over at P.T.

He patted me on the shoulder and said meaningfully: "The King is a king, isn't he Peter?"

Peter was the name I was using for the operation.

P.T. patted me on the shoulder once more.

"Leave us alone, P.T. I want to interview each rookie alone in the office." Elvis turned and pointed his head in the direction we were to go. As we departed from the gate at Graceland, it felt as if P.T. ceased to exist completely.

Elvis thought it an honor to welcome new employees at the gate. After all, he was the chief "mobster."

I walked at Elvis' side but didn't want to start asking questions or even strike up a conversation.

Elvis was silent and looked as if he were deep in thoughts. He glanced over at me after about every twenty steps we made. It was odd.

During our journey to "the office," when he looked at me for the third time, I ceased thinking about him as an ordinary person. I came to the conclusion an ordinary person would ask something.

But I was young, only twenty-six at the time, and the Elvis cult had an effect on me, whether I wanted it to or not. Regardless of what I thought about him, at that moment I still was forming my opinions based on what I read from a piece of paper.

During the short amount of time we had to walk together, I had enough time to notice his body language. He walked upright and proud, as if he wanted to say, *Look, this is mine, this is what I've earned.* His hands were relaxed. He didn't think about what to do with them while walking unlike other folks do when they try to keep their movement and facial expressions under control. His legs walked in harmony with his head, which is the way to put it when you want to say, "This fits, and women are crazy about it." He walked as if he were a model and he knew it.

I couldn't guess whether he was the person he wanted to be when he was on his own or whether I was seeing the man Elvis for whom his life, his lawn and even myself were part of the central stage.

Now I realized the urge, the ambition, the reason and cause why I was hired by the CIA. I wanted to find out, as much as I could, who Elvis was, what was really inside him, and what he might be capable of in the future. It was only now my own thoughts were activated. My internal clandestine system took hold, on this spot, just passed the gate to his paradise. The ancient columns supporting the roof of his home were nothing less than a classical imitation of a Roman temple protecting the door into his house, I thought and then stated, "You're my role model, I've always wanted to be at your side." I tried to appear honest, making use of my endless practice in front of the mirror in the hope only an experienced psychologist could see through my pretense.

Elvis looked at me haughtily, although I guess he didn't really want to make that impression. It was just that he was used to taking advantage of his success and power, and used these to keep up his personality. Which was just about to rebound on him.

"Many people want to stand at my side."

I thought he was going to say more. I looked at his face for a while and saw that I put him off a little by what I'd said.

The King needed to be shown devoutness and love of his greatness but not in words. I knew this from the report I received. To be honest, I didn't know what to say at that point. I loved dealing with people's destinies, with the human psyche developing right on the spot, right in the middle of action.

Only this way could I make the impression of being "honest." Maybe this was why I made a mistake and told Elvis what I shouldn't have told him at the very beginning. You know, people like me – who can act on the spot, who can deduce and create in mid-action – are the best paid people. But it's hard my friends, I can tell you, it's so hard . . . but whatever you choose to do, you've got to do it as well as you can.

"I know, you'd get a confession like that from anyone, I understand. But only few of those who graduated in philosophy . . . I'm the only one from my class who liked you. They laughed at me because of it . . ." I produced a forced smile, the smile of a person who tries to chuckle over his own words, in an attempt to drown in the nervousness caused by his idol being so close, just realizing he couldn't have said anything more stupid. It was ingenious and beautiful back then. I was able to relax by actually pretending to be very nervous for a while.

In retrospect this was – from my point of view – a really dumb beginning, whatever I was pretending.

Elvis looked at me, screwed up his eyes and grinned. Maybe I just wanted him to grin, that was all, but let's leave it at that, he just grinned and that was it.

"I've always been interested only in my own life philosophy . . . that's what you have to . . . They taught you nothing, did they? Nothing about how to survive, eh?" he asked seriously. He glanced over at me sideways very quickly and then looked straight ahead again, he started in again . . . "Go on talking like a philosopher who has no reason to listen to other philosophers anymore: That's life, philosophy starts inside you. I'm just a musician but I know much better how to survive than any philosopher."

Elvis preferred to say he was a musician, not a singer. He wiped his brow. It was hot, and Elvis looked up at the sky and started whistling a tune. He didn't wait for my reaction in the least. I felt a power in him, despite everything he'd said before, a power he had inside. Everyone who's achieved something has this. Regardless of whether a slave to their profession or not.

I hung my head. I knew I was supposed to show humility at this juncture. I knew it would make Elvis happy. Because a "star" always wants to prove something to anyone who's got even a slightly better education. And, so I continued walking and kept staring at the ground. I thought about how I could make an impression in a way that would make me seem effortlessly dedicated, while allowing me to influence the King. I wanted to find out what was on his mind and who exactly he was in terms of "experiencing social reality." Some things are just noted on paper and others are in the head. Clandestine operations worked solely with devices controlling the fall and renewal of personality. In my profession, we identified weaknesses and then exploited them:

> **Field Agent Directive 39275**: Identify weaknesses and faults. Don't assimilate the entire personality of the artist. Focus on faults and little insanities. The Company is seeking candidates with "potential" to influence and shape young minds. Individuals with the capability to impact young adults to an extent they'll conform and adapt to the intended agenda. This Directive doesn't apply solely to recording artists; however they are the easiest targets with the greatest viable outcome.

Working for the Company . . . as a Field Agent . . . the assignment was never to overtly manipulate people. Instead, identifying and exploiting weaknesses in order to maintain operational tempo was the primary intent. In this manner, adverse effects on society were being enabled to rectify a sweeping propaganda plaguing the youth of America and the world.

Like a virus, finding the weakest link, modifying it and then allowing it to spread was the overarching dynamic and believe me, this is how it's done even today.

Elvis was one of a few candidates who didn't suffer due to fame and success; at least, not as much as the others. Elvis reveled in his fame and suffered only when people stopped buying his recordings.

In the "here and now" of that timeframe, Elvis had begun to think about the world as a controlling, manipulative, monster. My task was to "not" allow him to write anything sending such an ill-gained message due to the harm it would have on America's and the world's youth.

It was believed that without social pressure and/or oversight artists, such as: Lennon and his Plastic Ono Band (Circa 1970) would eventually release material sputtering a lot of lyrics that would be against the system. It was expressed, the system has to remain more sophisticated and maintain oversight because anti-government Semitism would result in potential mayhem and there is plenty of evidence for this. We all know of at least one piece of such evidence. Each of us has owned at least one album in our lifetime that speaks about rebellion and civil unrest.

I was determined to remain silent and work in a sophisticated manner. Clearly, as a field operative in my training, I realized the timing required to get an asset of Elvis' caliber to be exploitable – I was on my chosen path.

Elvis opened the door to his home for me. It was a huge wooden door with scenes from the Odyssey displayed in patterns.

I gazed at it and looked at Elvis.

He noticed I noticed the battle. And, I could feel that he liked it.

"That's the Odyssey, right?"

Elvis smiled. Finally he smiled. He smiled so honestly, I could see his teeth, which weren't as yellow as they seemed at first sight. Still, they looked much more yellow than in the pictures on his albums, which was pure manipulation on the part of the recording companies. See, the social world of entertainment is full of manipulation, what matters is who manipulates and why.

"Yes." He affirmed. "That is my Odyssey." As he said it, he pointed at the interior of the house as we entered and winked at me.

**Field Notes Entry 103 – Arnold Lane**: It was obvious the Odyssey made a statement regarding Elvis' internal mêlées. In my mind, it appears, he is struggling and largely from the things and/or people he surrounds himself with. When surrounded with your own visions – which the miracle of success makes real – what is left? Elvis' art? There seems to be a void in Elvis' internal make-up.

Elvis liked saying he was a great artist. At the same time, he was drowning in his own insecurity with hang-ups for not being able to write ingenious memorable songs. He was drowning in his environment under the pressure of profit because someone needed to extract as much as possible from his vocal chords and stage performances.

And no one from the middle-aged generation running his recording company was interested in what the maestro was singing. Elvis' art was not assessed based on quality – it was based on profit. And, Elvis wasn't allowed the time previously to react to this dilemma. Even his recording studio, RCA still revels in the proceeds of the King's works years after his untimely demise.

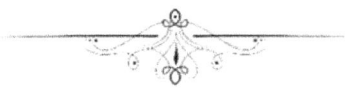

"I love the Odyssey, it's a story about life. Imagine that someone could set it to music." Elvis spoke declaratively. If Elvis wanted to set the Odyssey to music, we wouldn't have objected. An ancient story can do no harm. That story was verified by generations and contained the message of survival with nothing that would allude to antisocial ideas.

"You can set the Odyssey to music . . . You can . . ." Elvis continued.

"I know." I answered to let him understand I was listening.

Elvis looked into my eyes, as if trying to examine what was behind them. It was just my feeling, just another feeling, that's all. Almost everybody who doesn't know the person he's talking to wants to, perhaps even subconsciously, find out what's inside the other one. It wasn't anything extraordinary.

"It's funny how everybody, one after the other, when they see this they ask if it is from the Odyssey. Almost all of them. I know that P. sometimes tells people to ask me about it, that it will make me happy . . . do you know what's even stranger?" He wanted to say my name here . . . I saw it in his eyes . . . he didn't take them off me while he was speaking.

So I told him what my name: "Peter, I'm Peter."

"Oh, yes, Peter." Elvis smiled but it felt forced. His smile was coerced by the fact he had forgotten my name. However, he felt no shame in this and went on straight away, "You know, Peter, it sounds even stranger every time I say someone could set it to music, every-one tells me I should do it . . . it doesn't matter everyone keeps telling me this, I'm telling you on my behalf, I think it's a good idea. And, if everyone else says the same, well, it's proof that it, in fact, could be a good idea. Every artist needs support with an idea which is harmless but which could easily be just phenomenal! But I know that. What you're saying is . . . come on, let's talk about it too, but let's sit down first. I like talking to new people." He winked again.

Under normal circumstances, it would have been a bit strange how quickly Elvis finished what he started and left things unsaid, both by him and by me as if he were in a hurry.

*Yes, I'm ready* I thought quietly. I knew from a harmless little spy called P., Elvis enjoyed getting drunk with a new team member in order to have a conversation and feel he was connecting. He also liked feeling admired. I guess every star feels benefitted when a drinking partner adores their opinion, their world and most of all the opportunity to get drunk with someone great.

Elvis led me through the halls of his temple, his hiding place from the world. He was glaring straight ahead without looking at me for a long time. His behavior, though he didn't exhibit any visible uneasiness, was fairly uneasy during the very short time I was with him in my estimation. At varied points, he glanced over at me - as many as three times in thirty seconds he'd glanced and then again wouldn't make eye contact for longer durations of time as we walked through the gate to his temple.

# 5
# The Art of War

I had a very balanced, though unfounded feeling that said, *It seems the plan to blend education with working class and a dedication to the artist is starting to take exactly the effect the Company presumed.*

Of course, that's just the way it is - when one person makes an uneasy impression on the other – the result is an elevation in the other person's stance because they sense their partner's uneasiness. In regard to business, especially the business of subversive activities with psychological tasks to fulfill – the notion of uneasiness and imbalance extends an upper hand as it were. Even where the person may not necessarily feel unbalanced - hesitation and/or an overstated reservation is all it takes to curve the association toward the field agents dynamic. But this is the nature of "all" social settings.

In my field assignment, the laws of human nature and sociology remained applicable, *Social evolution is not real evolution because it has controllers – not nature, but people like me.* I thought to myself.

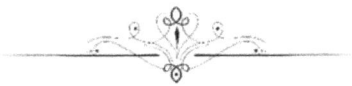

Elvis led me through what was an expensively filled yet empty house. I was surprised to see no servants. I knew most tasks in Graceland were fulfilled by "mobsters." Or so I was informed by P.

These men were somewhat like me, except they held no authorization to oversee "social evolution" regarding people thought to be winners.

If I had been just Peter. If I had been a fresh philosophy graduate and devout Elvis fan, surely he would have thought I was becoming a member of his clan during my visit. Which is to say the others thought so – even P; for Elvis the proof of a trustworthy teammate was their upholding the collective mindset. And, the conviction I demonstrated, no matter my degree of talent, left shards of clandestine affiliation – after all I was representing the Company and they were interested in Elvis and his environment. But, I felt I was holding to the reins of deception.

Social evolution holds certain victories . . . the act of dutiful, slow, subconscious tasking and fulfillment toward mass control through the greatest recording artists of a decade or set of decades does result in a subliminal oversight. And, as *stars* - societal role models once controlled extend a layer of management of the masses otherwise untapped because more is completed when a role model influences.

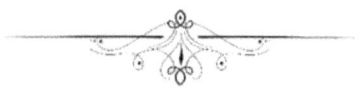

In touring the mansion, I thought to myself, *Man no women not even maids in Graceland . . . I really thought there'd be some eye candy on the grounds, be it real housemaids or ordinary groupies who certainly must swam the King. Where are the women? What is wrong with this picture?*

Of course, I knew Elvis was married but of all the rich and famous or achieving men and some women I'd seen . . . beautiful people were always a component of success and in short supply.

The Company trained us regarding the disintegration of values including the defiance of conformity and the application of social pressure to be an infidel. The nature of Elvis' business one would have thought would have forced him to become a one-night male with the most beautiful women. As a successful performance artist – Elvis was in demand. After all, he was a successful male – *So where were the women?* I was dumbfounded.

Oftentimes, my role may include the consternation of involving a tawdry women on the scene and gaining an upper hand through archiving facts; however, in the case of Elvis this would seem highly unnecessary. The nature of women, and the level of his success would seem to be a natural result with no need for the Company to be an integer creating such a scenario. *What would be the point anyway?*

It often happens a great artist – at a certain point of life – believes in maximal uniqueness which always brings along a decline in moral values created by humanity only for its own benefit in order to survive. Nothing more and nothing less, you cannot walk on without rules and solid foundations to rely on. You walk on to survive and perhaps even improve a bit – but my friends, this improvement was taking place under my own control!

At the Company we knew, those artists who constantly copulated with new partners annihilated many of their innate capabilities and often they'd lose their creative spark. Sooner or later . . . their inner voice let's loose. It was the observation at the ranch these artists go on to create a handful of great works of art, which aspires to send a message, but usually gets lost afterwards.

And, during their fall from grace – as it were – was the time where the Company could easily get those artists to do exactly what was intended in the field. If only it were so easy. The best artists, the most ingenious exceptions, always gave the hardest time. Dylan was a classic example . . . *but what about Elvis?*

*Was the world his groupie?*

*And, where was his wife?*

I wanted to know. At the time, I was hardly in the position to attempt to stick myself toward asking questions regarding Elvis' soul. *Not yet . . . not yet.* Reaching the soul is the hardest element of my work and yet . . . *the best paid job I tell you. In particular, if you enjoy the work and have a natural intuition and enjoy doing it – it is a good gig. But you do need to ensure your soul is not exposed – to gain acceptance takes empathy and it is not always easy to remain unemotional in those situations. Never, oh never, put your heart on the line and get engaged at that level . . . becoming friends with an asset is a serious issue. And that's what no one wants, come on, let's be professional!*

*The only thing you're allowed to use when getting stuck to the soul is a psychological hammer and a wedge which you'll have to use so skillfully that the victim will believe (quick-witted he or she may be) that you're offering them your own soul because you love them like something you won't find so easily. The victim should feel that you consider their soul to be the materialized grandeur of this life and its meaning. While in fact all you see is just a person like you.*

*And the psychological hammer and wedge, that's the cultivation of the artist's weakest points which can be even more confusing in reaching "producing a work containing the truth of creation".*

*For example, if he likes women, you'll* **sincerely** *support him in this. You will be fond of women yourself. If he likes drugs to chill out . . . if he "likes" to feel depressed . . . if he likes alcohol . . .*

*All of this you'll have to be able to use in your own behavior as an eternal part of yourself, as something you will use like your own virtues in your struggle against the cruelty of life in a stupid society, virtues you'll offer the artist as an ingredient of a sacred friendship which he'll be happy to trust, mostly when in isolation and alone. No matter how many women, drugs or alcohol he may have, you'll have to convince him that he needs you more than "all that shit". But in fact you'll be more and more an embodiment of "all that shit" in him!*

[19]

*You wouldn't believe what a person will do when you say, You know, this thing is by far not as good as what you did before. You should try to calm down and attempt something nice and optimistic.*

# 6
# Pool and Whiskey

I walked with Elvis like he walked with me. Maybe we were looking forward to the same thing. I have to admit although I'd really been assigned to all kinds of people, I was still looking forward to having a drink with the American boy.

We passed expensive vases as windows revealed the world the way Elvis wanted to see it. *Everything is artificial,* I thought, *even relationships.* Elvis had created a world trying to rise above a cruel society. But one man can barely beat the society. An artist least of all. As a musician, Elvis laid society's foundation in affecting everyone who was enabled to hear his music and **those** affects in turn shaped his life. And Elvis, of course, was and wasn't aware of this simultaneously.

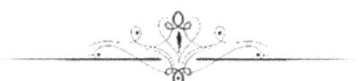

Elvis remained quiet. I remained quiet too.

The desire to have a drink with the King was increasing with every step I took. I was looking forward to it.

A drinking training was my favorite kind of training. The essence of drinking training is about staying in control. You feel you're under the influence and the only thing you have to do is stay in control. When you concentrate, it's surprisingly easy. Try it, try focusing on a task, work on your own and results will come.

Vase followed vase. Painting followed painting. I didn't know the paintings. At first, they were all pure kitsch . . . warriors who won their battles like true heroes but were killed in the end anyway. In each painting I saw Elvis. I saw his feelings filled with suffering. And, I thought, *sometimes people live in suffering because they can't get a maximum of feeling, love and friendship out of themselves, but they rarely realize it.* People like Elvis.

Elvis opened the door to his study. He let me in first.

In the middle of the room, I noticed a large pool table. To the right, about two feet away, was a small bar table – it was a small glass bar table. On it, a bottle of whisky stood like a mast suggesting anyone can play pool with whisky. And, it was an overstated reality Elvis had played this scene time and time and time again.

I realized I was going to play something I couldn't.

"Can you play pool?" Elvis' smile shimmered.

"No."

Elvis looked at me in a way which betrayed his inner satisfaction, as if he were saying to himself, "That's good."

"But will you play with me?!" He asked, incorporating a command into the question.

I glanced at Elvis with fear. The fear had nothing to do with my task. I was afraid of doing something I couldn't do and of humiliation. It was the fear of a man sporting with another man and knowing the outcome might be debilitating to his self-esteem.

"I'll play." *What else am I supposed to say?* I winced internally.

When two men play, the talk is usually very good. I relied on this.

Elvis opened the whisky. I think it was Chivas Regal. He poured me first, a good host.

Then he poured himself. His hand shook a little, but his overall countenance was self-assured.

He handed me the glass and smiled craftily.

"Let's play some music," he said, unequivocally.

"I'll play you a song," and he smiled at me again. In that smile I saw for sure he was relaxed, he was, at least for a while, the person he always wanted to be. A man who can live his life the way he sees it. And maybe he got relaxed just because he was holding a glass of whisky in his hand. Sometimes alcohol and ice can magically turn a man's soul into an ice king who froze before he lived to see his kingdom.

Elvis turned away from me toward the jukebox. He had an expensive device with vintage records where he could push a button and it would play an album, one of many albums. He could even play any song he wanted. And so he did. He chose the Beach Boys, *Pet Sound* album, *God Only Knows* was the tune.

Before he played the song . . . before I knew what song it was . . . Elvis added . . .

"I'm gonna write a song like this one day."

He never did.

As it played he started to sing *God only Knows.*

It appeared no one hindered Elvis from singing because he was able to. He just did it. He felt good when he sang. And, it gave him an opportunity to feel good, to experience the excitation of his soul when singing. His freedom seemed tampered by singing what he was required to sing in front of people at concerts, in his albums.

I thought to myself . . . *The only freedom Elvis has in life is free singing and that freedom is probably best recognized the here and now.*

I gathered these private concerts with people like me, where he sang what he wanted how he wanted set his soul free in a sense of solitude. Because even though I was with him – in essence Elvis was alone and it appeared he was alone far too little and I sensed his sadness.

I was looking at an honest and talented singer who was well paid for . . . to the whole of society he sang as if at one endless party. I realized there was actually little difference between he and I. He served society as much as I did. And, the fact resonated in his performance of, *God Only Knows* . . . I clutched the glass of whiskey in my hands . . . I felt lonely . . . although the song was beautiful and honest, I prayed for it to end.

Elvis was happy when he finished the liturgy.

I was still down but bottoms are beneficiary for spies. I approached the King and without any contact with his eyes, looked into my glass and drank a toast with him. Sometimes sadness is best conveyed as a repressed happiness. We drank the toast and only then I looked at him.

He smiled at me and knocked back his whiskey.

I joined him.

Our grounds of drinking the glass differed but we drank them together.

"So philosopher . . ." A bit ridiculous.

"What's so funny?" I did not understand.

"All the people around me are so like me. They have no education."

"I did not study philosophy for the dimension of power . . . Only few do." I reached for an answer that would be best received or at least I thought that I did.

Elvis smiled once again. He reached over my empty glass.

I handed it to him.

Elvis was no longer afraid of me, he felt powerful and that pacified him.

I thought he would return even to my philosophy but for that moment he was absolutely not interested in it.

"So what do you think of the song I played for you, Peter?"

"I know it is a brilliant piece."

"A piece of art."

"Art that works."

He put a full glass of whiskey to my hand. I looked at him.

I longed to know what means art in music for him. I longed to hear it from his mouth. Although I already knew it from the information received from various sources.

I tried to develop this theme, the whole album is great.

"Yes, you're right, it's brilliant work."

Elvis filled his glass and closed his bottle again.

He sat down in a black leather armchair next to the pool table.

He picked up his glass, so I picked up my one, too, and we drank.

As if Elvis wanted to avoid a longer conversation about music.

"Why do you want to work for me? Is it worth it? What?"

Although I was surprised with a quick change of the direction of the dialogue, quick even for me, I had no other chance than to adapt.

"Yes, certainly. Sure."

"Do you want to be next to me just because I have the dimension of your power . . ." he looked at me immensely scrutinizing "and I'm someone who can have any telephone numbers?"

I did not want to answer but I wanted him clearly to see that my eyes were saying "more than the truth" about its greatness:

"You are my idol, which I would like to believe, which I would like to help."

But Elvis surprised me:

"Aren't you an anti-drug cop? (Elvis himself expressed his interest in working in the drug issue. 21 December 1970 he even met Richard Nixon in the White House and suggested to the President that he would like to become a "Federal Agent-at-Large" in the Bureau of Narcotics and Dangerous Drugs!)"

What more could I do as try to overcome the shock caused by his question by sincerity as soon as possible:

I laughed. And it was really honest laughter I had rehearsed "at home" over and over again, so I knew I was honest before this world.

Nothing better I could do at that moment. This forced Elvis to continue to explain.

"Look, you wouldn't be the first. Sometimes I feel that somebody wants to get me. So I threw them out, even though I did not have any evidence. That's our way."

Elvis got up from his armchair but still while getting up, he looked at me somehow strangely.

"Fill my glass and yours, too" . . . he handed me an empty glass. Then he sat down again. He crossed his legs and stared at me.

I was filling the glass, my hands shaking a bit. My shaking was similar to that of Elvis earlier in our visit. I know he noticed. When filling the glass, an alarming idea crossed my mind.

What if Elvis had such good contacts someone warned him about me? In my field of expertise, one would never know. I did not want to return to the drug problem, to avoid getting any attention. In any case, I still took the risk. Today . . . I would have done thing differently but at the time, it seemed to be a good idea.

"Well, I think rather than trying to get into your head, folks would try to keep you in a state of mind to serve their interests as well as possible . . . so you would be, let's say, controlled . . . like Bob Dylan was. Why would they engage an anti-drug officer . . . when . . . you know . . . your drug abuse and drinking is good for them . . .?"

When I said "drinking," I looked at my own full glass and I laughed. The fact remains, I said what I said and pronounced my sentences with comicality, gassiness and exaggeration – then I handed Elvis his glass. During the filling of our glasses with alcohol, I lost track of whose glass was whose. I now held Elvis' glass and he held mine but it was irrelevant – only my last words were relevant. After my statement, Elvis remained surprisingly calm.

"What are you trying to say?" He asked with the mirth of a child who smirked at a practical joke. After all, a joke, which is true, is the best joke they say.

To make matters worse, I continued . . . "Elvis, after all you are "the" American golden-boy. You have amassed a great image ordinary people view as hope. It is the image of a good guy working hard and achieving the American Dream. Those people who can control your image like a puppet win if you are drinking and drugging because you are enabling them to seize greater control. You have created an image impossible to destroy . . . and to better control that image . . . drinking, drugs and other considerations give your handlers an opportunity to control you so that you don't destroy yourself or the image. I picked up my glass and drank without waiting for the King."

Again, I took a risk.

Elvis' face became neither red, nor new. He just smiled and with a smile he murmured, "I haven't heard this type of conversation in a long, long, time . . ."

As often happens to young people who believe something, I believed myself too much. "I'm here to help you from my personal conviction. You should no longer be a lackey to record movies that demean your character or to record music you yourself don't enjoy."

I spoke with a drunken seriousness minced with sincerity but I looked naïve as well.

As if just losing his confidence, Elvis appeared as if suddenly he did not know what to say.

I was scared.

He rose from his chair and he extended his hand to me. He squeezed it tightly. "Hello, I am Elvis Aaron Presley."

While returning the squeeze, tears appeared in my eyes. These were not crocodile tears. I was genuinely touched by his offer of a first-name basis - many of Elvis' mafioso remained on formal terms and never were offered a first name association. Maybe I approached to Elvis too fast, but the risk seemed to bear fruit. My tears made him visibly happy. He patted me on my shoulder.

"I felt from the beginning you will be someone I need; notwithstanding the fact that P. said me it before. "I knows people that is my gift. Artists see people clearly . . . you know" – he paused for a moment and then he hugged me. It was the most devout hug a stranger could exchange with a stranger. And, for me, his hug spoke volumes concerning the inner man. And, the fact presented itself . . . yes . . . Elvis needed hugs too. He seemed desperate to find himself in someone else as well. And, believe me, such people as Elvis can find only very, very, few people whom they trust with their inner person without fear of reprisal. Fame appears to be a victim-riddled lifestyle because the famous remain in doubt concerning their intent as well as the intentions of those they are in contact with. Theirs' is a world of virtual yes men and yes women.

"Man, you spoke directly from the soul. This is something that has bothered me for so many years. I do not know what to do. I don't want be a slave but here I am. I'm terribly dismayed by the weakness of everything I write due to the nature of fame and this business." Elvis' face contorted somewhat – a wrinkle line was exposed over his brow.

I felt his breath full of whiskey, and I could feel my first tear running down my cheek. But I could not wipe it because I was still in his embrace.

Spies cry, if crying remains in the plane of the mission. Spies drink, if they know where their drinking is headed.

"I would like to hear your own song," was my response.

Elvis stopped hugging me, fear appearing on his face for half a second and then he gained his composure.

"They are weak. All my songs are very weak," was his retort. Elvis clutched his empty glass in his hands as a rescue, as if he leaned his whole inside on that glass.

I saw Elvis' lack of confidence and wanted to help him only by a desire to hear his song. "Maybe they are weak, but it does not change the fact I want to hear your song Elvis."

"No." Elvis kept his empty glass in his hand. His face expressed internal struggle.

"I don't play my own songs even with my wife. Actually, I don't play them for anyone these days."

"You should overcome your fear." I mustered, feeling somewhat overstated.

Elvis got up and he did not look at me. Surely he felt to be in the room very alone now. He filled his glass. "Fill your glass when you wish, Peter."

There was a black piano standing behind the pool table in the corner of the large room. Elvis put his full glass on it. "Do you know how many times my glass has been placed on this piano?" It was a redundant question serving absolutely no purpose and I didn't answer it. It was just a rhetorical question, Elvis did not answer to himself, let alone me.

He lifted the cover on the piano, protecting the keyboard. He drank his whiskey, and he looked at me. He began playing a simple melody in G mol and continued in G minor.

I sat down at the place from which he rose.

*I cannot find my dreams,*

*I lost them somewhere,*

*but otherwise I sleep well,*

*I don't sleep for dreams.*

I liked the introduction indeed.

Elvis sang with even more expression than when he sang *God Only Knows*, and then I thought nobody could sing with more expression. Truly, it was as if the song rang from his soul and was unable to be emotively shared with any similitude in conversation. Truly, he was the best singer with the greatest expression.

# 7
# Music of the soul

Elvis' best music in my estimation were the songs, *I'll Hold You in My Heart* and *Loving You* as well as *Tomorrow Never Comes*. These seem to capture Elvis in my mind. However, he continued his own song and looked straight ahead with pinched eyes.

*And when also the dreamless sleep disappears*

*I'll stay here next to you,*

*you'll be my last disappearance,*

*either I'll go south or west,*

*you'll always see only my leaving back,*

*let me go forth any direction,*

*my dream that's you,*

*will remain in me as the sun goes down*

*and comes back, love.*

*I love you, I love you, I love you too.*

*But will you sometimes be my last disappearance?*

*We'll never be it together?*

*I love you, I love you too.*

*Believe me, that ultimately nothing will left over after me, just this song about love,*

*I long so much that my children sing this . . .*

*an anonymous folk song*

*from an anonymous author, love.*

He recited the final stanza and I suddenly realized I was witnessing something great the world would not experience. His lyrics were contemporary and his heartfelt singing . . . somehow lost in time. Never mind the lyrics were a bit slushy . . . full of present-day convention . . . the expression, the rich voice, the honesty, and dedication made the song extraordinary. Notwithstanding the simple melody, I felt honored listening to Elvis perform his own work.

He turned to me on his revolving piano stool. "Nonsense, right?" he asked in a voice that seemed to be still as part of his singing.

I felt I met someone who had endured a lifetime of talent and waste-- certainly there was more to the King . . . "I love it, Elvis." I responded in a heartfelt affirmation. Not everything has to be so clandestine in the performance of field operations – for the benefit of the case – we can deviate on the limb of realism.

"I don't believe you." Elvis was unable or unwilling to accept my praise. His self-confidence was really spot on in this moment. And, then I realized with greater clarity, Elvis lived the complexities of a life he could not overcome, because the images of his life were altered to such perfection – he couldn't reach those standards in his own soul.

"That's your problem – these words I would never say without a genuine belief – If it was weak, I would have said so, especially after these drinks." I shook the ice in my glass . . . and continued, "The lyrics, your voice, the sentiment, the rhythm . . . perfection my friend. Certainly, the pop songs are fun but you are wasting your talent here." I stood up, I was directed to Elvis' glass, I took it, I filled it (as I filled my own) and I returned them to their original positions.

"It's hard to believe you . . ." Elvis spoke thoughtfully.

"Stop, thinking for a moment, whether, what you are playing is bad or good or if it is better or worse than this and that. Just sing your own music . . . you can do it. Be yourself Elvis and sing your own song. Don't be a fan of your music . . . that's my role." My words did not seem to help anything.

"I think . . . I think that I should fill my glass more . . ." he said without having a look at his filled glass. But his hands naturally returned to the keyboard. His face remained melancholy.

I was hoping that he would play again . . . sometimes desolation makes for a great musical score. Was I able to encourage him? I do not know, I believed I helped him play on and I slowly began to feel a truth. Elvis was influenced easily.

Elvis began again in A minor – the score came more rapidly than his previous piece. He returned to G minor but soon to A and continued in the same key. He held the pace and expression. He accelerated and decelerated the intensity of his singing:

*My heart is like roses that have nowhere to bloom,*

*so I am alone,*

*your heart once used to bloom in me,*

*but I was not sure I was not sure:*

*get up, you someone,*

*Elvis, get up –*

*the world is over,*

*the world has nothing common with you anymore,*

*now you see, now you know that living is fun when the world is over,*

*there is nothing,*

*you are going nowhere,*

*but it is fun to live.*

He repeated his sonnet several times escalating and de-escalating speed and emphasis. It was clear the song was unfinished. Elvis sang with the voice of a broken man, much like his last full studio recording *From Elvis Presley Boulevard Memphis Tennessee* in 1976 where neither song was from his own pen.

It appeared Elvis did not feel a reason to complete his own songs because when he finished he immediately reached for his glass and washed down the feeling the song was not a success. "No one will listen to this song you know . . ." Elvis trailed off .into silence.

I looked at him and lost the desire to say anything further. He was convinced of his own inability so crazily I had to calm down. I sat there feeling sorry for him.

So little would be enough. He just had to meet someone else accidentally, someone really honest, who would try to get the most of him.

So Elvis never wrote a song that could win in hit parades? Or he just never released such a song?! All it took was just a moment hearing Elvis' own songs. He had such artistic empathy . . . in my opinion.

"The public needs a smiling, sexually attractive man. There's no room for a depressed underground artist . . ." Elvis voiced the limitations of fame. He closed the keyboard. Disgusted of himself without reason, Elvis got up from the piano and walked over to the pool table. He did not perceive me. It appeared to me I was not perceived. For a short time he acted as an unrecognized genius and even started to play billiards with himself.

# 8
# All-American Boy

I was surprised, just a moment before he was a completely normal person if you know what I mean. Now here stood this man before me whose own music declared a lack of peace. He played two successful shots on the billiard table then looked at me and winked. His winking was freeing. I did not want to be silent anymore. Elvis was faster than me and asked me a question I didn't anticipate.

"Say, philosopher, what do you think is the meaning of life we are trying to live here?" The question surprised, I cleared my throat. I had no problem with the question; however, the man standing before me was no longer the Elvis who had talked with me thus far – he was not the "All-American Boy" any longer. I paused, then came to respond . . .

"Everyone has the right to live as he wants unless his actions adversely affect others. And, everyone should live "freely" in their own goals whether doctors, teachers, scientists, economists, lawyers, laborers or entertainers . . . it is a simple fact - we are all manipulated in order to withstand the demands of living life. It is how we function in that manipulation that is ultimately the most important consideration."

Elvis paused at my response.

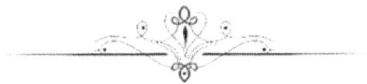

During this break in our conversation my mind whirled with thoughts . . . *Elvis' tragedy consists in the fact the public leans on him as they have since the very beginning of his career. It is part and participle of his role as an entertainer and the business surrounding him. The business of manipulation and control of his brand and trademark. Elvis reminds me of Coca Cola – he can't deviate to bitterness nor taste apart from the standard anticipation of flavor*

*upon popping that cap off the bottle. Elvis is his brand and "it" is more important than he is. Even if he wishes to change the taste of his story – the public and his business managers won't stand for it. Elvis is under control without an ability to grab the reins and redirect his chariot. His lot in life is to entertain the masses. The business of Elvis is allowing his demise. Ultimately, it will allow his death because a dead icon is better than a reformist or a transformation.* I knew inside, *Elvis is the saddest story of our generation:*

I felt sorry for him. I was trying to be empathic and keep my thoughts on the mission as well. I decided to answer his question with a question. "What do you think is the meaning of life?" For me, trying to figure out how nature works and how society works is of the highest importance and this referred to almost everything: Elvis, religion, etc. I wanted to continue, but I was uncertain because the struck my mind I might be better able to discuss love and human relationships. Moreover, I saw Elvis' expression – my thoughts would go in one ear, and out the other. He asked and did not want to hear my answer or I was too daring or at the very least my answer was not interesting enough for Elvis to reply. After my hesitation, Elvis interrupted me, his facial expression changed, to an expression of friendship and affection.

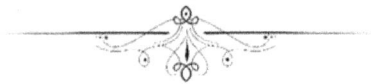

"Take your cue Peter – let's play some pool . . . and I am looking for the same thing; however, this helps more . . ." he did not finish, he concentrated on his cue he held in his hands.

With that said I realized he was set on automatic response - he was looking for the same thing – it was as if my answer suddenly ceased to exist . . . he finished his sentence as late as after his blow to balls with his mahogany cue . . .

"But none of that matters. In fact, all of this does not matter." Elvis drew in a breath. And, followed the path of his ball with a concentrated face. The ball did not hit its target. And, it did not send another ball into a hole for a score. It was then Elvis changed the meaning of his response giving it new charge.

"Balls are rolling Peter, they need not make sense." Again, his comment seemed to trail off - he did not finish. He watched the balls until they stopped. "I want the ball to obey me . . . now!" Elvis' voice moved from peaceful to demanding.

It was evident to me, he was not interested in my purpose of life. Instead, his demeanor was commanding as a fathers to his son. I remained surprised because this was the Elvis I had read about in the Company reports. This rendition of Elvis demanded control in order to cap the emptiness he felt. It masked the imbalance of vulnerability he felt inside. My mind shifted, *Those balls have ceased to move now and we should not drink anymore but I need his to drink more and expose himself while becoming better acquainted with me as his servant.* So I changed direction internally . . . *Fuck the balls, although I should not drink anymore, fuck the balls.*

Elvis shot at me . . .

"Play pool with me man, pick up that #&$@$ cue. That's what I want! Let's play pool."

I grabbed the cue and played. I felt like we were two drunken children wrangling with one another over the pool table of life. I wasn't a pool man, I couldn't hit any of the pool balls into any of the six holes on the table. I wanted to step away and allow Elvis to take another turn immediately. It was his turn now . . . however, he grabbed my cue and talked at me.

"Play the game Peter. Here, in my house, we don't play according to the rules of the game. Let's not be disturbed by rules. Play until you land a ball in the hole."

Elvis' comment was off-putting and somewhat harsh but riddled with confidence – so much so I could not take my eyes off him for a moment. *What kind of person is he?* I thought while presuming the act of playing pool. Finally, I hit one ball in the hole but that said nothing for me – I was being doubly forced into this activity – by Elvis because he demanded it and as a hired hand because my role demanded it. Elvis remained the beneficiary of these actions. And, seemed to have a good feeling he was manipulating and controlling somebody.

But I was getting a good feeling too - the longer I played I told myself, *I will play until Elvis stops me.* Well, Elvis was not stopping me, whether I hit or missed the balls. He just observed me. During this game I collected all the forces I was comprised of that had led me toward this role. During one insignificant action with my cue I asked Elvis another question in a certain voice.

"Didn't you want to know what I thought about the meaning of life? And how would it help me? I mean you asked after all. If you didn't care, why did you ask?"

"Play." Elvis stated emphatically.

"But I am asking." I pushed forward. Elvis avoided my gaze. I tried to connect with his eyes. He took the cue from my hands at that time. He probably told to himself he should stop my attempts at playing pool, which were looking very unprofessional. He acted strangely and I was wondering where the man who played nice songs to me just moments earlier was.

Elvis prepared for his pool shot when the cue fell out of his hands. He let it fall to the ground and clutched his head. He made two reeling steps and grabbed at the table that held his alcohol as if some unknown spasm hit his musculoskeletal system. Then he sagged down alongside the table. One of the bottles fell to the ground, but it did not break. In his fall, he did not seem drunken although alcohol was undeniably involved in his landing. He began to cry for what I did not understand.

"I . . . I . . . I do not want to live this way . . . my songs, my . . . I do not want to play billiards . . . I know nothing, I know nothing . . . I do not know . . . I do not know . . . I cannot even play billiards, its bad." Elvis' comments were rambling and resembled a child's banter in a fit of emancipation of repressed feelings.

I didn't want to play billiards either but my act of manipulating Elvis to a trust position was underway. I knew I did not have to say anything as Elvis collapsed himself. It became obvious Elvis was losing more and more of the real Elvis – his soul – his inner self. Although he was at the stage where even Elvis could hardly tell who the real Elvis was. He was sobbing now.

"Look at me . . . just look . . . see . . . I am a plain fool. You heard my own songs. They are terrible – you want to know the meaning of life?! Just look at me!" Afterward, he stopped crying as if a magic wand was waved and said Stop Crying. He stood up. His face changed.

"A ball. Normal ball. Where's the whiskey? Let's finish what we started." Elvis said.

He picked up the bottle from the ground. He held the bottle in his hands and opened it. He reached for a clean glass and filled it to the brim. He did not turn to me, he did not ask me if I needed anything. The King was a captive of his world. He drank and turned to me.

"So you think that there is supposedly any meaning here?" Elvis spoke in a withdrawing manner.

I seized another opportunity and stated, "In this way we get nowhere, Elvis."

"Answer me nothing!" He acted like a man needing to be king even in the moment when he would probably offer his kingdom for a single beloved carrion . . .

I replied coolly, as a manipulator on the top of my options. "And why, if you don't care and don't like my responses to your questions – do you take time to reject them?"

Elvis drank to the soul as if he wanted to wash away the pain of concepts. He smiled at me with the smile of a robot. It was evident an alcoholic nature was emerging . . . "I make the rules here Peter!" Elvis was stoic in his now evident swagger.

I thought, *I cannot stop playing billiards with him, there's too much at stake. I am close to his repressed inner person. I can feel it.* I lifted my cue to the table and played on, even though I didn't want to – I was provoking Elvis' opposition and becoming closer to him every second..

"Why aren't you playing? We stopped playing! You don't believe you can be free, do you Elvis?!" I pressed him for more.

But Elvis did not feel well . . . "What . . . what are you trying to prove here?" Elvis leaned his arms on the pool table. His voice was broken, however, was surprisingly without any sign of audible reproach.

"You act like a child who did not mature. You act like an adult who desperately needs a companion in his proximity, nothing else. He is not great enough to exist. You have no personality. If I was your manager, I would like such a child and such an adult . . ." I replied with self-confidence, with the highest possible one, which I then found in myself.

Elvis continued, his hands being supported on the table, he suffered, but he tried to fight. His inside was fighting with himself, with the alcohol and with me:

"What right do you have to tell me all this the hell? Do you want me to give you a job?!"

"Yes, I do." I answered convincingly.

"So what should that mean then? Stop your antics and convince me you are applying for work."

I stopped playing, but I did not stop holding the cue in my hands.

"You have no right here . . . but I'll give you much right as you want, if you'll respect and act honestly!"

"You sound like a corrupt politician." I retorted.

"You're naive, terribly naïve." Finally, he stated madly, "I don't need you."

His "I don't need you" gave me even more confidence and certainty. "As your fan I have the right to tell you my opinion. I have the right to try to get the best of you, if I'm with you and I'm not shaking knees. I have the right to hear from you a really good record. A sincere record. It is my right. The right of a fan . . . , yes, a fan!"

Elvis sarcastically smirked - I knew I had won. After all, he loved himself so much even if I upset him sooner or later he would realize he needs such commentary.

"Get out of here!" He shouted in frenzy of humiliation, for he knew himself for a long time he did nothing to support his feeling of being a great artist.

I looked at him and again with confidence, convinced that I could not be wrong without any sign of loss of self-control, "You know I am right."

"Get out, I don't need such as you." He was attempting to laugh in my face but it did not work.

"There is only one Elvis . . . and forever will be." I said calmly while smiling.

"Get out! Now it's too late kissing my ass!" He breathed in: "I am crazy of all the sages like you! What do you, know?!"

I laughed like a man who has just been fired from work and has nothing left to lose. I laughed as the winner, who reached his goal. I needed only a while and I understood who Elvis was in his essence.

# 9
# Don't Let the Door Hit You

I knew my training resulted in an expertise I could not disclose to Elvis Presley or any member of his Mafioso or anyone else for that matter. I was one of the "best" in my field. And, it was obvious, my new friend; however, short-lived our consideration of one another was totally unaware of my training and I knew the management need not be afraid of Elvis.

He had played me songs, which meant nothing but confirmed Elvis could become someone else – he only needed a bit of pressure. In one aspect of his personality he loved his status, he loved the freedom of doing nothing by schedule – of having money to spend and had acquired a sense of arrogance. The other part of Elvis was eager to reach for more – even the level of composers of popular music. And, it rang true, as "King" he was compared to Jesus; who wouldn't want to be compared to him?

Elvis demonstrated a potential for volatility. Even in the pangs of despair he could be one person one minute but unable to suffer despair in the next. He created songs of his suffering but in doing so lost his self-esteem and could only suffer.

I returned my cue to the place where I had taken it from. I glanced at Elvis.

In the meantime someone knocked on the door.

"Enter." Elvis sounded off with a hope in his voice. For me, it was the hope of escape from a bad situation.

A large man stood in the doorway. He had a mane like a lion and looked like a fox.

"I heard screams, is everything okay?"

"Yes," replied Elvis. "This one is leaving." He was confident in his resolve to remove my questioning nature from his presence. The man looked at me in consideration.

"Leaving as an enemy?" asked the man, and he winked at Elvis.

"No, no, no lesson. He's just a poor fan."

I had a taste to say something . . . and I not the slightest reason to contain myself. "Poor Elvis, I'm afraid this will end badly - it's a pity – you have the strength to change your path." I did not shout, I spoke calmly instead. I was aware of my hidden strength. I spoke quietly to his conscious that I understood spoke the same words to his own thoughts daily.

Without Elvis' order, the man approached me as quickly as possible. In two to three seconds he stood next to me. He looked into my eyes and I saw a great void in him. Hard to say what he saw in me because we were really the same character but on differing playing fields. I knew he wanted to hit me because he probably hadn't gotten to hit anyone that day. The man was almost touching me as he readied to escort me out. I knew outside the compound he would not avoid touching me.

I was saved when Elvis spoke up, "No, no, you know what? Let him be, I want to ask him something. You can go. And call P!"

The man gave me a look and I knew I was lucky, although trained in self-defense it was best avoided.

Apparently, Elvis' "Mafioso" gave him new zeal because his voice was more fully animated back to Elvis' original presentation. He started as the man closed the door. He was speaking as a man who understood he is the strong man here in all circumstances.

"I really did have not met someone like you in a long time. You make me angry! You tell me things I want, and don't want, to hear."

The man closed the door quietly, even if his face was bursting with anger.

"And I wonder why . . . It's so simple, because of you, Elvis. I tried to calm down – in any case, I am just Peter . . . the philosopher." I spoke as a young servant of a great king.

Elvis shook his head, expressing his disbelief rather than rejection.

Now, I wasn't surprised at all, when he I once again asked the question that apparently had nothing to do with the storyline of our dialogue.

"Do you believe in fate, the predestination of the world?" Elvis inquired.

I did not answer. I stood before Elvis with empty hands I was shaken by fear and anger provoked by the Mafioso (who probably remained stationed outside the door) who wanted to strike me.

Elvis looked at me clearly in surprise, for I dared not to reply.

Apparently the words "you will end badly" overcame his anger. Yes, they definitely overcame his anger.

"Why do you not answer?" He asked.

I shook my head but this time it was an expression of sadness. I consciously manipulated Elvis' emotions and feelings because I needed to provoke him again. My facial expression clearly expressed disillusionment and sadness from what I'd seen thus far. Actually, I was not pretending. If I were standing in front of Elvis for myself without any deeper role I would behave reacted differently. I would certainly try to hide my disappointment. Now, however, I did not need to hide anything.

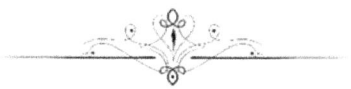

When consciously destructing personalities, agents such as myself don't hide negative emotions regarding our observations because they are a driving force triggering self-doubt within the victim. Using techniques such as *Propaganda: The Formation of Men's Attitudes* (1965), we train our assets toward the betterment of mankind as a whole. I spoke once again, remembering my station.

"Elvis, if you saw yourself, if you heard all the things you said today, what you sang, how you behaved, you would not understand yourself better than I do now . . ."

"I understand myself better than most out there. I need love, to be a little in touch with how I am loved there outside that much is true."

"You need people . . . who see in you what they see in themselves. A human with everything that constitutes a human."

I thought quietly, *It is always gratifying to tell people what they know themselves, especially when they dare not to pronounce it.*

Elvis looked a as if he really did not need people "in his world." He proved this will his follow-on question, which once again changed everything.

"Why are you not influenced by my strength and my greatness?"

"I am. It is just that you're so impressed with yourself you cannot see my admiration."

"What?" He snapped.

"You need help, I think. Not so much in your music as in your soul."

Elvis laughed as a king and I smiled at his laughter.

"You're crazy," he managed to say something he could not believe but said it as if he believed it.

I laughed, the way he said it made me smile and I also laughed to relax.

Elvis laughed convulsively as if he had a mental spasm.

I felt well for the fact Elvis laughed even if just to protect himself from the pain. Every second near Elvis I was more and more certain his behavior demonstrated a capability toward the greatest sincerity and subsequently largest affection, which left him vulnerable and this weighed on his thoughts as to whether such consciousness would be "good" or "bad." Even his consciousness was an instrument of his greatness.

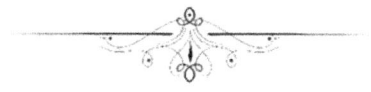

The "meaning of creation" didn't have a lot to do with Elvis' glory or lack thereof in his personal life; I believe everyone experiences similar alienation from time-to-time. For instance, alcoholism has nothing to do with "the spirit of creation" but it does bond people until it wreaks havoc on their lives. Elvis experienced too many alienations probably due to the fact he was Elvis. He experienced them in everything: alcoholism, marriage, music . . . and often at the same time. Would that not kill you? If not physically – then at least proverbially?

Over time, alienation seemed to have become natural to Elvis, as much as human sexuality converts from taboo to repetitious in each of us. Our own alienations, or guilt, is removed by the repetitiveness of any act.

When Elvis lacked personal belief he was something more; for example, he was compelled to greater inappropriate behavior. When Elvis was a demigod, he behaved as he did with me, in a disturbing somewhat maladaptive manner. It was as if fame and success abolished his personality and relinquished boundaries normally set in place to remain appropriate. Elvis no longer knew what was common and what was not.

When Elvis felt like a demigod he was loving. He hated when he felt like an ordinary man because he sensed his own innate weaknesses and became vulnerable – even though he desired to be ordinary more than not. And, in his own compositions the convention of his managers was to suggest he was unable to compose a "hit."

Either inferiority wins or the individual suffers until they overcome it. In the vein of fame . . . already glorified it is difficult to overcome inferiority when it is aligned to the inner being rather than the public figure. Elvis was compelled to live what he felt was a lie - even if his compositions were just a tip of the iceberg. He was crucified by the lack of ability to return to the ordinary and achieve success on "his" terms. His life in the material world made a tragic poetic misappropriation of justice.

I wondered, *Did Kafka write his books in this way? Did Lennon compose his music in this way?* The ideal connection for an artist would be to achieve on their own terms, using their own music, true to their inner voice. In that manner – success would be less of a drug and more of a statement. The demigod is more aligned to success as a drug. Eventually, the drug forces them to work on anything to keep the success-train rolling. *That*, I thought, is *exactly what happened to Elvis.*

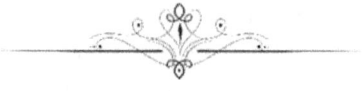

I laughed. Elvis laughed, too.

We staring at one another keeping eye contact and I knew what I knew and suddenly I did not care what Elvis knew. I realized I had nothing to say to the man before me because he had no faith. It was apparent he didn't believe in his music and didn't believe in his life.

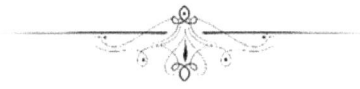

"Get out of here . . . Get out of me . . . You . . . boy . . . you will truly not help me!" Elvis was hysterical . . . his face was tense . . . his hand outstretched toward the door. It was a simple gesture – he cried get out at the same time he pointed out of here.

He was not laughing. He reached a "Himalayan" height of shriek with wheezing concerning the self-mockery I had previously perceived as a kind of laugh. Instead of laughter there was a fearful shriek resonating in his soul. All my consideration of his childish demeanor was in error. Elvis was angry like a child who believes he is right because the whole world is his.

I had no reason not to abandon him. For brief moments, in drinking with the king I made quick probes into his personality and found an insecure man. He was an abandoned king within the ramparts of his kingdom, with dedicated servants who served the king but not the man. In taking leave of Elvis, he surprised me once again. He changed the angry tone of his voice to a calm and even depressive one . . .

"When you go, serve yourself from my whiskey, so I'll feel better . . ."

He said it like a tired river flowing neither ironical nor derogatory. After all, I would be able to discern it. I did not perceive any irony in his voice. The tense situation between Elvis and me could not be a mockery – it was a sincerity with Elvis . . . A sincerity, whose quiet and fluent depressiveness did not disturb the moment of rejection, rather delivered pathos of incredibility and Elvis' bifurcation. Elvis realized he was expelling the only man who said in recent months and years, what ordinary people were thinking. And, it was ordinary people he cared the most about.

*Attraction has many forms; it is always about the id, the ego and obsession,* I thought to myself. *Am I wrong?*

Our eyes met again - Elvis avoided prolonged contact of the pupils; the immediate turning away of his view reassured me . . . *I must have one more drink.*

I walked over to the second open bottle of whiskey and filled a clean glass. I filled the glass fully!

*Drinking other's drinks is the best, you're right, I will gladly tell my grandchildren about this* – I said aloud, but my voice continued in the Elvis' depressive campaign. I was not ironic. Calmly and serenely in the sadness of life I saw in Elvis, I still raised my cup to Elvis and drank

[43]

it facing him in one gulp. I'd never drank so much before "that day" at once. I was determined I would master it. And, in the end, I realized – most importantly – the faith in my own capabilities to master alcohol rang true. I drank heroically - I still wanted to impress the King. And, to do so, I pretended to drink full glass of whiskey free of consternation...

I quickly put the glass back on the table, I closed my eyes for a moment to handle the pressure of alcohol, and without looking at Elvis again . . . I said very dryly, "Thank you." I walked to the door. If *Knocking on Heaven's Door* (Bob Dylan sang in the movie score from *Pat Garrett and Billy the Kid*, 1973) had been composed at the time, I would have sang it in spirit. I was completely empty inside and my emptiness grew commensurately to the alcohol releasing in my blood.

When I was approximately one meter far from the door, just one meter from the end of my action, I could not avoid a quiet (but audible) reproach to Elvis – he surely heard it . . . Together with the alcohol, the remorse had audible character of alcoholic haze of mind (now even I do not remember whether I've played it or not) . . .

"He that will not be counseled, cannot be helped."

I do not know if I was waiting for any reaction or not, I just walked to the door to leave and left a parting remark of consequence. How much time does a drunken man need to move a meter on his way out the door? Nothing happened during that meter. I had not heard any responses from Elvis. I put my hand on the door handle and something whistled along my right ear. It was a question of centimeters, if not millimeters. It took as long (or as short) as a drunken man needs to move one meter to the door – he threw an empty glass of whiskey to me. I'll never know if he wanted to hit me or not but the fact remains he didn't.

The glass hit the wooden door and broke. I was very lucky none of the fragments hit my face, hands, or chest . . . after all, drunkards have good luck in their bad luck, because they rarely focus on back luck and do not realize it as soon as if they are sober.

That is exactly what happened to me. I realized the fact Elvis threw the glass at me as late as when the last fragment fell to the ground. It took about two seconds. Before I managed even to look back to Elvis . . . the door, whose handle I was holding, opened. The door opened in a direction away from me otherwise it would hit my forehead. While the door was opening, the door handle receded and my hand hung in the air for a brief moment. The man stood in the doorway with whom I had previously gotten acquainted with together with P.

Only then, when I saw their surprised eyes, which immediately met with my eyes, I gasped out loud . . . "He threw his glass at me! The King . . ." With whiskey breathe I half whispered, "He . . . at me . . . the King . . ." I'm certain it was a sight to see for each of them. Despite all my temporary amazement . . . I noticed their eyes moved somewhere behind my back certainly at the face of Elvis.

"What is this, what happened?!" The man asked hastily with a hoarse voice while still looking somewhere behind my back.

"I am playing! I love these games!" Elvis exclaimed and immediately started to laugh wheezing a little as he had before. His laughter a mockery was rather gleeful noting he had startled everyone. Each of the two men looked at me differently.

"Simply playing, guys . . ." Elvis added. It seemed Elvis was really fun. He loved the opportunity to prove his strength.

"What did you do to him?" P asked me with an agitated voice.

The man who would probably still like to hit, slapped me on my shoulder and smiled. He added, as if he just won some dramatic competition, "This is our king and we love him it this way." I knew he meant it sarcastically and half seriously.

P. entered the room bypassing me. He did not wait for my reply. He did not expect I would express something. He went to Elvis himself who was in his place from where he threw the glass.

I stood near the man who gave me a smile as he bent over to me and whispered, "Elvis is our God, and who will not accept it, he will end up in hell." His smile turned into a grimace.

At that moment, nothing made sense - I was not capable of making sense of things for a while because I felt drunken. After a short interlude, the fellow patted my shoulder once again and left without being explicitly instructed to do so. He closed the door behind him.

And under the influence of Elvis, under the influence of my role, I felt as when you come home from work. I turned knowing I must return to my role – the love of my life – one I believed in. If Elvis did not believe anything . . . it was my big advantage I had faith.

P. embraced Elvis and Elvis embraced P.

I stood at the door and watched the hugging men. Elvis wept. I heard his cry and I felt nothing. He threw a glass at me, I did not feel like forgiving him but Elvis was crying. When you see a man crying in the arms of another man you know that man is suffering.

I need my pills now, please, now! Elvis spoke declaratively. I heard it.

"You could have hurt me." I stated

The King answered, "You're still here?"

"You should go." P motioned toward the outdoors.

"No, let him be, he endured till now. Let him see what wreck he wanted to help."

The depression in his voice gave me a green light. I forced a smile.

"A wreck?" Elvis managed to smile, while he ripped right corner of his mouth. He had the symptoms of addiction. Glory and pressure, isolation and fear of nothingness, of the largest nothingness, of living his life without deeper meaning on top of the society pushed him far. Elvis, the king of success, could find nothing more in that success. An adored and loved individual as he, still lived without meaning. He served as a slave to his success.

I returned to the middle of the room and our game of wits. I walked around the room and Elvis stopped hugging P.

P. addressed me immediately, as a man who felt a bit of responsibility for the condition of the King. "What were you talking about when you came to throwing glasses?"

I felt that the question is directed at me, but Elvis answered the first. "He told me the truth . . . but what . . . who cares . . . It will not change . . ."

P. and I looked surprised at Elvis. He said "the truth" and from our perspective that was strengthened by the fact neither one of us immediately responded to what Elvis said. It was special that someone throwing glasses at people desiring pills for an artificial calm kept a matter-of-fact realism regarding life but it was a sad statement none the less.

P. responded, "It isn't too bad Elvis . . . you have stood next to your Judas and because you are free as the King . . . you have taken the higher ground." A strange poetic justice from Elvis' teammate.

"P. bring my pills now." Elvis turned and looked at me.

"Parker won't allow me to employ a philosopher – he'll say I'll be influenced in an unintended way. But . . . let it be . . . Just give me pills . . . I want my pills."

"But Elvis . . ." said P. His words were a quiet resignation and P. stared at me briefly for a fragment of a second. *I thought what kind of character as a close friend of Elvis is P. when he arranged this meeting for the Company.* I thought *something similar must have crossed P.'s subconscious in the fraction of a second when he looked at me.* And, my mind furthered, *So who is the real friend of Elvis? Or does he have real friends?*

Elvis did not answer the words of P. directly, he just shook his head. "Am I the King?!"

I pondered, *if even Elvis can't be free in this world who can be free?!*

To me, Elvis suddenly showed a romanticism to the heroes of Dostoevsky's novels! Although he most likely he never read Dostoevsky's novels.

If it weren't for the fact I stood in the room with the two men, I would not believe Elvis' next question . . .

"Aren't you a bit of a weakling P.?" His question irritated P. and it crossed my mind, *His irritation is stemming from the fact of his betrayal and is in synergy with his prior feelings – both stabbed at P.'s inner consciousness.*

"I myself, I'm not a weakling. I am the King. And this can be understood only by another king, but I cannot see anybody like that here."

Silence followed. If someone was listening, he could hear only my breath because I had a nose full of mucus due to the situation I had not blown my nose and it was audible.

Elvis stared at me with dogged eyes. Surely he didn't know P. stared at me with similar eyes. Two dogged eye expressions glared at my face. Elvis, however addressed me.

"I need Elvis. I hate Elvis!" He laughed.

It was pleasant to see him smile again and for me, to be near to him. This man who had risen from poverty to riches … who had the clarity to understand the words of his manager, music publisher and others regarding his need to entertain and be entertaining were both vigor and poison. He longed for the life before the fame, especially after becoming famous!

It was evident, his inner circle had persuaded him that everyone in his station longs for ordinary living and that his voice was the icon of ordinary people. Even Bob Dylan believed this for a moment. Elvis appeared afraid to be himself regarding his talent from God, from creation that chose him to be "King".

P's embrace of Elvis apparently ceased long before this physical one. "Elvis you have to always be playing with someone and attract attention. You are something else my man."

"What, in God's name did you talk about?!" P. attacked me pulling me to the side. It was evident P. felt bad, he seemed to really like Elvis. One of the few loyalists it appeared. I thought before speaking, *well . . . P. did betray Elvis for money . . . after all, Elvis was eventually betrayed by everyone he knew for money – even himself.*

"We talked about what we had to talk about." I answered P. It was my first sentence after a long silence and the alcohol had begun to process from my brain.

"Indeed, we talked about what we had to talk about . . . the path of the world cannot be influenced." Elvis added Elvis. "Sometimes the stars try to be so thoughtful, although no one cares."

I looked at him. He looked as if he knew more than he did. The problem was only in the fact who knew what Elvis knew? Even Elvis didn't know what he knew. It was apparent he *tons* of pills in his body.

Come on, P. go and bring my pills, that's what I want right now. You promised you're undying devotion to me . . . now get a move on." Elvis' voice changed and his enunciation were clear – apparently the alcohol wore off on him somewhat as well. He motioned toward P. and gave a wry grimace. It was apparent this was a private acknowledgment the two shared.

I was a little confused. If there was anything I was sure of, I was sure of something when he was playing piano, if I was sure of something when he switched topics, not I was not sure of anything anymore. At least a momentary deliverance.

P. recoiled toward the door and backed away from Elvis. He saw the table and two opened bottles of whiskey.

"You drank?" P. pointed to the plenary. But no one answer was uttered.

I was not interested in P. I had no reason to be interested in him because what he knew was said by him some time ago. I looked at him with contempt - the man left out immediately knowing even though I was on assignment – I still judged his weakness toward what now appeared to have been his friend rather than employer.

"Go and bring the pills P.! Elvis did not say it this time as a friend says something to his friend. It was an order from a boss, even if the order was against P.'s conviction he had to comply. P. did not say a word. He no longer backed away, instead he looked as if he longed to save Elvis from his inevitable demise – there appeared to be no hostility in his view, rather a regret. He then looked at me with disdain and I looked at him but he said nothing to Elvis.

"He that will not be counseled, cannot be helped . . ." I thought I heard him mutter in his departure. When he said it I looked at him surprised. *Why did he say the same thing as me? Are we indeed repeating in each fragmentation of thoughts just as "here and now"?! Or is this room bugged? And why immediately after pronouncing these words, he looked at me?* I became a little insecure or concerned, P. surely noticed it. He smiled underneath his moustache and made stepped out the door.

Elvis' reaction he had heard only moments earlier from me, was surprisingly calm.

"I don't need help. I think that in this moment I'm really free because I can take my pills, which I want." He grinned an ironic grin of a man able to get over his suffering through whatever means necessary.

Elvis was ready again to bask in the light of his own reality even though it was like a black hole to me as an observer. As he watched P. leave, he said, "P., you know what you have said and that it was said a while ago by our philosopher here. You should appreciate the fact I appreciate you because . . . when he said it (Elvis pointed to me) I threw a glass at him. And, I'm not throwing anything at you brother . . . hurry back." Elvis looked balanced and happy once more and his voice indicated it. He knew his medication would stave off the inconveniences he felt – much like a salvation.

P. stopped momentarily with one eye focused on me and then the satisfaction disappeared from his face – he left to perform his duties.

In that moment of hesitation I gained back my confidence. P. was not disconcerting at best. He lost his ability to prove to himself to Elvis . . . he may have meant his repetition of my statement that drew the glass from Elvis' hand but there was a difference in it for Elvis. The difference was I provoked Elvis to consternation; P. shared the feeling Elvis needed help and that he desired to do so. Both of us seemingly cared. In my caring an attempt toward liberation was shared and Elvis recognized this as such but knew P.'s heart was in his concern for Elvis' health. It was important for me – because he was under my control and wasn't until that moment.

# 10
# The Talk

Moving forward with our meeting I considered the role of Colonel Parker toward Elvis. *Was he ordinary scum or an ingenious entrepreneur?* I figured he was both. He performed a a role in the decomposition of Elvis' career and life, whether paid for it by Elvis' fans or by the very glory of his charge.

I was alone with the King once more. He sat on a black leather armchair, he was sprawling more than sitting.

"Give me more," he said, as if I were already his companion.

I was pleased; especially since I again felt a little closer to his broken inside. I filled his glass and also my own.

I brought him the glass and drank a toast. I remained standing before him and he didn't invite me to sit down. Instead, his soul retreated to a slow alcohol confessional.

All the better for me in my role.

"I don't know why I live . . . but . . . I am not bothered much about it but my entire body is in pain. I need to know why my body alive. But I even don't know why I am saying this to you."

"Philosophers say a lot of things easily. Maybe all of us are a living form or something like that."

"What do you mean?"

"I do not need to compose deep philosophical treatises when I stand in front of you Elvis."

"Why? Is it offensive to do so?"

"Do you feel you need to hunt for something in your life?"

Elvis bowed his head for a moment reflectively while looking at the ground. "Look, my art Peter . . ."

"Would you say that it is not you anymore?"

"No, it is not. Actually, it never was. I never hunted for anything, I wanted to be famous." Elvis drank in a sip of the vintage from his glass but his face did not indicate he had absorbed even a drop more of alcohol.

"I don't understand."

"I'm missing something and I don't know what it is."

"Are you trying to find it?"

"Not really."

"Not really?"

"Elvis shook his head. I guess it was his answer to my question. Why? Look at me – do I appear to need to find anything?"

"So what, you don't have any physical needs but this sounds more spiritual or philosophical to me Elvis."

"Great art does not exist anymore, no one needs it." Being said by Elvis, the thought was informative. I looked at Elvis with great suspicion of his fan, who is dependent on the art of his idol. "I'm not an artist but my life is art." Elvis surprised me.

"What do you mean?"

"There are many people with a voice like mine who wanted to be greatly admired and respected. When I was young, I was driven by a force within me. And, that got me here. Along the way though, so many asshole moments arose. This sort of effort is paid for . . . No one becomes great without drive or talent and a lot of blood, sweat and tears . . . you know?

"I came up in hardship. I understand the ghetto, I lived in the projects. I've been booed on stage before – all musicians experience something like that . . .

"I'm known as a man who borrowed music and moves from black men but I'm accepted as the King of Rock n' Roll. How many black men remain unaccepted with the same talent? He was somber.

"That may be true."

He continued. "I did not risk, I just played and played . . . ha . . . . ha . . . Businessmen packaged me . . . They know how to pack goods in order to sell and make the artist as big as possible. It works . . . Getting to the businessmen is so hard but once they are onboard it is liberating. Then, one day, you have to admit you are just . . . done, you know done . . . Once you've made it – what else is there to do?" He smirked and shook his head; he was destroying himself by his own words. "No, no, I don't see a way out of this hell." He ridiculed himself. "You see it is like a reflection in the mirror. My reflection. I'm good, I'm successful, and I'm often happy but the drive . . . everything may be right but not everything."

"What?" I presented a quizzical face.

"What is further in this business? I mean the irony. Great art is formed by critics and moguls . . . it's true . . . it's really true . . . I think so . . . The media too. It's clear. Even those critics and moguls are only in power because they were trained to do what they do – we gave them the power – we gave them the information. We allowed them to get rich right alongside of us and to whom do they belong? He asked with explicitness – he was already a case study. His, was the philosophy of a drunken man.

I answered Elvis. I was not deterred and used the mindset of a seventeen-year-old wjp responds quickly and incoherently to someone appreciated while wanting to manifest himself. "Bad and good art belongs to its creator. And, to the people who have the opportunity to receive it. It's the life that forces us to behave the way we do and our choices. How? You know, the average survives, as simply as possible. What does not make sense for ordinary people ceases to exist. Whether it is good or not. The good emerges and is beneficial to the people. And, that drives us toward hope. Living in itself is success. Elvis you are success. You enable ordinary people and people from the ghetto toward the hope for something more. Dreams are freedoms and in your dreams are fulfilled. You know Van Gogh, Kafka, Warhol, each of them demonstrated essential features of art . . . Each emerged and captivated their season of living. Each delivers truth and eventually embraces others. Art must perform . . . You know yourself how "the King" was created. You simply hit the mark and used courage with intention."

"How Elvis was created? Even I do not know how I was created. And, Warhol doesn't count, I'm greater than Warhol. You want the truth? Who are you? Listen to me, society doesn't care. You have to be successful and then society cares. He took a breath, still not abandoning his smirk. "The Beatles arose because somebody wanted them to? No, they became famous and then society wanted them and business drove them to success. Business and a lot of hard work on their part as well as timing and luck. And, timing . . . now there is a concept Mr. Philosopher. In twenty years, they'll be quite a few Elvis' out there. Performers who have visited my shows, learned my presentation, paid attention to my vocals and they'll have their own rights of success but they won't have the moments I have had. That is timing – and who determines timing? He grinned and I could see the underpinnings of his Assembly of God upbringing.

"Without society being ready the artist would never arise, is that what you are saying? Without an attraction for the songs . . . I mean songs for ordinary adolescents . . . you know . . . songs that could not spoil anything . . . that bring harmless fun . . . artists wouldn't become what they are today? And, due to this, artists are increasingly controlled because their naivety and ambition to be more than mere entertainers."

"By whom are they controlled?" Elvis was amused.

"You said it yourself, profit and success. " My reaction to his amusement was less cordial. It was essential under my Directive to make certain Elvis' anti-artistic would result in his being glad he was where he was and seeming irritated would tie him to defending his post. Elvis should prefer to stay on top – the silence again broke.

"You know Peter, who is that, how did you call him? The system of mine? Well, that is just my . . . Colonel." Elvis performed a face of hellish suffering. Religion probably makes drunken when drunk man likes to confess to anybody: "I used to think that he had the right to tell me what I should sing. He called it "my moral right of your success" but today – I am no so certain."

"Well, it had to . . . beat you down. Did it?"

"Yes, it did but I think he had that right . . . Yes . . ."

I looked at the Elvis from my standing position and finished drinking off this whiskey in my glass. Elvis went on with the thought of telling me something new. "I'll tell you and everyone will realize it sooner or later . . . freedom is not success in life unless it serves something greater. They taught me this in the military. Without discipline and management, it doesn't work. I accepted it. Therefore, I do what they say. I'm still at war with this world, or so it seems to me . . ."

I stood above Elvis. I thought about where things stem from in his mind. I didn't want even to mention he had basically said the same thing twice. Even better . . . I didn't want to tell him I was speaking about the Beatles, so I inquired further.

"I mean, you don't want to improve your art so that it has more in it of and about you? More of your personal message?"

"I might want to but why should I? What's the point?"

"It is truly hard work, I understand now." I said thoughtfully.

"Like what?" He asked surprised by my reflection.

"Trying to create something and still find a reason, sometimes it must be disheartening."

Elvis had a honest smile and shared it we me. And, he was in control and felt no remorse in doing so . .

"I did not come into the music like a man who wants to create something, really . . . I did not want to change anything, not me . . . not me . . . When I was young, and perhaps even quite naïve, I only wanted to entertain people as well as I could. I really enjoyed it. Now it is not enjoying anymore because sometimes I can see the fun began to be purposeful, yes, purposeful and stupid. I see it and feel it and it hurts. Here . . . here, boy, here" He pointed to his heart. "It is as if someone stole my youthful sincerity over the years."

"So what's next then Elvis?" No other question crossed my mind! I said it as a tipsy fan, who is satisfied . . .

In his condition, Elvis accepted such a stupid question well. "I am longing for a return to the time when I was entertained and nothing more bothered me. Then I felt free, yes . . . that's when I felt . . . free and magnificent."

Oh, just this was the reason why he was taking the pills whole that time? Otherwise, I was very pleased!

Elvis constantly changed what he wanted; however a return to the benign period in spite of the fact it was unwittingly triggered by Elvis' boyish insolence extraordinarily marketed by General Parker, would help . . . he added, "People are getting older every day and each day they learn something more. Again, it comes down to timing. The past is, well . . . passed."

Elvis quietly confirmed Rock n' Roll was nothing more than entertainment for hard-working people who were surviving as best as they could.

"To be honest, if it makes you feel happy, it's a pretty good idea. I would encourage you as a fan - I still like your first album and if you talked about the joy and sincerity . . ."

"I hear you Peter. At that time, I was a village boy that indulged in beloved songs. I'll never repeat those years . . . I've just gotten tired of success."

His sincerity rang true but as the King of Rock n' Roll such conversation couldn't continue for a lengthy period of time. Elvis had to maintain the role of the King of Rock. I was certain, in spite of his quiet fortitude he had worked to be as good as the Beatles, Rolling Stones and Dylan. He loved to entertain the masses like no other and that was work.

"Imagine you could do once again what you did as a young man only introducing your own works. Imagine you'd still be the big thing contained in it over the years that your greatness, and more would still have happened. Just imagine your songs bringing your expressions to the world!"

Elvis stared at me for about two seconds without ceasing. "But you heard my songs yourself . . ."

"I did."

"Thank you."

I smiled.

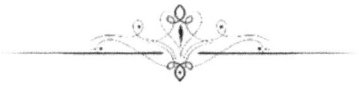

As indicated . . . planning a clandestine career development on behalf of the Company would result in great global achievements with a brilliant ease! After all, why not take a career destiny into their hands coinciding with the entertainer's desire to entertain. His expressed sincerity under the control of the Company would not suffer in imitation because the singer would deliver the kind of sincerity the Company intended. He had just said it.

**Field Notes Entry 104 – Arnold Lane:** I have decided it will go best with Elvis if we do not destroy him – rather we can use him more than anyone else. He is an asset we should mold his future successes toward promotions of morality even if they seem anti-social, such as the song, In the Ghetto. Elvis has a dream to elevate ordinary people more than just entertain them. If we offer him hope, assurance that he is someone more, he will latch onto it. No matter his education.

"The time has come to persuade people around you, your publisher, Parker and others you are the King. You are the singer of singers. You have the right to choose Elvis, songs for yourself! You know the songs with the right messages. The time is now Elvis. No one can make you make compromises because of your stature – you have the artistic freedom to rule your kingdom! You got it at your fingertips!" I delivered a genuine devoted fan speech of faith to the King. "Elvis, you are able to give everything you have in yourself to your album that you will trust with all your heart. I'm telling you this as a fan, which was long ago moved to tears when you sang as a free man. While then, during your singing I felt like part of the singing, as a free man in a free America!" I gave so much "sincerity" to my words it moved me to tears and basically in the moment I was saying it I believed it.

Looking into my sincere face, seeing sincere tears, Elvis clutched an empty cup and probably could not believe what he heard. Maybe he felt like a king who got the opportunity to finish reigning people whom did not believe anymore. It was the sensibility of a new chance.

"Where did you come from Peter? First, you make me feel like a courtesy to a fan, then you make me think, then you make me angry and now . . . you utter the first words I've heard in a long time that talk about meaning something."

"It's time to act, Elvis. The Beatles are no longer what they used be, Dylan is in isolation . . . It's time for your comeback. People love to hear the King and in a new language of hope they'll elevate their lives."

"Will they really need me?"

"Yes Elvis, people love certainties, icons, and new meanings."

"And I wanted to throw you outta here." He muttered to himself for a second. "What did you think when I threw the glass at you Peter?"

I straightened and without long thinking used the greatest sincerity I could muster; of course, alcohol was helping me . . . "That you suffer alone and you are happy with your suffering because you feel you cannot change it."

Elvis fell silent. Elvis looked at me. I need to embrace you. He got up and made one step toward my body and without waiting for my consent he hugged me with his whole body like a hungry man who hugged nobody for many days.

I dropped my glass during the hugging by accident caused by the weight of Elvis' body. As a matter of fact, I lost balance a little bit. Elvis squeezed me even harder. I was certain he thought I was returning his embrace as well as I could. Maybe he thought I felt the hug the way he did. The glass did not break. In fell on the carpet and it and it rolled for a while and moved away from us.

At the moment of the impact of the glass on the floor, the door opened. There was P. with an unidentified man standing in the doorway. At first glance he was completely different than all of Elvis' other cronies. Hair accounted for only small islands on his head, it was gray and I could barely assess whether he was smart or not – whether to care about them or not.

The man had intellectual glasses, a marked forehead but not as marked as to immediately trigger doubts whether you will have something to talk about with the intellectual. When he saw Elvis, he put a smile on his face, which may or may have been sincere. His teeth were yellow. In his left hand was a cigarette and he was smoking it. He held a small bag in his right hand. We quickly stopped hugging. I felt the break in hugging was as if Elvis was ashamed to be caught hugging me.

The man, who otherwise was not unusually tall – average height. He had a Greek belly. He theatrically put out his cigarette by pressing it to his shoe as a genuine comedian, which didn't make sense to me. It was far from being fully smoked. He put down his black bag and he literally fell on Elvis. His way of putting out his cigarette made Elvis laugh.

I later learned from P., the man behaved funnily because he was four days separated from Elvis, attending a pharmaceutical course. Elvis' good mood I had added him in achieving was improved even more. The man stretched his hand out to Elvis, his whole body being prepared to embrace. I stepped back one step from the place where I had stood and watched with an incredulous facial expression the typical South-European embracement of two men. The man kissed Elvis on the right cheek and then the left.

In the meantime I looked at P. who had an uninvolved expression on his face. It was as if he suffered seeing Elvis hug someone else. By his facial expression, I would assume P. was not usually hugged by Elvis. I forgot to mention the man with the belly and almost no hair had the most significant charisma of all the people I'd met around Elvis.

Of course, I was impressed.

And with that, I immediately knew who was before me. He could be none other than Dr. N., Elvis' personal doctor. The Doctor and Elvis ceased hugging.

Meanwhile Dr. N. took the small bag and placed it on the table with the alcohol. He did not open it. Without being asked as if he were at home, the Doctor filled his glass but not that glass, which he lifted from the ground with a bottle. He filled his glass with whiskey.

I guess he was depressed, when looking at me while drinking what he had poured. He closed his eyes for a moment and let a free flow of the liquid gift which helped him to open his eyes again.

I lost interest in P., because Dr. N., with a smile of a man on whom everything depends, walked over to his paradisiacal bag and asked, "So, Elvis, what's bothering you today?" It was a serious physician to patient question. He asked with a little hoarse voice, which resembled the voice of the man who had wanted to strike me earlier in the afternoon.

Elvis looked at me and smiled. "I am OK, Dr. N. Finally, I am free of bothering by what normally troubles me, my depression and pain. I feel well thanks to this guy. You were actually not introduced." He pointed to me with his hand. Elvis was excited and said, "This is Peter." He shifted his hand in pointing to Dr. N, "Peter, this is my doctor N."

The moment in which we met with his eyes, I felt I made Dr. N. nervous. We gazed at one another and I felt Dr. N. was nervous due to Elvis' statement "thanks to this guy I feel good."

The trouble was most visible at the moment in which we shook hands. He looked in my eyes again when shaking our hands, as if there was the question in the eye contact, I sensed he wondered, *what are you doing here, boy?*

Standing aside quietly after drinking the poured whiskey, P. observed the continuation of the undercover operation, he was informed about just as well as we were.

Immediately after shaking our hands Dr. N. turned to Elvis.

"How did he help you?" His voice was indeed that of a doctor, which revealed it was a very close companion of Elvis.

"I know what I need to do." Elvis replied serenely.

Dr. N. looked at me like a secret agent who has no idea with what role I came to his play but in the next second I felt increasing eye attacks toward me presenting a clear message: "This is my man."

I replied accordingly and I looked at him as he was looking at me.

Dr. N. just received two answers he did not understand. For a man who usually understood everything around Elvis and had everything under control it appear threatening.

"Elvis, and you have to do?" He asked curiously - while emanating some fear of losing the man who profited his business activities in the provision of good drugs.

Elvis surprised both his close lackeys when he said, "I must learn to love my singing again . . . to love it as I loved it when I was singing and I was glad of it . . . like a bird. You know." I pleased him indeed, because he took the freedom of joking. "I need to work on myself, they still love me out there . . ." Elvis was immersed in his words, using wonderful feeling in them, which did not differ from his feeling he was still able to feel when singing.

Dr. N. looked at me, he slightly narrowed his eyes, but he said nothing.

P. was pleased by Elvis' words.

"This is the Elvis that I love . . ." Finally he smiled. He even continued in his smile and once again briefly looked at me.

"Doctor, now I need something to support my euphoria and joy, because today is the good day because today Elvis was born back to life!" Elvis was so happy Doctor N was flabbergasted. Elvis' words he needed medication to make his joy lasting as long as possible, calmed the good doctor. Even Dr. N. smiled for the first time after his hugs with Elvis. It was as if he was aware he had to deliver every day what the King needed in order to survive in his world of isolation. That this was his mission in creation.

I was very happy, I felt like a winner. Elvis' joy was also my joy.

Elvis had no inhibitions. Maybe this was caused by luck - maybe by his life – so he did not consider it anything special waiting for pills, which should make him well again. Elvis believed he needed medication to help his sick soul and body. He wasn't doing anything illegal against God. He was happy taking his medications - after all, it was neither heroin nor cocaine.

Elvis sat in the black leather chair again.

"Sit down, anywhere," he said to P. and me. He finally said it! Elvis was happy and he immediately began to think about the others.

P. found his place the first, he sat down on the piano stool. I did not have much choice if I wanted to stay close to Elvis. I leaned on the pool table. It was something between leaning and sitting down. Elvis said nothing. P. looked at me with suspicion in his eyes but it certainly was not for my position at the pool table.

I was still close to his Elvis . . .

"But what, guys? A lot of successes is still waiting for me." Elvis' satisfaction and joy erupted. "And . . . why . . . not make it even better a bit? Let us spoil with the last fun before the hard work . . . yes, let us," he added, while his voice did not change, it was happy – like a little kid who thinks he found something he can live for tomorrow.

During my presence, till now Elvis demonstrated the longest internal stability, which was a good sign. Elvis wanted to work, he still had that that power in him, it could be felt of him!

Meanwhile Dr. N. opened his bag he'd placed on the table with the alcohol and he prepared something. Obviously he did not listen us. He face, even when Elvis spoke as a definition of a momentarily happy personality, remained constant and focused on the task at hand in the preparation of his concoction.

Half a minute later, Dr. N. finished his work and took some pills in his hand and with a smile returned to the sitting King.

"So, Elvis. Can we start?" Asked Dr. N., as if it was a case of some chess game.

"Of course," replied the King happily. One was sure, in that state of enthusiasm Elvis certainly did not look as a junkie or a misfit. Elvis was finally Elvis. This was the condition in which Elvis managed to enjoy a bit, whom he became.

Dr. N. showed him his fist and he smiled. It was a smile of a winner who offers something memorable. P. did not smile, his face was like a stone. He could be happy when his King was happy but the happiness for the happiness of his King visibly lasted only a few seconds.

Elvis laughed when he saw the fist of Dr. N.

"Today, it will be somehow mysterious . . ."

"Today, we will have premiere, we have special anti-depressants here, which even have no name still . . . yes, they should relax you . . . How much did you drink?"

"Not much, about two glasses," Elvis answered speaking with raised voice while winking at me.

Dr. N. (victoriously again) smiled, he could not help but notice the wink.

P. was sitting on a revolving chair but he did not twist at all. Maybe his soul was twisting.

"I've done my job, can I go?" He surprised everyone with his question, addressed to Elvis.

If I focused on him as I did on Elvis, I would be angry. But "now" I just knew he wanted to get rid of the burden of his soul, which consisted of observing Elvis as he madly and successfully enjoyed his opportunity to relax . . . at least once, for happiness!

"And why you should go?" Asked Elvis surprisingly. Probably he noticed P. was not entertained at all and his face was the opposite of happiness.

"I'm a free man, I need not be here."

"I do not know, are you free, what you think?" Elvis replied, his voice missing any sign of irritation.

"Please do not talk about my freedom, it is not . . ."

P. just shook his head.

I looked at P.

"Today Elvis already knows everything he should have known, P." That was what Elvis factually said instead of me, his voice indicated he was looking forward to what Dr. N. had before him in his fist! "Now I know only one thing, but it should be enough . . . I know that I need to work on myself and I love music. At last, an album will come that will mean something more." Elvis looked at P. but his glance indicated P. was much less important for him than Dr. N. and the medicine.

P. grinned wryly. He had courage.

Meanwhile, Dr. N. opened his fist, offering a great view to Elvis. It was Dr. N's view for the gods. Those who wanted to be deceived in their high places. Small gods deceived by greater gods. From that moment P. including his request to leave was not interesting anymore to Elvis.

After opening his fist Dr. N. could not miss P. grinning wryly because he carefully listened with one ear to the entire discussion between Elvis and P. It was obvious he felt like a winner as the most important person in Elvis' proximity. Probably it was reason he looked at me. For a moment, just a brief moment, I felt that he understood the situation quite clearly.

At times, field agents suffer such feelings. There is only one remedy for such a situation - to achieve greater confidence in the action.

Elvis was the only one of us who was still looking only at the open palm of Dr. N. The pills did not melt in his warm palms because they were wrapped in paper tissue. If Dr. N. was truly interested in Elvis' conversation with P., the more he was interested in Elvis' face. The longer the palm was open, the more escalated all expectations in Elvis and attention paid by Dr. N. to Elvis' face grew accordingly. At last, Dr. N. ceased to be interested in me and P. The longer Elvis looked at the paper with his pills of happiness and success, he seemed like an excited dog who is waiting for what his lord offers him.

I thought, *some drug dealers really feel irreplaceable.*

"It seems Elvis you feel unnecessarily . . ." My broken sentence directed toward P.

"I know but . . ." P. retorted.

With a low voice I was trying to get rid of P. I spoke in a whisper Dr. N. heard my words. "And Elvis?"

Again I used tactics from my training. *Offer P. what he wants anyway himself.*

P. looked at me with a challenging look for a long time nothing was said.

I wanted to ignore the departure of P. but I would have greater certainty if P. left.

He was the only one who knew me. Who knows, maybe he wanted all the time to stay sitting on his revolving chair to attract attention. If this were true, he must have felt worse than he did before his request. Because he could easily see Elvis gradually conquered by his drive to give up under Dr. N's watchful eye.

# II
# Helping the Medicine Go Down

I looked at Elvis and saw I was right in what I had thought. He did not care about anything more than the hand of Dr. N. not even himself. At the moment of Dr. N's entrance, Elvis forget his happiness and what he wanted to do and what must be done to feel needed and loved as the artist of artists in the pop religion.

On the other hand, Dr. N. – as an opposite – experienced a kind of mental orgasm when he felt Elvis become his chemical child. Every day, over and over again. What more may receive a doctor of his patients, if he is able to believe what he does, he does for the good of his patient? But Dr. N. was certainly not naive.

Elvis thought the game that kept him alive again in another world was truly medication he needed. The game was a transformation toward compulsion. It was becoming part and participle of his body – it was enslaving Elvis. It happens that every game has something to do with reality. And although drugs don't have a lot in common with reality of the soul; in the mind and body they do. Elvis was not only a social slave – he had become a chemical slave as well.

In the classic ascription, pimps know devoted and good performance is created from a need to fulfill an addiction. Create an addiction and momentarily the freedom from human consciousness occurs, which is an artificial freedom and the fastest portrait of freedom every man, woman and child craves – freedom from cares and wants – freedom of spirit and soul.

The fastest illusion of freedom can make slaves out of the most dedicated people. Elvis was in this situation. Who knows, maybe it already happened in his past that he recorded a song in the daylight to have the opportunity to devour a soul tranquilizer in the evening.

There is no greater enslavement than the substitution of a right for freedom through the illusion of freedom through bondage. Elvis did it. With pills in his body he felt cool about life. It worked, his pills still performed as needed.

P. stood up, leaving his little piano stool. "I'm leaving, I'm not needed here anymore. If you need anything, I'll be outside. They should bring a new car." P. behaved like a professional. If servants understand they have nothing to do in the vicinity of the King, why should they stay unless they asked by the King?

I knew Dr. N. didn't wish my presence in the same way as I did not wish the presence of P. The rejection of my person was clear. Every dealer can better relish himself the effect of his work with the victim.

Dr. N. turned his head to me asking, "You are staying?"

I did not want to answer directly. I needed Elvis' response. I avoided Dr. N and cast a rescuing look toward Elvis. He ignored me altogether and scrutinized the novel feeling within his body. A few seconds later he assumed a robotish appearance – he looked extremely unnatural. His eyes were motionless without blinking. He appeared to be a slave to medication while he felt he was experiencing freedom!

In any case, I was lucky because Elvis looked up for two or three seconds on my face and he said very quietly. "Let him stay. He deserves it." Saying those words he stopped watching me. He looked briefly toward Dr. N. but did not seem to be interested in him too much.

Dr. N. looked at me for a second, his grimace saying, "OK, nothing happens, what the King wants – the King gets." Without any visible moodiness he returned to his patient.

Although I did not know how exactly I should explain his phrase "he deserves it", I was pleased, sparks of professional success emerging in my eyes.

So I remained at the pool table looking at Dr. N. as he unpacked his handkerchief with more pills. He did so just a moment, Elvis opened his hand and Dr. N. put five pills in it from his handkerchief. Two of them were the same color (blue), the other had multicolored representation. Orange, red and black.

I did not move but one thing I knew, I never in my life have taken more than two pills at once in my life, without feeling ill.

Elvis looked up to Dr. N. and asked him with a very peaceful face, "How should I start?"

"We must be careful."

"What are you talking about? They are supposedly dangerous drugs?"

"The more effective medicine for your soul, the more your body has to be careful."

Elvis grinned. "Let's start, doctor." Elvis encouraged the doctor to his work.

Dr. N. tried to act relaxed but something was not right. I have not read a lot of historical novels but one thing I knew then . . . if I had to assign administration of poison to any face I would even now assign it to the face of Dr. N.

The whole time I was looking at Dr. N. and I was watching his every move, every change of his facial expressions.

"First – we will ingest these blue." Dr. N. smiled at Elvis. "They should not be rinsed down. Their effect will be even better then . . ."

So Elvis ingested the two blue pills the first. He swallowed them but he did not rinse them. "They have no taste."

"Why should they have any taste?"

If I was a pharmacist, I would be inventing pills with as good taste as possible.

Dr. N. smiled again. "If it was so easy, believe me, Elvis, each product would taste amazingly."

"Eventually they will taste good." I joined the debate. My voice indicated I was trying to join the debate using any words, even stupid ones. And, preferably using such words that would go at least a bit against the words of Dr. N., at least slightly . . .

Dr. N. looked at me. His eyes told me, "What do you want? What can you know?"

You can answer such a look in a winning way, if you use relaxed – even victorious smirk. I smiled relaxed and my hand caught the ball that remained on the table after the unfinished billiard game.

"Elvis never was anybody with us when I was helping you before." Dr. N. tried to restrict my freedom in Elvis' office.

At the moment at which Dr. N. asked Elvis to limit my freedom of speech, I increased the pressure on the billiard ball. I wanted very much to throw it at Dr. N. but believed I impressed Elvis enough and he would express in my favor.

"Doctor, today he done for me as much as a few people have done for me . . . Now I'm doing well, when I see him . . . really . . ."

Already much quieter but clearly with even more anger of a man trying to control of their doctoral position, he asked, "Do you mean he can say what he wants, even if you require peace and quiet when our work begins . . . when it starts to bear fruit?"

This time I just could not just produce victorious smirk. Even I did not think about what to do, what to say, "If I am intruding, I don't mind I can wait outside." I decided to try the alternative of departure where I longed for Elvis' to stop me – like a fan who understands he is a disturbance.

After all, I had nowhere to go, I just came to form a religion! I jumped off the table and while jumping I was looking at Elvis.

For a short while, Dr. N. had a winning look on his face, *I did it*!

I looked at him just for a second and could not miss it. But I decided to leave, now really only Elvis could stop me. I was hoping the two blue pills he swallowed had not begun to work. I stood straight and waited for the voice of Elvis . . . I knew he would say something as late.

Standing still – I did not feel awkward. A lean back was out of the question now. I had to the first step toward the door even though I did not want to in the name of my religion. More than ever I longed for seeing Elvis under the influence of pills. I took the risk, I wanted to have dominion over Dr. N. and for the first time in a long time I felt I ventured up too much. The first step, the second step and Elvis still said nothing. No response to my departure. I bent my head to the ground. For about two seconds I felt like a man who stupidly beat himself because he wanted too much.

"Where are you going, boy?" Elvis taunted me.

"Well, finally! Elvis saw my back, Elvis saw my slaughtered soul." I turned around and while I was turning, I wondered what to say so I could stay. "I wanted to go. I feel your doctor does not want me here. And actually, I think that he is right a bit . . ." Oh, what did I say?!

Now Dr. N. grinned triumphantly.

"Come on, boy. I want to have you here. Today, I talked with you the best I did recent months. So you stay. You see, still today we will continue."

It was a victory!

Dr. N. did not want to pose as a man who got an inner hit from Elvis. As if his unambiguous peace rejected Elvis' sentence "Still today we will continue."

So I felt it then since I could stay and everything in me wanted to stay. I felt necessary and irreplaceable precisely because it was the feeling demanded in self-confidence of an agent in this legendary role.

"See, guy, I would just like to ask you, sit down for a while meanwhile and hold on a little bit. Well, I need quiet, some concentration you know. Elvis likes these moments. He is here to serve his fans and so he likes simply likes . . ." Elvis spoke in the third person and his voice was a little thick, then he leaned his head on the chair.

"I can feel it. And it's nice."

"That's right . . . that's right . . ." Dr. N. continued praising his drugs. He looked at me and winked and then nodded his head toward me.

His nod surprised me. I don't know if it was a gesture of superiority, the gesture of the strongest man in space or another gesture of victory. That nod was so unexpected I missed his facial expressions. He surely felt I was taken aback because from that moment he personified total relaxation as a man who is absolutely sure of what he is doing. He was proving it with every movement.

Elvis opened his eyes. There were still no visible signs of the effect of drugs visible on him. He felt, especially mentally, much, much better. He smiled continuously.

"Time to swallow the black, Elvis." Dr. N. patted his hand, which held the hard-earned and sung pills.

The pills started to melt slowly in his hand but nobody cared. Certainly not Elvis. I was so impressed by the fact that holding pills in his hands somehow magically helped him.

"May I rinse it?" he asked the doctor as behaved little babies do.

"Yes, this one yes."

"Please, pour me another whiskey." Elvis turned to me . . . his pleading voice sounded innocent. I'm not a woman with maternal instincts but I felt a shiver down my spine – so childlike and looked at Elvis in his petition.

Immediately I looked at Dr. N.

"Elvis, you should not combine it with alcohol." Well, after all he behaved at least a bit like a doctor.

"One drink after so many one won't kill me now . . . uh . . ."

Dr. N. remained surprisingly silent. He just nodded as a sign of approval of Elvis' requirement.

He surprised me, but I did what Elvis asked me for. I did what a doctor allowed . . .

My firm hand gave Elvis a glass, which was half full. Elvis did not look at me and he did not look even at the doctor.

He put a black pill into his mouth of and rinsed it down in one gulp. Near the King, I could notice his right hand, where only two pills were remaining now was completely black now. Elvis closed his eyes and leaned back on the chair. He looked as a man on vacation at sea, who exhibits his face to the strongest sun. A glow was coming from inside. The heat, the certainty, life is worth something came up with the belief even I could not provide to Elvis while trying to convince him he still had a lot to offer. Convinced that was chosen. "Now I feel the way I always wanted to feel. I feel to be myself . . . at least once. Today is a good day . . ."

Dr. N. grabbed Elvis' his hand and he returned his grip. I stood over them and I did not know what to think.

"Did Elvis really not know what he wanted?"

When he was as-so sober and so without drugs, although he never knew exactly what he wanted except permanent success, something rushed him forward, a kind of restlessness. Well, all of us suffer with this. Indeed, rarely we name the unrest. Elvis was no exception. Now, when I looked into his face, it seemed to me he got what he wanted, he got it, after which he searched during his whole life.

I knew where was he going and I think that Dr. N. knew it, too, and it made him happy, *We are flowing nowhere but to our deaths and it is too little time for our souls!?*

I understood Elvis' situation. Indeed, despite the fact I gave him new hope he hadn't been able to overcome his interior. He had to disperse for a moment and spoil himself with an artificial peace that all too real. Sometimes there is nothing worse than when starting to feel you have artificiality in yourself but need the reality of that artificiality without any depth in order to survive in the real world.

"Elvis, still have these last modern pills and everything will be fine." Dr. N. still held Elvis' hand in his left hand, while he opened Elvis' right hand and took the two pills from it.

"Well, he is . . . it's all right now," whispered Elvis. His muscles were relaxed. He did not resist at all when opening the palm of his right hand. Without opening his eyes even a little, he let Dr. N. insert the pills into his mouth. He did not need to rinse them with anything, his smile was rinsing with magic after ingesting the medications as a "free man."

"Nothing is more beautiful. I feel so calm and happy. What . . . what else do I need? Please . . . please, play *God Only Knows* . . ."

Dr. N. looked at me. I understood. I walked over to Elvis' jukebox and it took some time for me to get oriented.

"So . . . so . . . come on . . . put it on . . ." Elvis said - his voice sounded as if behind some wall.

Finally I managed to play the song that already sounded in this space. I wonder how Elvis received it now . . . initial tones sounded, of the song which I still love, and Elvis spoke slowly, obviously trying to give a new dimension to the song but it probably seemed just to me.

In any case, he said, "Guys, I feel, what the meaning of life is and it's nice, guys. Why should I know what is the meaning when I feel it . . . uh . . . I wish you sincerely . . . yes . . . to experience such beauty and greatness. I love you and I know about it. I want you to know it."

Dr. N. smiled once again. Doing so, he uncovered his teeth. There were not only yellow, there was so much tartar present, you would not expect from a reasonable and prudent physician. He uncovered inside of his maw, so we can say it was his most feeling ridden smile performed at that moment.

"Oh, Elvis, Elvis . . ." He shook his head but there was happiness and satisfaction in that twisting of his head.

"This should experience all people, everyone should have that right." Elvis went on, still continuing with his eyes narrowed and voice behind the wall. Elvis defined Pink from The Wall full twelve years earlier, without even Roger Waters knowing it.

"But how many such hidden definitions of the various films are happening here every day, aren't they, actors-people?" Elvis suddenly opened his eyes and without volition, in which he would be looking for me around the room, his eyes lite on me. "Thank you, Peter."

He said my name as if he was not quite sure of the name and he pronounced it with difficulty.

"Um . . . thank you, today you saved my life, thank you." I could hear the will in his voice to get up and hug me but he did not move a muscle still sitting in his chair.

In the first moment of Elvis' thanking me – I wanted to accept his thanks only such an exaggeration under the influence of drugs I was uncertain of. I could not avoid it but who knows maybe Elvis was thinking more seriously. In the second moment, I felt his comment was factual because it suited me because my mind accepted it so gladly! When Elvis expressed his thanks, he closed his eyes in a slumber.

Shortly after the moment of Elvis' confession and thanking, Dr. N. put his hand on the arm of the chair. Throughout the mental operation he knelt at King's side. Probably this was the reason why he stood up slowly. Perhaps he had cramps in from kneeling so long.

Again, I had the impression he had just done what he had to do and thus it ended for him. Perhaps the thanking from Elvis hurt him a bit, since he was not included.

Our gazes met again. *How many times did they before?* He was standing and wiping his right hand with his left hand. This time he turned away first. Dr. N. focused on me and I focused on Dr. N. The main colossus regarded who was moving with our worlds remained unnoticed.

Suddenly Elvis appeared as though he would vomit. He made the familiar sound of a man who was vomiting some food and gastric juices. We both immediately leaped toward Elvis. He deposited the vomit next to his chair. He appeared to be aware of his circumstances as his facial expressions reassured us while he vomited, "Everything is fine. I love this world" he declared. And again he vomited most of what was in him. He clutched the armrests of his chair. I looked at Dr. N. whose face was surprisingly calm. He exhibited no concern.

"Is everything OK?" I asked with mild concern in my voice.

"Oh, yes, it's always this way."

"It's always this way?" Dr. N's words and reassurance stunned me. It sounded as if the doctor spoke in to my soul. *In any case, Elvis is feeling well, and when the patient feels well, let him even die . . . at least he does not suffer, and that is the issue of our lives, to suffer as few as possible.*

Fortunately, to me, the doctor's face reflected some anxiety.

I had a desire to cry.

Elvis furthered, "Everything is fine . . . that's fine . . . I'm . . . I'm fine." It was as if he was saying: *it is just my body that once again cannot endure how well my soul is.*

I thought, *Elvis surpassed Pink from The Wall a long time ago.*

Elvis' breath was hoarse. In the first few seconds of the hoarse breathing I felt he was crying. *God Only Knows* was finishing, and I thought, *this man is a true definition of thy song.*

When I found out Elvis was not crying, I nearly started crying myself. I did not care for Elvis as you do for someone close with whom you have known all your life but believe me, it was a heartbreaking sight.

Finally, Elvis' body settled a bit.

"Now he'll just be . . . only better." Dr. N. relaxed. I had no way how he could accept such a smile. The first sentence served only Dr. N. to overcome what he saw, to overcome what should simply cause mental spasms, as it should cause any sincere doctor seeing a patient who suffered so much.

"I long to sing, I long to imagine my return." Elvis quietly expressed his request.

"So sing, you got your audience here . . ." Dr. N. supported him.

I was so taken surprised by what I saw that I could not respond.

"I will invent . . ."

"Do so, Elvis, do so . . ."

Till today I am surprised, why Elvis' vomited juices didn't make me nauseous. But I focused on something else, after all, I was working. I was in a new environment. With the strain of his last forces Elvis stood up. His taut muscles of the hands we visible very well, when he was rebounding from armrests of the chair to be able to stand on straight legs. He stood up more quickly, as you'd expect from a man who drank as much alcohol and swallowed as many pills. He opened his eyes. His pupils were large and dilated.

"Where is my wife?" He asked as a man who had just been abandoned. Was it just a game or was Elvis experiencing something really painful within himself? I couldn't judge. Elvis stood and his balancing resembled a person who does not have anything to fight with, even not with gravity. He didn't last long.

"Love is like my life but it does not matter . . . I want to feel like a little boy . . . Little boys feel love, yes, they just feel . . . They don't ask what it is." He smiled.

I'd never seen such a dramatic change in an individual from a sad adult into a happy childlike man. Elvis was childlike and smiling now. It was not all he was feeling, just about then his smile transformed to an equally childlike bout of laughter. But what started it – I couldn't tell. During his childlike free laughter he lost his balance.

I wondered to myself, *Is this a happy free little boy who is laughing at himself as a stoned adult?*

In any case, he was lucky because Dr. N. was quick and caught Elvis' body, which was falling to the ground without the will of its owner, who was still laughing.

I jumped toward Elvis' body and helped Dr. N. prevent his fall.

"Let's put him back to the chair," said Dr. N. a little nervously.

For a brief moment, Elvis' soul and consciousness became opposites for his body and the fact of survival. Was it only the drugs that made his consciousness and soul seemingly unite? When Elvis was in a position where his widely open eyes could see a world free of the threat of collapse of his body, he looked like a man who found true happiness and freedom. *Could it be that he could only feel beauty, beautiful simplicity and beautiful complexity of the world?*

*Could it suddenly neither need nor want to know why was he born, why is he Elvis and why there is love?!*

His smile was irreplaceable, it made me laugh inside, because it relaxed the atmosphere. "Well, guys, why did the music stop?"

"You wanted to sing, didn't you?" Dr. N. asked, very pleased with what he saw, pleased with his smile from ear to ear.

"Must I sing when I'm happy?"

"Some people sing only when they are happy," Dr. N. replied with a broad smile, so his words were a bit lost in that smile.

"It's a joke, doctor, it was a joke. Yeah, I want to sing! I really want!"

Tired of so many changes, which I was losing orientation in, I sat down on a revolving chair at the piano. I was not spinning, what I saw and heard spun me enough:

Elvis threw his head back, Dr. N. leaned on the pool table for a while, Elvis opened his mouth and a scream sprang from somewhere from his soul that should be heard by his fans:

"I love this world!" Elvis may have thought that he sang but he just shouted something, something very short.

Dr. N. laughed out loud, a little affectedly, as an actor during a rehearsal.

Elvis repeated what he shouted.

Dr. N. ceased to laugh.

In a second, Elvis changed from a laughing man to a tired man. A man tired of his fortune. He closed his eyes.

As he closed them I saw the soul of a man close with them. Momentarily I felt maybe Elvis was really getting what he needed. After all, he loved the world and appeared to feel he was just beaten and trampled into the black earth for it.

Dr. N. looked at me and, as if wishing to justify himself and stating in a low voice, "Any new medicine takes time for him to adapt." Dr. N. did not even finish the sentence. I assumed he realized how nonsensical it sounded.

"Maybe we should go. He will sleep. He will just sleep," he added rather quickly but his expression contained a degree of uncertainty as he gazed at his patient. "But maybe I should stay here. For sure I should stay," he added.

I had a feeling he was trying to get rid of me once more. I saw in his eyes a sadness and depression, which ruled him and that he needed to be left alone with Elvis. Well, if not for the fact I was at work, I would have probably wanted to leave right then . . . it's true. I spoke without hesitation, "Are you making an addict of Elvis?"

Dr. N. retorted, "Who are you that you could ask something like that?" He immediately added "I wouldn't do such a thing." He questioned me, "You are from Parker, aren't you? Are you from Parker?!"

I smiled feeling victorious as Dr. N. was on the defensive. I only say what I see Dr. N.

He answered, "Every one of you mentions Parker over and over."

I shook my head.

Dr. N. paused for a moment. He looked at Elvis and he returned his look to me, his look expressing dissatisfaction and anger, "All of us are doing only what we must, you understand, all of us."

"Pardon?" I did not wait with my question a single second. My voice was louder than usual.

"I'm not doing anything that Elvis would not want me to do. I'm just his slave," Dr. N. was furthering his defense.

Because he now appeared full of himself by defending himself I presumed my brutally fast commentary upset him as an arrogance in his voice erupted.

This provided me immediate self-confidence, "Maybe each of us is doing what he has to do, indeed."

The doctor paused. Have looked confused.

Maybe you thought "you are still too young," maybe he thought "you are too marginal to know something" and maybe he did not think nothing more than "I don't want to talk with you about medicines which give Elvis at least a little joy in his Odysseus' journey, I need not confess before you."

"New people are screened here more than anywhere else. The fact that you got so close to Elvis, already means something, boy but I'm doing my job here – the one Mr. Presley requested of me." Dr. N was quieted a moment.

Dr. N. and I continued our banter back and forth for a few minutes until Elvis's breathing changed and drew our attention . . .

I duped you both . . . you thought good ole' Elvis was gone. I like to play so much. Hah, you foolish lugs. You guys are my crazy guys." Elvis stood once more for a brief moment as the King of Satyricon. He was happy now. If it wasn't for his occasional vomiting, I'd think he planned everything out in jest . . . absolutely everything!

At this point in our getting to know one another, I was uncertain when he was playing or pretending and when he was serious. Everything seemed genuine though. In my opinion, he woke up on top of the effects of the drugs and pretended from there on. Maybe he did not know, maybe he thought he was telling truths . . .

Elvis smiled. If you saw him it would be clear to you he was another man on his medications.

He confirmed just how much different by the next words he uttered, I couldn't say if he was serious or joking. It was apparent the best aspect of medication is the ability to talk freely without repercussions and that was the state we were experiencing.

"You have to know about it. I'm one of the chosen ones. Up there, chosen by God." Elvis pointed skyward. "Still I cannot take one decisive step." Elvis went to take one step and then laughed it appeared as a scene from a botched adolescent play. It was an unnecessarily embarrassing tragic comedy that he believed was entertaining.

"I'm so happy now, I have to think about God. It is strange, I only do this when something hurts me – never when I'm happy. Oh, I have found something here Dr. N." He breathed through his smile with satisfaction.

The awakening and conversation from Elvis when we'd believed he'd be asleep the remainder of the day surprised both Dr. N and I we stared puzzled at Elvis.

His narrowed eyes opened more and more, "It's true. It's stupid. It's stupid and true." Elvis surpassed his own apathy with a debilitating new apathy. "It's just so . . ." he pronounced half singing, half-serious, half-ironically. "Who knows?" His words echoed off into the air and he appeared to be making fun of himself.

From my observation, Elvis appeared much paler – he was falling asleep again. I thought to myself, *it is a shadow of paleness of Elvis who said I'm fine just moments earlier.*

I believed though, he really meant it when he said, I love the world even if he said it sounding kind of crazy. He didn't need us to remind him of what he had said. He didn't need us to grill the facts of the conversations. He needed us to just be human beings whose presence he could feel to whom he could demonstrated what a king he was.

"I'm here alone. There is nobody else here. Just me, just Elvis. I'm here alone, you know? This is a concentration camp. I'm here alone. I can love you in this solitude. Do you now that? Can a man like me love anybody? In solitude? Can Elvis love? I can love. Uh. Just. God . . ." he asked his questions and answered them loudly. He laughed again and again. He spoke very quickly.

*Did Dr. N. managed with his drugs more than he originally thought he could?* I wondered. *Did he give Elvis feelings of megalomania? Does the good doctor know what he is doing here?* I was suspicious.

"Elvis and God, no . . ." Elvis continued talking to himself while shaking his head.

Suddenly a change overtook him. Like a cat taken over from lethargy, Elvis looked into the heavens and shook his head. It was as if he did not agree with something. Then he looked directly at me. His expression was as if he only needed to see the face of another human being alive and well and with him. I was certain of it. I'm not saying Elvis looked at me haughtily but despite the fact he was pumped full of pills and alcohol, at that moment I just knew he presented himself as someone who felt he was more than I was. It was like some-one who was something more gazing upon me. He began, "Tell me, why should just me be such a sad savior? When I love only God, he wants me to love all. God overestimated me. I do not think I would like to be a savior but nobody cares. After all I only do what I must do. And you . . . and you . . . will you do this with me?"

I was speechless. I did not know what to say or how to answer. Finally, I said something that wasn't thought through and something that was absolutely not meant as a provocation. I simply answered with what I believed to have come to me as God's will. I was honest and I answered him, "I see you have fun. So have your fun. I wish you'd continue to just have fun Elvis."

Dr. N. looked at me sternly, he didn't seem to approve.

I'd already attempted to speak to Elvis without making him angry but as an agent I couldn't' help myself.

Elvis pleasantly surprised both Dr. N. and I by his response, "I just want to know why I have to bear all the sins of all those idiots out there, you know? I didn't want to be such a situation . . . I didn't want to be this Elvis! You just don't understand – you can't understand – it is something only I can understand." Elvis and his body seemed to come back to reality in the moment. He almost cried and calmed down once more. It was miraculous Elvis for a second flew into self-control. He shook his head again but this time he did not look to heaven but to earth. He quietly whispered, "God, I want nothing more or nothing less than to know why I'm Elvis." He was sincere and vulnerable and he found no response within himself on in our eyes.

I pondered, *We never know exactly, what can break a man. Is Elvis broken by not knowing the answer? Is he just beginning to think he is entitled to because he is Elvis?* It remained unclear.

Elvis raised his head looking at Dr. N. "Thy will not exchange the Kingdom of Elvis for . . ." he looked sternly at the doctor and added, "for what you are responsible, heh, heh, heh."

Although his comment was mild, his message could not be doubted. It was bitter irony. *Can a person under the influence of chemicals mock himself?* It was beginning to appear so. *Perhaps, though, even more when taken sober . . .* I presumed. At least, in my profession, truth serum worked best if not clouded with alcohol. There was a part of me developing admiration for the dear doctor and his capabilities with his doses.

Elvis was exhibiting the Lamb of God syndrome and when he said, "I do what God says for me to do" I felt like an angel guarding him in "God's elections." It was in that split second I felt most satisfied - it was such a strong satisfaction. I saw Elvis doing much worse than I thought at the initially. *Can a man insult himself?* The irony of the exchange of the Kingdom of Elvis made it appear so. Elvis wanted to be sincere and he tried to get rid of the flash using the thoughts of a child. *Could it be so that he could not bear the futility of his life?*

He began to quickly twist his head from side to side. I thought that a next attack was starting, caused by organic and inorganic compounds contained in the drugs he received. Yes, his next reaction started, this time more violent.

Elvis clenched his fists.

I thought to myself, *This is how a warrior looks, who does not know what is he fighting for, but – he is fighting.*

Elvis suddenly fired his gaze toward Dr. N. like an arrow. He stepped and grabbed the doctor's shoulders yelling at him, "Crucify me alive. You stupid people. You are useless. You are talentless cowards. Confess! I want to know why!" He shook Dr. N. It was an attack of greatness woven with nothingness and fear. It was apparent he was conflicted by his greatness and somehow felt it was unrelated to his soul. Elvis looked like an addict. His drugs brought him to the brink of despair and elation. He looked furious. His face tensed, his muscles were uncontrollable and he continued to shake Dr. N.

Dr. N. caught Elvis' shoulders and stopped him from shaking him. While holding firmly to Elvis' shoulders he said very loudly, "Calm down! Listen to me, this is not what you want, this is not what you want. Calm down!"

"You want to continue singing," I chimed in and the piano caught my gaze. I became caught up in my thoughts.

Elvis, however, did not listen to anything and anyone, he did not stop to ask, he did not stop to try to pour his inside into the squeezes of Dr. N., he went on, "Will Elvis be crucified?! He must be, just as Jesus was. Just, please . . . please . . . let it make more sense then it did with Jesus!" It was a culmination of his words and actions – exhaustion seemed to kick in. !

I could not bear anymore without saying anything on my piano chair. I stood up and, without fear, I said as a "social agent" who knows when he can afford to be more honest than anyone else in the world, "He will be crucified if it continues in this way." I shook my head while thinking, *He will be crucified, if he misses purpose in his life.*

Elvis ignored me because he never ceased to be entertain by Dr. N. After Dr. N. began to shake Elvis he became bored with shaking the good doctor.

I observed the useless struggle of their souls and how it resolved nothing. A wave of anger overtook me noting I was being ignored.

Elvis turned to me after mildly throwing Dr. N.'s hands away from his body. "Huh, huh, huh. Only God can judge me! Only God! Do you understand?!"

As soon as Elvis left him, Dr. N. made two steps backwards, so he again touched the pool table.

"Power belongs to people who are wanted by God to be powerful!" Elvis was speaking quite nicely, comparing with the restless and hyperactive appearance of his body.

Dr. N. put his finger to his mouth as a sign for me to be silent. In any case, his face yet manifested neither fear nor anger. I think he was beginning to be pretty entertained. In spite of the fact less than thirty seconds passed since he was a bit scared with Elvis.

*Why should I be silent?* "Say, Elvis, tell me now, why do you live? All sentences, questions, you research and determination is so you can get lost here?"

Elvis looked at me like Satan himself. "I love music, I love music"

My eyes fell on a moment to Dr. N., his face was appalled. His index finger was tapping on his forehead, sending me the message, "Are you crazy?"

Elvis changed his posture. A shadow of sorrow covered his face and his hands slackened. It is difficult to live for nothing. To have no sense. Maybe he had some but it appeared to be expelled from him in the moment. It was me who was persuading Elvis to record an album where he could use the force he hadn't used in a long time. He seemed to mostly waste away the day – like he was doing this day. Why couldn't I force him to do so as I wish, if my surrounding permits me to do so?

"No, no, no . . . No! I don't love anymore. I hate! I don't want anymore. No this, I wish to feel good, only good. Don't take it away from me." Elvis looked around seemingly only now realizing where he actually was, where he was actually standing. His hands were shaking.

I imagined his world in my eyes, *He was standing in the desert, wind was blowing sand in his face and he did not know he was in the desert. He did not know which way he should go, he did not know whether he was alive or dead, because they could not even look at his body. He covered his face with his hands and he wept. He cried like a baby again. But at least he wept sincerely. He cried like a little boy, men even cannot cry otherwise, when they lack the essence in their souls, the essence, why they are actually alive. I know that he would not cry if pills did not tear his inside and did not offer him to such vultures as for instance I was.*

"Elvis, this is not the way of getting back to the top." I spoke earnestly.

"What the hell are you doing?!" Dr. N. asked surprised.

"Shut up, you have done enough." I answered angrily.

"I know, Peter. I know it. Gosh, I know it. After all, I know it all but you don't know how hard it is. Finally, they crucify you alive . . . this whole . . . whole . . ." He didn't finish.

I smirked as a man who laughs at the man who gives up without even beginning to fight, I smirked as soon as I abandoned the gaze of Dr. N.

"Why are you smirking? Mocking sad and lonely people is the easiest, isn't it?" Elvis spoke like a child.

"Sorry, it was stupid, you are correct Elvis." I responded.

Dr. N. probably appeared as an abandoned shadow now with no one paying him any mind. When a doctor sees his patient suffering he has administered drugs to in order to avoid suffering I wondered, *How does he feel?!* As Elvis and I talked I thought *he should feel humiliated.*

"Let Elvis alone, he must have a rest." The doctor returned naively. As he spoke he seemed to convulsively hold the pool table. He looked up. He face was as salty as a salt bed. His eyes and his soul in all probability couldn't accept what I said with an imperative tone. I was well-prepared for Elvis. I knew he needed commanding. He needed controlling. He liked to adapt to what he believed he would eventually do himself.

Dr. N. stared at him wishing Elvis would look at him.

Elvis – as if he was blaming him for something, as if the doctor done something wrong - ignored Dr. N. He just concentrated on his piano. Suddenly he was able to pronounce words, which, were easily audible once more. He spoke slowly.

"I am longing for what you want, too. I am longing and I know that there is still the same predestination in me. I am longing and I know.

Yes, it was so: even now, when he was under the influence of drugs of Dr. N., every-thing in Elvis was constantly changing. His interior did not know any persistence. It seemed just a "subject" could become a permanent goal for him. *How can the man Elvis find any meaning in life, when minute by minute he is someone else, someone who required a completely different meaning for his survival than that who "lived" in Elvis in his previous state?* I felt sorry for him.

Dr. N. narrowed his eyes. He looked at me once more and then at Elvis who was just opening the keyboard. We looked once again at one another. The doctor and I locked eyes and then turned our gaze equally toward the vacant armchair. I made the first step as soon as I realized the space was free. By making that step I conquered the doctor's intention to sit in Elvis's spot. I knew it, I knew I conquered the occasion and it made me happy.

When I sat down I could see the doctor's disappointment, which he tried to hide.

I turned back to Elvis in time to savor something that could not be seen since the late 50s. Elvis sung "That's All Right Mama." It was one of his first songs that helped him to succeed in the music industry. It made him a revolutionary and I wondered, *How often do revolutionaries know that they are something that will not be forgotten?*

Perhaps it was the drugs that aided him to reach his youthful exuberance in a state of relaxation as natural as his speech once again. He played with life. He was playing with a power he had within himself that was often hidden even when he played his own songs. His power was not uncontrolled. It was a power felt to the core. Elvis again became one with the song he loved. Now it was visible. How important it was to love what he sang was palpable.

Dr. N. was remote and disgusted. He seemed to be drowning in personal humiliation. He had to be touched by what he saw. I looked at him and saw a small, barely perceptible smile come across his face.

Sweet arose on Elvis' forehead during his performance. He played the piano as an amateur who loves piano rather than a professional. We had no reason not to believe his sentiment.

"This is the will of God!" Elvis screamed before returning to the song.

I was not considering his shouting something about the will of God. Instead, I heard and viewed his voice, the full expression of his body, which seemingly hovered and rippled above the piano.

Now I could have been anyone from the masses. My power didn't enter this realm. This was the real Elvis. His bare and naked and honest talent. Even though it was deceived and misled by life of Elvis "the King" it manifested from time-to-time. You could see predestineation. Sparks flew and entered the souls of his audience. I could only think, *This is beautiful and true.* In that moment, it did not seem real to me! With each touch of the keyboard Elvis appeared to find himself. I saw the man before me. In this moment, he knew who he was and what he wanted. He even winked for us, smiled, and leaned his head back.

Dr. N. began clapping to the beat, so I joined. The music conjoined our contradictory souls but the connection could last only while the King was playing.

We applauded. I believe Elvis was closer to what every man desires. He approached his mental awakening, orgasm, enlightenment, and excitation.

*How could I think so?*

The song had to end but Elvis began to improvise and gave to it only what was in him,

*"I love the world and it is my sense, my friends!*

*My sense, I found it with you, I love my singing!*

*I love flowers, I love the soil, I love clouds.*

*I love the wind in my singing,*

*and my singing, it is the life itself,*

*yes, yes, yes,*

*it's the Life singing, it is the sense flowing off me."*

He sang and meant it. This was his legacy. The genius of his singing could be performed only by a few individuals in the era. He had what every artist desires whether or not anybody is listening, Elvis sung exactly what he wanted at the moment in which he longed.

"That's All Right Mama," was followed by a no-name song. It was a kind of mono-jam, which led him to mental excitation that demonstrated his devotion to his art. In this mental awakening the King barely wondered whether singing was a success. He just did it! Maybe it was a night, maybe a day, we were impressed by his voice and its creations. Sunshine was contained in Elvis as much as it is contained in the dimensionless expression of every genius able to express themselves! The last note came too soon.

We applauded, truly, applauded. Suddenly I did not need anything more than applauding and admiring the King. I forgot for a while why I had come to his estate. Elvis freed me for a moment. For a moment we became just people with Dr. N., who were equal. He did it! We applauded some more. After our last clap, Dr. N. and I at one another and caught our eyes; without Elvis' music our souls had nothing to say.

Elvis stood up from behind the piano and suddenly looked tired. He appeared damaged. It was as if all the sparks abandoned him. He gave his all and supplied us with his energies. This strengthened our understanding of loss a genius experiences in giving their all to the masses or even just a couple humble followers. There stood a white man from Tennessee. The room though still ringing with the chords of his music also contained a gloominess, which wasn't going to get lighter.

I understood Elvis was describing his condition better than any biografist could. The older and more unsettled he was – the more each brilliant performance drained his full glory. Even when able to do shine - immediately after the trance - he suffered enormous losses of personal energy. He was, after all, only one of us. I saw him standing in front of us and appearing weak, stoned, and tired having just performed one of the best performances of his life. I thought quietly, *This is the man who has changed so much. Did he give to the performance more than he could afford? He gave so enormously much into it, and only for two people. Something important is missing here.* I having inner dialogue about his performance and our enjoyment of it while a devastating mental awakening arose after the end it all. *Why? I wondered.*

Maybe he really put as much power, as much wanting, as much resignation into the performance that there was simply not a bit of energy remaining in him. Maybe he put so much of himself into it, he could not continue even in the positive state induced by the maximal excitation of his soul.

I pondered the question now underlining his future and my involvement with him, *Could he do it without the supporting and incentive drugs, or not?*

Elvis lost his balance and caught the keyboard with his right hand causing a cacophonous sound. He literally fell back into the chair from where he had stood up only a moment ago. He landed on his buttocks. It was as if an invisible force wanted him to suffer for each peak performance he provided. His head fell onto his keyboard, adding another cacophonous

sound to the first one. If I wanted to be ironic, I would write that Elvis kissed the keyboard without being aware of it at all. He definitely appeared defeated by the helplessness of being a man and an artist. He still did not lose his metaphysical contact with the piano however – it shone resolute.

Elvis had fainted.

Frightened, I looked at Dr. N. and perceived in his face the same level of fear I felt. The King wouldn't be any good to either of us dead. In that moment we again looked into one another's terror-stricken faces. Nothing was said. It was as if we knew we were both thinking, *Just a few seconds ago we applauded him together.*

Dr. N. was at Elvis's side first. I sat in my chair. It took me a little longer to stand up and move toward the now nearly lifeless genius. In the moment I did rise and then bow toward Elvis' face, the doctor had already checked his pulse and vital signs to understand whether he was okay. "He's unconscious – probably from exhaustion of performing while under sedation. It certainly is not an overdose."

I returned, "We drank about five or six glasses of alcohol."

"But he told me only two," Dr. N. returned without appearing scared, rather he was more obligatorily. He held Elvis' hand and checked his pulse once again.

# 12
# Off to Bed

Dr. N. acted as if nothing major had happened and his peculiar peace helped me to resolve myself to the belief, *All is well at Graceland.* The good doctor stated, "It is not healthy to pump stomach and it is not needed. He needs rest."

"But what should I do?" I retorted.

"Stay with him. If he would like to vomit, turn his head." Dr. N. stood up, straightened his hair with his hand and a familiar glimmer appeared in his eyes "I know what I need to do." Dr. N. walked to the phone, picked up the receiver and dialed a number.

In the first moment, I thought that he was calling an ambulance. But then I realized, before anyone sounded on the opposing telephone, Elvis could not be rushed to the hospital with an overdosed or due to continuously falling. Such an event would cause a sensation nobody in Graceland would want.

"Where is P?" Dr. N. inquired. "Okay. Have him bring a car immediately. We will transport Elvis. Now." He hung up and looked at me. "No worries, this has already happened several times over the last year. It's nothing."

I was thinking about saying, *How can you allow this to happen?* It wasn't the time or place to do so.

"Let's catch him under the armpits." The good doctor commanded.

I could only answer his command, "Yes, sir." But not being under the good doctor's military command I answered with, "Okay."

We caught Elvis' armpits. He showed no sign of life. His was totally unconscious. It he died now, he would probably even not know about it. We were carrying him (rather dragging since his legs were touching the ground) to the door, which was opened by Dr. N. Upon doing so, he nearly dropped Elvis. I had to exert maximum efforts to keep him supported; however, his head uncontrollably hit on my chest. In that moment a strange sound became audible from the King's neck, as if his neck were harmed. I prayed at that moment we wouldn't break his neck trying to muscle him around. Immediately, I remembered drunken unconscious people tend to be more flexible. I presumed Elvis' guardian angel was watching over him and this presented another internal dialogue of irony.

As we bore the weight of the King through the corridors of his castle, we moved between sculptures and paintings I had seen only once before. The entire estate, our place in it, and the rooms we were passing seemed surreal as if they did not exist in my conscious-ness. We were carrying the King. We were slaves saving the life of our Lord.

We continued on into the out of doors where the sun was still shining but was almost setting. At that moment I remembered how much I had drunk alongside of Elvis. With each beam of the sun, I felt the whiskey surface. It was as if I were an animal myself. One I did not have under control. I looked at Elvis and a little madness surfaced.

I envied Elvis. In his deliverance, which pointed nowhere he knew nothing about the sun and how much he had drunk. I envied him. He could bring himself to collapse again and again and again. He could bring himself to the edge of his existence and there would always be someone trying to save him.

The concentration and strength I had to exert to prevent Elvis from falling, was making me relatively sober.

A Cadillac was waiting for us in front of the entrance doorway to Elvis' palace; P. was sitting in it and the door was open. It appeared as if someone was sitting in the back seat. This became a reality when we loaded Elvis into the back seat. A woman was sitting there, but no one, neither P. nor Dr. N., felt a need to introduce us. Under the weight of the moment they probably forgot we should be introduced.

Immediately, after we deposited Elvis into the back seat of the car, the woman took his face into her hands. With tears in her eyes she became . . . "Oh, Elvis . . . Elvis, what's wrong with you? What are you doing to us?" She sobbed. She was a very pretty woman, with big décolletage I'd noticed while loading him into the car. I had looked at her for about a second. I regained my wits though and stopped. *Surely she did not notice I looked at her,* I thought upon releasing him into the car.

She kissed Elvis' face leaving a tear on his cheek. She grabbed his hand but Elvis did not respond. He was sleeping. Dr. N. sat in the car with Elvis. Together, with the woman, they caught his head and the woman lightly touched him. Dr. N. shut the back door. I tried to move to the front door as quickly as possible but it was locked. P. had locked them on purpose as Dr. N. instructed. As P. set the car in motion, Dr. N. called out, "You do not need to go with us." The car did not go to the main gate, it went somewhere into the inner realms of Graceland, *Maybe they have an onsite hospital?* I thought to myself.

# 13

# Colonel Parker

I stood. Dr. N.'s reproach becoming increasingly deafening to my ears. As an agent, I was failing in the current moment; however, Sunday does not come every day. Coinciden-tally, I thought, *today is a -forgotten Sunday.* I didn't know what to do in the moment and my eyes wandered toward the gate, which in the meantime had opened completely. I saw a Cadillac coming toward me from further up the driveway. It was a white Cadillac this time. My heart skipped a beat. I had hoped to see Colonel Parker. It appeared he was coming.

Parker was one of the most important people in my action. His car stopped in front of me. I didn't mind the small amount of suspended dust brought with it. The front window opened and I saw the face I had hoped to see.

"What happened?" He spoke intentionally.

"Elvis fainted. Probably overdosed." I shared unequivocally.

Parker even did not let me finish my words and he opened his door.

Get in.

He extended his hand to me. It did not surprise me (I will explain shortly). What first intrigued me about the Colonel was his white cowboy hat.

I sat down and closed the door.

Parker was a man in years. He had a pudgy face. If you met him, you would hardly be concerned by his appearance.

I'd met him before so I knew what was hidden under his hat . . . baldness, a lot of it. And, his large expressive forehead. There were wrinkles of wisdom there too. He knew how to use them to his advantage. He would shrink them in a way that the viewer would believe he was sensible and well-read; while he hadn't finished primary school. His eyes were small. They were also exaggerated and often super-pragmatic due to his thick black eyebrows. He had a serious double chin. And, the big belly of a *fast food* lover. The Colonel's legs were a little crooked as if he'd rode one too many ponies. They certainly appeared too small for his body and oversized belly.

It appeared Parker loved white because he was wearing all white and driving in an all-white car. He had an ironed white shirt with short sleeves and white shorts with a Playboy bunny on his right side pocket . . . the only off color item was his slippers, which were black.

From time-to-time people I'd meet people who resemble Colonel Parker. The money and success is cleverly obscure but obvious at the same time.

We met two weeks earlier in Vegas.

Shiny hotels, and black women and white women in the streets. Many cars with people who appeared to have conquered the world in freedom . . .

I came to Vegas just to meet the Elvis' manager – to explain to him our mission and that his room was bugged; in fact, his whole world was bugged at that time.

He's sent a *supposedly secret message* he wanted to meet with the Company. I called it supposedly secret message because he thought it was secret and was unaware he'd been on our radar for many years - first through the economic sector . . .

And every man with some secrets found by you can be utilized; so Parker had no choice, albeit Parker needed to be assured he still had choices. He was living in one of the most expensive apartments in the Vegas Hilton.

I didn't make special preparations for Parker. I knew who he was and who he became. He didn't know who I was. He just knew who I worked for. Parker thought when he was paying for tracking and protection services, he was protected from us. To be honest, even then, most services passed the best information for a compensation to people like me.

It was grand, Parker paid good money resulting in better control by my Company, not less because the more security services and secret agents the more we knew without lifting a finger. Isn't that genius?

In this manner; for example, P. received allowances from Parker and from us. There was just one difference between the Company and Parker – he did not know we were giving P. a little more money than he was.

I entered the large hotel spying the noblesse reception desk. Gorgeous women stood everywhere – I approached one of them . . . even before speaking she watched me and took stock of my person from head to toe. I wore casual-blue jeans and a rather old shirt with old black boots. There wasn't a lot of branding going on. The woman didn't appear to gingerly when I approached her after registering my attire. Since, the Hilton has a worldwide reputation – she smiled hard.

"Hello, how can I help you?" She mustered in my direction.

"I am looking for Colonel Parker." I stated my answer seriously while staring into her beautiful blue eyes, which resulted into furthering her forced smile without a break into a sincere and respectful one. Noting the request for Colonel Parker, the sparkle in her eyes changed and she suddenly looked pleased to address me.

"Yes, sir. Colonel Parker is living here. Should I announce you?"

"Of course, we have an appointment."

"Your name, please?"

Her smile was beautiful and uplifting. "I'm Mr. Lane." I answered.

"Thank you, please sit down. After a moment I will come for you."

I sat down on the nearest armchair and watched her walk. Her legs, her ass, her waist, her shoulders and her neck. I sighed. *I'm at work.*

She returned about a minute later, her laughter was not lost, this time it was she who was looking into my eyes almost constantly, even I had to duck with my eyes. I knew already by her conduct that Parker accepted our appointment as agreed.

"Follow me Mr. Lane," she said somewhat provocatively (maybe it was just my feeling). I stood up and I followed her on the way to the elevator. I followed her in the way of an elevator and on the road through one of the many passages of Hilton until we stopped in front of a room with an impressive number 313. Our eyes met again as she knocked.

Her knock was ordinary. I read into her nature by the power of the knock on the door of a wealthy, powerful, tenant. I didn't gaze back at her.

Colonel Parker opened the door. He did not impress me as much as he did my companion – she appeared extremely devoted for those few seconds. I saw an elderly man who cast an insignificant look at me and immediately transferred his gaze to my companion. He liked her, he would surely prefer to invite her in but that was understandable.

The front desk assistant looked at me. I knew she wanted a tip. I gave her ten dollars. "Thank you." She said in a manner where I presumed she'd expected more. As she turned, she cast a last smile at Parker and then at me. As she walked away, before our first handshake, both Parker and I looked at her ass. And generally, at anything, she could offer us. The woman disappeared leaving only thoughts of her in our minds.

"Come in Mr. Lane." Parker instructed me.

I entered. There were rooms of rooms. Everything appeared to be similar to a Hollywood movie set - very luxurious. I was surprised it did not bother me – all the excess. It was only when I looked around the room, I noticed Parker holding a glass in his hands with some alcohol. Comfort versus attention.

"Would you?" He noticed my eye, so he asked.

"Yes." I replied as simply as possible.

It's a very important answer because when a man is getting acquainted with another man – there's an anticipation for verbal sparring – like a game. The best thing to do is to agree if asked about having a drink with the host.

The Colonel filled my glass and put it in my hands.

"Oh, I forgot to ask whether you put ice . . ." He trailed off.

"No, thank you." I did not care for ice at all.

It was strange the room impressed me more than the person for I came to Vegas to see but locations can be that way. I had no reason to be afraid of Parker. I knew his personality from an initial observation. I knew where his maximum was. At times, one look is all you need to know someone. I wasn't certain I cared for Parker at all. He was an avenue of access and that was all that was important but Parker didn't know. He considered himself an important person. And that was my advantage.

"You like it?" Parker queried about my drink – I hadn't acknowledged it yet.

Parker's eyes narrowed. He drank his glass that was almost empty and put it down. It landed strongly and heard the blow of glass on glass but it nothing broke. Finally, the Colonel extended his hand and I extended mine.

His grip was strong. Each of us attempted to have the stronger grip without making it wholly for the other.

"I'm Colonel Parker."

"Yes, and I'm Peter Lane." I responded.

"Well," he started as if he felt my name was not essential. "They call me Colonel because I once fought for the United States Army." Parker obviously did not realize who was he was speaking with - I had the accurate information regarding his past. He had never fought for the US Army. His statement amused me. The Company has found he was born in a caravan of a carousel owner in West Virginia or in the Netherlands in the town of Breda. The year of his birth remained a mystery – it was either 1909 or 1910.

"Well that's interesting." I said as if it wasn't interesting at all.

"I see you don't have problems with sincerity." Parker retorted more to himself than to me. He jerked the corner of his mouth and I smirked slightly.

"So, Mr. Lane . . .?"

Yes, Colonel . . . I realize you must not be happy to be bugged and to know you are being watched?"

"Of course," was his response.

"But you know why if I'm not mistaken."

"Perhaps. Perhaps I do, Mr. Lane."

"I know you have a good indication."

"You know a lot." Parker used irony.

"Well, so do you, Colonel."

"May I know why you're hunting after the gold lamb?" The Colonel stepped up his game. "Mr. Lane, why don't you let us alone?"

"Well, this is America. Land of the Free. And, while you are clean or perform what you have to perform, Colonel . . ."

"You know Mr. Lane, I know many senators. I have strong contacts. Bugging me and Elvis is a disgrace. It could be very bad for you."

"So . . .?"

"Pardon?" Parker was taken back.

"You know, when somebody is dirty and robs taxpayers who buy records?"

"You probably have not understood me." Parker furthered.

"This is not about words, Mr. Parker, this is about evidence that cannot be erased."

"What are you talking about?" The Colonel raised an eyebrow.

"I am here sir, to reach an agreement. This depends on you Colonel Parker."

"If you have something to tell me . . . tell me . . . so we understand one another Mr. Lane."

I smiled a winning smile. "There are too many tax havens is the world, Colonel, aren't there?"

"Too many." Now he shared a winning smile with a certainty of victory. "Everything is clean, everything . . ." He added.

"Are you certain?" I highlighted the *are you* and minced it with a little mockery. I succeeded in unnerving the Colonel.

"I am certain Mr. Lane." He answered struggling to convince himself.

"Why did you move to the Bahamas Colonel? Was it to have some money laundering company access?"

The Colonel's eyes narrowed. "It cannot be proven." He answered. "With the help of banks in the service of the government there anything is achievable. I mean . . . if someone wanted to . . . you know . . . but not me. You have no clue about how it works. You are too young to have . . ." his sentence trailed off bearing a seed of uncertainty.

I smiled. I didn't need to answer. "You know, some forces can't be reached by even senators Colonel."

"Are you kidding me?"

"No." I replied wryly without the slightest doubt I was misleading my asset.

Parker looked me over another time. This time, as if he'd just met me. It appeared he had hundreds of questions running through his mind but he remained quiet instead.

I had to get him into the conversation once more – after his initial shock subsided I continued … "But, Mr. Parker, we need you, because, in spite of everything, you have a simple truth."

The Colonel did not know how to feel and asked, "Which simple truth?"

"You were right, Colonel, when you talked about the golden lamb." I purposely didn't finish the thought. I lifted my head a little firmly looking at Colonel Parker. Then raised my eyebrows and opened my eyes wider so my forehead knitted as much as possible.

The Colonel's reaction was exactly as I'd anticipated, "What but?"

"Well, if you have something that is tarnished and you want to make it clean again, it depends on you, doesn't it? It depends on what is asked of you. You know the tabloids affect listeners. A lot of those are taxpayers. Even if only such a minor thing as buying records."

Parker's interest rose, "Well, go on …" He filled his glass once more but didn't ask me whether I wanted another drink.

"We've got information our American Boy – the golden lamb as you call him - has some issues lately. I believe you know what I mean. His career has to continue on a positive path in order for us to make the best use of his talents. Elvis has to remain an American success story and you need to ensure he does. We cannot lose him or his credibility as a solid, stalwart, America's son."

"What do you want me to do?" The Colonel's voice was much more saturated and fuller voice than earlier in our visit.

"America needs Elvis to continue to put on his best face Colonel. We don't need to talk much, it's just for the benefit of our nation and the worldwide society at large we need our golden lamb to remain, well … golden – without any tarnish."

Parker ran his hand across his forehead narrowing his eyes, "This will never change …"

"I assure you Colonel, this is in the best interests of the state."

He returned with a grin. "In the interests of the state? Well, gosh. Your business always uses young guys who work to trick you." He stood and shook his head. "If I understand you want to hear from me I will not make any trouble?"

"Yes, that's it, no trouble – no problems for you or me or any of us … right."

He continued shaking his head but smiled. "When would you start?"

"Within the next two weeks. I will be getting a position as a security guard. In this manner I'll have direct contact to Elvis."

"And, how will you approach him? Without me, it won't work you know."

I nodded.

"From the commercial aspect you'll be satisfied with my security work. We need Elvis to make a new, wholesome, good album. This will introduce the new Elvis, Colonel. And since you do nothing …"

"Any warranties, Mr. Lane?"

"Elvis will not be presented in the media as a man who robs America Colonel, and you'll be enabled to continue in that role and live the life you like to live."

Parker shot his innovative look at me. This time I did not know what to think, I did not know what was going in his inside.

"May I have another glass?" I preferred to ask so I didn't feel insecure, so I didn't wait with empty hands. He filled my glass but I did not know what to think. "We'll see. When I am on board, support anything I try with Elvis - indicate you agree." I got a taste to leave after this statement. I said what I needed to say. More words were useless. I drank the remainder of my drink and with a stone-face I closed . . . "You are in agreement with my offer." Parker smiled like a prisoner the day before execution and then extended his hand. At that moment Elvis' fate was sealed.

I extended my note of departure and opened the door not looking back and only sent a solemn, "Goodbye." I closed the door. No one was in the hallway. As an agent I had successfully completed this phase of my assignment. I stood alone in the Vega Hilton hallway where the richest people in America and the world visit from time-to-time. My thoughts were drawn back to the woman who introduced me to Parker. As I rode the elevator, I thought about her. I stopped thinking about Elvis and Parker. And, the music played in the elevator.

As the elevator door opened I saw many faces and then there was the woman I considered on my ride down to the lobby. Suddenly, I knew what I wanted. I walked around her. She was standing near the exit I was headed toward. She noticed me walk around her and pretended not to have done so. "Goodbye, Miss. Another time maybe . . . " I said in passing.

She said nothing.

"There is nothing more meeting someone ever so briefly and feeling a connection you cannot act on.

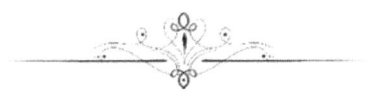

# 14
# A New Beginning

Sitting in the white Cadillac, the Colonel drove onward. I did not know to where but I was happy to be on our way to Elvis.

"How much did he take?" The Colonel asked.

"Enough."

"He looked bad."

"Yes, he did."

"This is your tactic?"

For a long time I did not answer.

"Why don't you answer?" Colonel asked irritably.

"I told you in Vegas Colonel what we wanted to achieve; this drug activity is not what we want."

The car stopped in the dust somewhere on Graceland but we didn't leave the boundaries of Elvis' isolation. The moment where the Colonel opened the door, I breathed in slight disappointment.

The Colonel departed quickly. I opened the door after he closed his. I followed him and headed toward a small house, which from the outside looked like a tool shed for storing horticultural equipment. It was a small bungalow. It could hardly have more than three rooms. Its plaster actually did not exist. Its color was faded. Everything in Graceland I'd seen was impressive and beautiful and well maintained. This bungalow was just the opposite.

The door was closed. There was an old rounded handle, which could not be turned so it could not be opened even if not locked. The Colonel had keys; he opened the door and looked back to see if I'd caught up to him.

"See what you can do to help." Rang from Colonel Parker who now appeared to be a father of a child in crisis.

We walked into a hall and there were no windows. One lone bulb shone; it was enough for us to see two people who stood in front of us.

The woman who had driven off with Elvis was there and also P.

I realized I hadn't seen a car on the access road to the bungalow and wondered where it had disappeared. The special beauty of the woman grabbed my attention. She turned to-ward us.

P. had turned too but he didn't interest me as much as she did.

The woman greeted Parker. It was a polite greeting but I could not help noticing the greeting was kind of salinity seared with rejection. It could be seen in her view, on her lips, in her beauty, in her sensitivity.

She looked at me, and continued with what she was doing. As I came up with Parker, apparently she considered me his ally. She did not greet other than a nod. I answered with a similar action, while looking in her eyes.

I think approximately at this time Parker realized he had to explain why I came with him up to the hidden chamber of the king:

"This is Peter Lane, I hired him to help Elvis."

I threw a wild look, full of surprises, at the Colonel. He smiled at me aware of his power. My gaze immediately changed to a look of recognition and gratitude. I replied to his small smile with my own small smile.

The woman interrupted us when she ironically, while also sadly asked Parker, "How to help, Colonel?"

"To get him out of those shit, honey . . ." He answered.

The woman settled her gaze on me. She focused on my eyes where she shortly began and also ended looking into them longer than usual. She returned her gaze to Parker.

After Parker's words that he hired me himself to help Elvis, P. knitted his forehead but didn't say a word . . . He was a wise man and probably realized Parker knew something about me, although he may not have really cared at all. I felt his momentary glance at my shoulders, but I was satisfied with P.'s silence, he fulfilled his role as he should. He was not tedious, he was silent.

Parker suddenly recovered and appeared enlightened with social recognition. When looking at the woman he realized I didn't know her. He nodded in her direction while sharing, "Priscilla, wife of Elvis."

Again I nodded in return. She did not smile. I extended my hand to her and she extended her hand to me as well. I pressed gently.

"Are you another psychologist?" She asked inquisitively.

I looked at Parker and my eyes touched on P.'s face as well; I noticed he grinned in return. Parker's face remained constant without any response to the women's another psychologist rhetorical question. I hadn't read anything about psychiatrists or psychologist around Elvis – and didn't know what to think about Priscilla's question but I answered her anyhow, "No, I'm a philosopher." I mustered a serious voice.

"A philosopher? At least someone is trying to make me laugh tonight. You know because each of us here is a philosopher. Are you something like Nietzsche? Are we living like nihilists with Elvis is far ahead of us?" A sadness strained through her exaggerated voice. It was obvious she was making a joke of my comment. Her voice was spicy. I glanced at her in a more studious manner, she was sad and worried about her husband. I could only think of how engaging she must have been to have cornered the Kings' attention. Her one sentence relaxed me resulting in a mental chagrin.

"I graduated in philosophy – really," I retorted with the ego of a wounded man.

"Oh. Well, I don't think that changes anything." I felt her tired soul speaking silently.

This was interrupted by Parker, who questioned . . . "Where is my king?"

"He's in the next room." Priscilla responded. She appeared to be certain Dr. N. was the only source who could inform the Colonel Elvis was once again gone for the moment but I bet on P. who shook his head whilst bending it to look at me.

"I'll rather wait outside. There's bad air in here. Should I keep the door open? The air here is outrageous." Nobody responded the question of whether he should leave the door open. P. appeared to be a close confessor for Elvis' wife.

The moment at which P. shut the door behind him – the Colonel walked toward the door behind where Elvis was parked.

The woman said nothing.

Being P., I would try to help Priscilla as much as I could, and I would not depart noting her reliance on him but . . . I was not P.

The Colonel opened the door. Rays of sunshine penetrated the hall. I stood to an angle seeing Elvis lying on the bed with Dr. N. still standing over him.

Parker entered the room and I decided to join him. As I approached, I passed the woman. Her fragrance was alluring. It refreshed me.

What Parker was observing in full view was extremely depressive. Having someone else there, even me, seemed to help. He did appear to care about the golden lamb after all but what we saw would move the guts of any person. Elvis was panting on the bed. He sighed painfully. His eyes flowed with tears. His hands trembled in spite of the fact that they were put on the bed next to his body. He didn't see us. He appeared to be in a trance of pain at the bottom of his soul.

Dr. N. held a syringe in his hands. When he noticed us he was not frightened. He did not expect us but he visibly didn't care whether or not he could see us. At least it appeared that way when looking at him. He held no expression.

He spoke up catching my stare, "There is nothing here to interest you."

"What are you doing with him?" Parker asked without any sign of despair in his voice.

"This is just to calm him. He needs it, poor guy, he needs his stomach pumped out twice a week now. This is too much even for a bull." He said it as if he were a village veterinarian.

"Doctor, I guess you are not doing your job as well as you are paid to do. We are paying you to avoid something like this." The Colonel sounded adamant.

*Was Parker honest?!* I wondered quietly.

The Colonel's words did not disturb Dr. N. He answered with a gaze that clearly said: "Guy, if I did not, but I do . . ."

"What is the matter with you all . . . what is going on . . .!" Elvis' wife joined the flow of emotions. Her voice was and her demeanor was immersed in sorrow.

Elvis' eyes were open but he didn't see to see anything. He looked toward the sky.

All of us were looking at Elvis; I thought to rank the levels of heartlessness at that moment as follows:

1.  Dr. N. – he was administrating numbness like Elvis was an inanimate object
2.  Parker – he was using human feelings devoid of conscience while exploiting a man who needed to be loved
3.  Me – they gave him drugs, while I wanted him to return to his music campaign
4.  Elvis' wife – I could see the fourteen year old girl somewhere in her. The more I returned to her a kind of coldness spread, of a woman who was just one step from abandoning her feelings. She seemed to have lost her fight for her husband and an ordinary life.

She spoke up, "I needn't see this. Finally, you'll all kill him," she said with a certainty. And, in her statement was no sign of pain, rather anger and disillusionment. Here and now her beauty and charm did not mean anything at all to anyone. Even her words did not interest anyone. She was aware of the fact – it was all Elvis. She didn't catch Elvis' hand, nor gave him a kiss. Instead, she left as a woman whom nobody needs who needs nobody. She walked away without tears and without a scene. No one reviewed her departure. She left her suffering husband behind. I assumed she'd stayed with him more times than she dared count and now – it was just better to leave.

Elvis was wheezing with open eyes.

"It will not be long, I'll soon bring him to his feet." The good doctor shared. It was as if a real life Frankenstein was standing in front of the Colonel and I.

Parker didn't say a word. He seemed to perceive the passing time with Elvis as a manager needing results.

Dr. N. devoted one medical view of faith in the new injection.

They both appeared to enjoy their control over Elvis. I saw it in their faces. Parker perceived the injection as beauty. In that moment, I described him as a perverse man who felt pleasure when he saw someone become a victim of more and more drugs. I think they both of them gave to the destruction of Elvis something of their personalities. Maybe they loved him and didn't sense the destruction. I saw these two people in front of me and they were like viruses behaving intelligently as they sucked the life out of Elvis Presley believing they were giving him the cure.

"A little adrenaline never hurts. I'm sure that this specialty will help him." Dr. N. looked at Parker with a self-confident smile.

"The more pleasure in the blood of Elvis, the more adrenaline in my blood doctor but if it helps him . . ." Parker patted the doctor's shoulder – he seemed satisfied the doctor was working some magic.

Although Elvis' eyes were open all the while since our arrival – it was only now that they moved. He winked as his eyes began to return to life and look for something in the room to focus on body.

They found me and then turned away from me. As his head turned away from me, it also turned away from everyone in the room. Elvis found a space where nothing could observe him. He looked at the wall and cried. We could hear him crying and it was a real cry. The kind that rises from the pit of a person's soul from some deep place inside your being that is beyond rationality. Actually, he sobbed. This was the sound of a man who lost everything that could be lost.

Dr. N. appeared content with his results. He licked his lips and smiled in satisfaction. He packed up whatever he had used to rescue Elvis from his nothingness.

"Well you know, art simply cannot be done round the clock." The Colonel snapped.

"My life is not honest. This is not my life. My God, I do not know who I am. I cannot stand it. Help me. I cannot bear it another day. I cannot endure myself, my body and cannot stop lying – and . . . you . . . are helping me do that." Elvis was clamoring to make sense of his insensibilities.

I thought to myself, *Elvis is honest; what an injection they gave him and then suggesting he'll be better.*

"Elvis, no one is deceiving you here. You are deceiving yourself." Colonel Parker was defiant.

It seemed ruthless but maybe he thought he was right in what he was saying – it was a difficult scene for all of us.

Dr. N. had even no reason to join the dialogue. He packed everything up and just stood in the middle of the room. "I'm hungry, gentlemen, if you please, I'm going to eat." The good doctor didn't fire off any pretenses – he didn't pretend but was his statement a private message to the Colonel or better yet, to Elvis?

Parker's words fell dead ground.

Elvis turned – his face exhibited small red spots.

Both the Colonel and I looked at the doctor who was waving his hands while saying, "Its okay" before departing.

The atmosphere in the room was unbearable.

Elvis became more and more reserved, he turned toward the Colonel, "No, no, I need your hand . . ." Parker seemed to be waiting just for that. He clasped Elvis' hand and their palms were immersed in one another's. The Colonel's countenance altered while holding Elvis' hand and accepting his suffering.

Suddenly I I was hungry too but I didn't feel like eating. About thirty seconds passed without words.

"I'm leaving. I'll be waiting outside. This is a little much for me." I spoke in a broken voice – I allowed myself to feel the suffering I was witnessing. Suddenly, the doctor stuck his head back in the door and asked, "Is there anybody I should give a ride to?"

Parker nodded at me. Neither I nor Dr. N. said anything further the afternoon's events had emptied us. I was happy neither of us had to acknowledge one another, until the doctor spoke up . . .

"I allowed myself a break, I worked enough for today . . ." Dr. N. was resolute in his own regard.

P. sat quietly in an old chair staring and quiet.

As I opened the door to the out-of-doors the last rays of the sun liberated me somewhat. Elvis' wife sitting in front of me.

She was alone – perhaps enjoying the freedom of solitude. I knew I had to make a choice either to address her, sit nearby to talk or go for a walk or leave her be. I decided that it was not the time nor place to address Elvis' wife. I opted to walk a bit and leave her in peace but Priscilla surprised me and began to speak.

"Do you really want to help him?"

I turned around and met sad attractive eyes, "Yes, it is my mission." I smiled without a hint of insincerity on my face knowing full-well she wouldn't understand the "mission" part of my statement and how absolutely honest I was being..

"You are doing this for money?" She asked. It was obvious trust wasn't a thing she invested in.

"Maybe you'll not believe me, but I love Elvis' music." I responded.

She looked at the ground and shook her head. "You know he has a bad conscience – it is the reason for this madness."

"Maybe I do."

"Yeah, maybe."

"But I'm here to help the real Elvis rise to the surface and create work he believes in – not just for the marketability."

She shook her head again.

"I don't know whether you are naive or just another fool employed by Parker but you don't know how serious this mess it now. Are you being paid a lot?"

"Depends on the album and how well he recovers."

"My God, you've seen him. He'll die soon at this rate." Her voice and facial expressions indicated she needed to speak more for herself than to me.

"Die? Well, we'll all die eventually." I answered with a straight face.

She raised her head and looked me in the eyes, "I'm not ready to love a dead man Mr. Lane."

"You know I like that Priscilla – that's a good statement."

"Pardon?"

"What you just said, its positive, a good statement. I think you know only a naive young woman was allowed to love Elvis."

"Why are you with Elvis?" She breathed in while adding, "I know why I'm with Elvis and maybe I was naive but I'm not today."

"So, do you think he isn't wasting his talent?"

"There are many people who waste their talents and Elvis has given so much

"Do you think Elvis is dying for the life he dreamed as a kid?"

She smiled. "Well, if you think he is wasting his talent, how is he doing it

"He is wasting his talent because he is wasting his life – he appears lost halfway between his youth and his dreams. IF he doesn't restart his course, he'll die a wreck . . .

"He is dying as a wreck." Priscilla declared, while adding . . . "You probably are a philosopher but let's talk rationally."

"From my perspective in the short amount of time I've been with Elvis, he is unique. There probably are not a lot of individuals who are like him. But, he appears to feel lost in his own discoveries. I noticed there is nobody like him and that is a lonely place to be."

"I think that you have seen well," she responded.

I looked at her and she only noticed my gaze only for a second before hanging her head once more. She bit her lip but not in desperation - rather as somebody trying to think of something more to say.

"He is not himself anymore – aren't all kings are like that – they lose themselves?" Her voice was low and cautious.

"I've seen him perform in the past and now – I agree – things have changed." I sighed.

"Although I love him, perhaps too much, part of me is wanting distance. It may be a defense mechanism."

She looked at my face seemingly seeking an answer . . . whether to continue or not. I was a stranger and people tend to bare their souls to strangers. I was all too content to listen.

"There is nothing worse than when you love someone but it doesn't work. A lot of animosity develops."

I narrowed my eyes and asked, "So you have a love / hate relationship now or do you hate yourself for loving him."

"I don't know for certain – you seem to understand what I am saying. I love him but it is useless he doesn't recognize me as a joy in his life. It has become pain and more pain."

"You regret your marriage to Elvis?"

"You are asking too many questions now." She winced. "Yes, I do regret a too early marriage as a child and I do regret this situation. I'm a mother now. I need a human being, husband, and father than I need a king. Especially a king who believes normal life is sinful and futile. Eventually, all of us want to be ordinary, otherwise only misery waits for us. I want an ordinary marriage and family but I'll never be able to have one."

"Maybe it is your age Priscilla – a stage of development more than the entire situation."

"There is a big age difference between us and you, Mr. Lane are younger still. I am the wife of the king of rock n' roll but he's not ruling the castle very well. And, as the queen I don't have a lot of power to change things."

I had the feeling that we should move forward and asked a final question, "Priscilla . . . when did he actually began to decline? What started his path to the person he is today?"

She finally laughed while adding, "You are a piece of work Mr. Lane."

I answered, "You make me talk strangely I guess." Gently I smiled an honored man still waiting for his response.

She began, "I knew him as a girl. I young. I was innocent. He was too. I feel in love when I met him and believed it would remain like it was forever. I was too young to think other-wise."

"So then your baby – this was due to being young and innocent as well – believing the family plan was the best way to go?"

She lifted her head . . . "No, I was somewhere else. I have talents. If you are asking if I wanted to have Elvis' baby," she swallowed . . . "definitely not when conception took place but, of course, I wanted my baby. I mean I was only 21 when I became pregnant but you know I began seeing Elvis at 14 and a half years of age. I moved to Graceland at age 18 and then we married when I was 21 and I was pregnant six months later. Of course, I wanted to be a wife, a mother and a homemaker but Elvis is always gone and when he isn't physically gone now, he's mentally gone."

"Well, for a woman, you are a complex thinking Mrs. Presley . . ." I wanted to make her laugh.

"Is that supposed to be a compliment?"

It wasn't the reaction I'd intended.

Our eyes met with a short silence somewhere in the middle of our dialogue.

"So you are suffering, I hear that. But the suffering is something you can defeat, I believe he can get better. And, you have a beautiful daughter – so you have gained a lot."

"Yes, I love my daughter, she is my deliverance."

"When you see her, do you see Elvis?"

"Of course. I see the Elvis I fell in love with. I try to block out the bad. I'll go crazy if I don't. And, I'll tell you one thing, I want my to protect my daughter this situation – there is nothing worse as far as I can see, than a man who thinks he is so exceptional that he forgets the real miracles in his life."

"Well, Priscilla, I am here because Elvis wants to return to his former self. As of yet, he isn't capable. I'm here as a last resort. I believe he has a chance."

She peered at me in a stark manner.

"Well . . . why not. He has nothing else. All that is left is his faith in the music. He had a dream to sing sincere music. I think he lost that in all the glamor. He believed, you know and if a person believes something they survive the impossible. But now, I'm uncertain he has the strength."

"He needs you Priscilla and *you do still love him.*"

"I know these things. I just feel he may die soon. Nothing is holding him here – not me – not his daughter. His fame and success are not real enough for him and haven't made him feel free. In his case, his beloved music, is the last thing that has remained true to him and he occasionally can't bear it and he hates it, which makes life difficult with him – as you can see. And, he is afraid of it. He was afraid of loving me at one stage of our relationship. He thought he was going to destroy me."

"Okay, I hear you but how did believe he was afraid of loving you? Maybe I can understand more if you explain this to me."

"He told me once he should not love anyone because he was not able to do so."

"Was he?"

"Well . . . he tried but he seemed to finally give up. I'm not angry at him. I understand him. You see, how can someone living in an unreal world believing in too much . . . how can a person like that love ordinarily in the real world?" She breathed in. "Still . . . it makes me sad. He wants to be just Elvis. He wants to be the King but he also wants to be protected from the world. And, by the King I mean the Elvis in his heart. I tried to use my family as protection but it wasn't enough for him."

"Well, this is a dilemma of even ordinary people without the complications he faces. Sometimes a quite ordinary person has a problem living in this world. It is not all that uncommon to be uncomfortable in one's skin."

"From day-to-day Elvis can choose to escape from reality or live it. The people around him don't sleep with him or live with him. And, they simply encourage him to live his way whether it is good or bad for him. If he just opened his eyes a bit. When he is clean and sober he's quite a different man. He is the man I love."

"Aha."

"What!?"

"You're saying when he's clean . . ."

"He wants to love me but he cannot do it in this world he has created or that has been created around him."

I pontificated. *Here we are sitting on the steps of Elvis' home where he is existing as a virtual zombie version of himself – sharing a philosophical discussion about him – while he remains unaware of these truths."*

"Priscilla, why exactly are you sitting here? When I saw you leaving, I thought you were intending to disappear as far from here as possible."

"I still need to support my husband and I don't have the strength to walk away now. I just needed to be alone and away from seeing him in that way."

"You'll don't really seem to want to live with him anymore from our discussion, Priscilla."

Our eyes met again. She nodded reluctantly – it was obvious she was intending to leave.

"Yes, I've actually left already." She took a deep breath. "For a while I tried to live with him believing the boyish sincerity still existed. It took quite a while for me to realize it wasn't. I've already left him. I am living next to him but I'm already gone. I never thought it would happen. Never thought it would happen to us. Never thought it would happen to me."

The door opened. Parker came outside. Elvis was behind him appearing refreshed.

"Any autographs?" He asked abashedly.

Parker gave us a wink. He was visibly satisfied.

"Do you think you're on a concert tour?" Priscilla's question had a humorous undertone minced with sarcasm and bitterness.

"It's hard, you people, come on." Replied Elvis. In his response he looked at Priscilla as if he hadn't seen us.

I looked at Parker and he just shook his head. I could read in his eyes . . . No more questions today . . . .

Elvis made notice of his wife sitting next to me. "I've never had a wife, have I?"

"I'm your wife."

"I know you are Priscilla. Where have you been? I can have as many women as I want but where have you been?"

I saw a new side to Elvis on display now.

"Come on, Elvis. Just come. You need to take a break. No women. This has been a challenging day." Parker barked at the scene.

"I don't know. All women. But I needed and never had . . . love . . ."

"Yes, you did. Yes, you do. Just come on now Elvis. No women right now. Only us men. All right?"

Priscilla's face was corpse-like in color, she remained stoic.

Parker embraced Elvis and Elvis did the same. They walked to the car.

Meanwhile, P. approached us. He looked at Elvis' wife.

"I thought you've already gone . . . I'm sorry."

"It's okay P., I am used." Her response was cold.

P. looked at me askance. He said nothing. He returned his attention to Priscilla.

"Here are the keys. Take him. Give him a free room. The car is behind the house in the shade. I'm going with them. If by chance something . . ." He trailed off after speaking as a man who knew her well.

"Will he sleep?" She asked bravely.

"Probably not now – we are going to look around somewhere . . . you know."

P. put his hand on Priscilla's shoulder. He nodded at me. He ran to catch up with Parker and Elvis in time to catch the other side of his shoulders. They were a trio marching toward the sunset.

P. seemed to be a slave for both men. Elvis seemed to be a slave to Parker and Parker . . . well the Colonel was the Colonel. As far as I knew, Parker seldom entertained with Elvis. Most recently, Elvis' entertainment reached different contours to Parker's tastes. The worst part was there were many women who loved Elvis in his current state. They loved the King and the strength he represented as an icon. And, those women didn't ask a lot of questions or make a lot of demands. They'd never know the real Elvis. And, the woman who did, she remained suppressed on the verge of a mental breakdown but there was a degree of tranquility in her voice. In any case, I was certain it was extremely hard for her to control herself. The pain she felt had to be eating her alive.

"Come on. I'm hungry. I think you should be too." This was a way to break our silence. Neither of us were hungry after the recent events. We climbed into the car and went back to the main house.

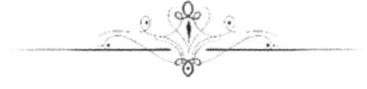

# 15
# The High Life

After everything I'd just seen - Elvis didn't appear to be desirous of performing any great anti-social work. However, in my line of work, one could never know for certain. I thought of the album, *How Great Thou Art* and realized it was proof how an artist works for the establishment even when supporting a religion.

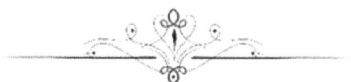

If I said our ride to the main house lasted a minute I would be telling the truth. Priscilla's door slammed and her hands shook so much she couldn't hit the ignition keyhole but then she floored it . . .

She swore for the first time . . . "What a @@#0$ life."

I remained silent. She attracted me and I felt it best I remain quiet. I did not want to make love with her . . . I felt for her. Therefore, I remained silent as if I was ready to listen.

"How can I bear this?" She stated without a desire for a response – it was more of a validation.

*Many people suffer similar kitschy* . . . I thought to myself, I did not want to talk. I could tell her suffering was nothing compared to suffering of people in Vietnam for instance – I knew it was a fleeting sadness – I knew she'd survive it and philosophizing it all wouldn't help *her today while she suffered the most from her perspective. That's* all life is – a matter of perspective, I thought again while I peered out the windshield. But again, she surprised me . . .

"You know, the worst part is, I suffer because everyone thinks I am living off Elvis and I'm not here for that."

I knew I should remain quiet . . . "Elvis is living off the . . . too . . ."

"Well, thank you. You'd better stop there. We better just be quiet."

The car stopped. Priscilla stopped talking and waited for me to get out of the car.

"Come on, Priscilla. Let's go inside. Its life . . . you are living life. It will get better."

"I can't be alone. Not now. I've had enough solitude for a lifetime. I need to talk. If Parker is paying you, I intend to put his services to use."

"Priscilla, I am here, it is fine with me . . . okay . . . with pleasure." I answered but has a sense of surprise.

There was prolonged silence. She led me through corridors some of them I'd traversed earlier in the day. In any case, I noted a disjointed journey and felt my interest wane more toward this woman walking beside me.

She was not very tall. Her black hair was not well-arranged. Her makeup was missing. When quite close to her I noticed her teeth were not completely white – there was a yellowing and she hadn't recently brushed . . . nothing unbearable . . . despite it all, she really attracted me. I was a little uncomfortable. A little nervous. My mission, after all was with Elvis – not Priscilla. She didn't speak while walking except one sentence, "I cannot stand it here anymore."

At that moment I felt like telling her the truth . . . my truth. She had charisma and sparkle undoubtedly because men tell the truth to women with charisma and sparkle when it comes to them – I found myself malingering to tell all; however, I controlled myself. Instead I retorted, "Perhaps you are not the only one here with the same problem."

She looked at me rejecting my statement. "I'll tell you something but when we sit down to talk." She spoke persuasively.

I believed she wanted to tell me something I certainly didn't know. I smirked. My mood was improving. We walked for about thirty seconds longer. Sometimes I looked at her face but didn't see signs of release. She opened the door to her room.

"You don't sleep with Elvis?" I queried.

"No. I don't sleep with him anymore. We don't sleep together."

Her room was simply furnished. A bed opposite the window with a cot next to the bed. I had the desire to ask where the baby slept but changed my mind. She replied to my look.

"The baby is with our nanny." She didn't speak like a mother. She said it as a woman who wanted to her room just for herself. I didn't find her statement appealing but I wasn't talking with her daughter.

"Sit where you want."

She left to her bathroom. I looked at her ass as she departed. Even though she'd given birth she was quite attractive and fit. When she opened the bathroom door, I noted it was covered with wallpaper like the walls. Anyone who wasn't familiar with her room would have a time finding the door – it seemed to blend into the wall.

Her room was equipped with a television and only one picture. It was of Elvis from 1955 or 1956. The image appeared reminiscent of a Presidential photo. In the room where his unsatisfied wife lived - it was more than peculiar.

The wallpaper was a pattern of roses. They were red on a white background. My eyes fell toward the carpet. It was very expensive. I touched it with my fingertips because where I stood I could feel its softness under my shoes. I touched it while sitting on the bed.

The bed was violet with various ornaments and resembled the Distant East. As I raised my hand, still sitting on the bed, Mrs. Presley walked out of the bathroom without any visible signs of arranging.

"The painting, I must have it here. If I didn't hang it here, Elvis would be very angry at me."

"Angry?"

"I am still living from his money." There isn't any coercion – it is just a respect thing.

She sat at the opposite pole of the bed.

"How does he accept you're not living with him?"

"Hard, very hard."

"And isn't his condition a bit a result of your moving away from him, while still living in the same house?"

She did not respond. It was obvious my question disconcerted her.

"You are asking as if someone who cares for the improvement of his condition. Just to let him issue great music that means something more? Or to let him live a fulfilling life?"

"I'm in your room. Why do you think I'm here?"

"Am I attracting you?"

"Yes, you are but I did not come here because you attract me."

"Oh . . . men do not speak so too often . . . so . . . so why are you here?"

"Even in this room while I'm with you - Elvis is here. In fact, Priscilla, he's right there." I motioned to the wall.

I was working to avoid a debate regarding what was a seemingly mutual attraction – we could make love together – even if nobody would forbid it. However, it wouldn't be beneficial for my mission.

She added, "You are kind of like talking with a woman." She grimaced.

"Like a woman? Maybe . . . or maybe like a principled man."

She smiled in return – it was a painful smile.

"I just need a hug from someone foreign. You think I would make love with you? I'm not that kind . . ."

I didn't let her finish her statement, "You don't appear to be coming on to me – I understand. I respect you Priscilla. It's been a difficult afternoon."

I was sorry our dialogue shifted so dramatically – I truly felt she'd wanted to have a heart-to-heart but she was distracted now.

"Do you think that I'm an attractive woman?"

I did not like her question – every woman still knows how men perceive her, doesn't she. "All women know if they are felt to be attractive Priscilla – don't you know?"

"You would be surprised. Marriage makes a woman insecure."

"Well, only those who allow it do so."

She shook her head. "Elvis never liked strange men looking at me."

"Is he very jealous?" I inquired.

"He used to be."

I swallowed. "You've mentioned lovemaking – perhaps you miss love and the man you love."

"I hope not."

She looked at me. After a few seconds I worked to look elsewhere.

"Yes. I miss it because I'm an ordinary woman. There's nothing wrong with it we're both adults. You know what I mean."

"Yes." I swallowed. I seemed a little nervous and uncertain in the proximity of her body. "I'm not acquainted with the circumstances here but what you are saying terrifies me somewhat." I added.

She was smart. She understood my nervousness. Any woman notices when a man is nervous of her. Concurrently, I wanted to avoid dialog on sex and sexual life.

She looked at me. She was obviously becoming more confident as my discomfort rose. Unfortunately, she did not cross her legs. I would have preferred her legs crossed. In her eyes I saw she was interested in me but not in a sexual manner. She saw something mysterious in me. I was sure from her look.

Our eyes met again. This time I didn't turn my eyes and asked her, "Does Elvis love your daughter."

She stared at the ground silent for a moment and then answered, "He loves her. If she is crying or messy he doesn't want to be involved but it is that way for many men I believe. You don't mind discussing my daughter?"

I shook my head.

"Well, you know, when a person does not talk for a long time – the sincerity is often questioned."

"Do you doubt whether there is any sincerity at all?"

"I do. I have nobody to talk with, so yes."

"Sorry but I noticed P. and you – it appeared as if . . ." I trailed off.

"Oh, P." She retorted.

"Just on speaking terms with him?"

"I think I attract him but I do not know how honest he is when talking with me. I'll tell you the truth because I'm a bit worried about him" – but she did not finish.

"What are you worried about?"

"Relations among people . . . now that's a stumbling block."

"Talk . . . just talk . . . I know, honesty hurts, if you are afraid of it. After all, you wanted to about P. and about you. If . . . I feel . . ."

Her gaze change from a look of a women to that of a suffering little girl. "Keep this secret please. The few honest people among us I still recognize. I want to believe you came here to help. I want to believe you."

"It's the truth." I was an agent and no more than a liar notwithstanding how much I'd like to be truthful.

She breathed in. It was a painful inhalation. "I am having an affair with him."

This surprised me indeed. I didn't think they had that sort of tryst.

"An affair of loneliness?" It was her turn to be surprised.

She answered quietly, "Exactly, exactly."

"Are you sorry about it?"

"Sorry? That is the question. It hurts. You know I love him but not like Elvis. You know. I should be having an affair because I see the good of Elvis in him. I don't know. I guess it must sound a little psycho."

"No. Not really."

"It's not about the sex but the sex is . . . well . . ." She blushed. "I need the human contact and we connect."

"Perhaps you are just sad and striving to manage a tough situation."

"Yes." She agreed.

"Do you want to quit?"

"Whenever I see him, especially when standing next to Elvis, I feel a kind of satisfaction and no pain. Then it's okay."

"And ... Elvis?"

Her eyes narrowed. She settled her gaze on me as a woman who was just going to ask a serious question. I did not understand her expression until she asked, "Are you in a relationship?"

"Yes, I am."

"Have you ever hated a smell, a whiff of a person who passed by?"

"No but what are you getting at?"

"The relationship with P. began as an ordinary courtesan. I could not endure Elvis' moods, his ego, the humiliation, and the pills. I couldn't be with him. A long time ago I needed a man and he misused it a little. He saw it. He could read it about me. He listened to me. I could cry and knew he would listen to me. It was good and nice. It was something I had not experienced. I always had to listen only to Elvis and his laments, his hatred of anyone who was better. He always strived to be the best. P. delivered me from that."

"So P. liberated you a little?"

She grinned.

"Well, you know, every coin has two sides." She shook her head once.

"I don't love him love him but I love him as I said earlier. We sleep together – sometimes out of necessity and other times because we love to be together. Maybe he is happy to have someone like me. I don't know. I am taking it as it comes but sometimes I feel poorly about it."

"What don't you agree with?"

"With my life here. That I'm nobody. That I'm striving for nothing. I thought having my child would be enough but I'm disillusioned something is missing here. I don't know if I'm quite like other mothers."

"Other mothers?" I sat in silence repeating what she said.

She was impressed and without deeper sensibility reiterated, "Other mothers ..."

"But you have indicated you wanted to leave?"

"It's hard. In a way, even though I hate it here. Everything's here, as a kind of protection against the real life out there. Although sometimes I feel it is even worse here. That it's terrible here."

I paused. I was thinking what I should say. I didn't want to be unnecessarily philosophical but in pausing and thinking I could not avoid it. Simply, I did say the following sentence naturally but I have it consciously invented. "What is artificial, is sooner or later destined to extinction." She was caught ... the sentence as if even helped her.

"Well, that's precisely why ... but, after all, all of us are so, aren't we? Any relationship?"

"It is not as bad . . ."

"All I have is artificial except for my child. I love her. I do love like a mother but . . ."

"What but, Priscilla?"

"I conceived – do you understand!?"

She slumped in emotional pain. Such a pretty woman. Do I behave as I should behave? I did not blink. I strove to listen and keep myself sincerely involved in her conversation. It was a sincere effort. Indeed, I was dedicated to the effort. My devotion shown in my eyes. She probably did not realize it at first but it definitely held some impact on her subconsciously - because she opened up her Pandora's Box further . . .

"As a matter of fact, when I last made love with Elvis I clenched my teeth and prayed for a child. So the sex would end. It was horrible. It was disgustingly awful.

I was deeply impressed by what she said. It was cruel, sincere – and? I knew she was telling the truth. No one would lie about this sort of isolation, I believe it even now.

"It was my worst lovemaking and yet, I became pregnant because of it. Do you understand!?"

She got me. I felt her pain. I could only imagine how she must feel. I never made love with maximum resistance. I'm a male after all.

"The pain I can feel it from you but it just happened."

Such kind of truth uses to be useless on the top of pain, but nothing else occurred to me.

"The pain remains. Whenever I love myself . . . since then . . . I can't be like before . . . with anybody." She bowed her head and a tear fell from her eyes onto the expensive carpet. "I am very honest and it hurts . . ."

I knew what I should do. I moved closer. Women don't like to remain alone in their interpersonal pain when pouring their heart out. I grabbed her around the shoulders. I strived to be a comforter. The moment I grabbed her around her shoulders, I thought I am grabbing the wife of the King around the shoulders. I had nothing to say. The grabbing around her shoulders was enough. She leaned in. She began to weep.

"I've never cried in front of anyone like this . . ." she mustered through the sobs.

"It's okay." I responded. I was proud she was crying with me and that she could lean on me. I felt good inside.

"Do you know, when everything breaks?" She asked me with feeling in her voice. She was reflecting on the condition of her situation.

As soon as she said it, I realized it was a rhetorical question and desired to continue. In any case, she was also pushing me away simultaneously – the feeling of loss was a feeling, which had nothing to do with "our" reality.

"My life was broken. Like today, I am here alone. I am fighting alone. My whole life has been this way. I'm afraid. Terribly afraid I can do nothing that I'll be alone. Because I'm alone, I'm alone when making love. Oh, God, how much I'm alone. I'm scared. Very, very scared. But I can't go to anybody anymore and cry. Actually, I can come home to nobody. I can't do this anymore. I know that I can't." She breathed in. "I know, now I know it . . . life broke me. I'll tell you. Finally, we must understand we are all just ordinary people. Otherwise, there is no way to escape this sort of pain. Otherwise we only suffer even more but how am I supposed to believe in myself? How should I manage now? I don't know. I know nothing. I was pegged for marriage at 14 years of age. Now, here I have a child, what can I do? I was even allowed to breastfeed."

The fury flew from her lips like a hummingbird flies. You can't see the wings because they wave to fast. Her words flowed like the hummingbird's wings waving too rapidly to see. She was being honest and pouring a river of pain onto my ears.

"Your confession is the proof you want to survive. You are fighting to survive. Although now you probably are not aware of it . . ."

"Am I looking as someone who wants to fight with something? Oh, just look at me."

"Oh yes . . . I'm expert in reading people Priscilla." I disclosed.

"Thank you." She accepted the statement.

"Are you hungry?" She asked as if continuing her remuneration.

"No. Not so much but if you are hungry . . ." I was hungry at this time but I didn't want to take her from her moment of personal revelation.

"So, you are?"

I did not answer. I only smiled.

Her face changed to one of hope. "So let's eat. At least I'll show you the dining room. We'll order something."

She stood up – the empty cot was disturbingly stark next to her hip. She went to the phone and dialed a number. Meanwhile, asking me what I would like to eat. I replied I did not care.

"Good evening. It's Priscilla. Can you prepare fast? Something light. Is it? A soup is already ready . . ." She nodded to me. "And the second course? Late evening. For two. Thank you." Then she turned to me. At that moment a shadow fell on the room. The remainder of the sun had set. The day was lost forever.

"I have to rinse my face. I'll be right back."

I waited and paced the room." There was only one bedside table. It appeared expensive. There were two chairs. *Why did we talk on the bed?* I thought impromptu-like.

She returned quickly. I stood in the middle of the room but felt her perfume. It was a beautiful fragrance.

"Come." She said excitedly. I could not help feel it was exciting. We were walking. It seemed to me we were returning somewhere. I remained silent. It occurred to me some of her stories and emotional games might be invented. I had a talent to know when people were inventing themselves and when they were not but there was one problem; when someone attracted me as she did I could be fooled. I tried to analyze the situation as we walked. I looked forward.

She bowed her head to the ground, "You know, when he bought this house, when I came to it . . . I was proud. We were together. Now I feel so alien here. Would you believe it?"

I stopped a moment. "Maybe seeming unhappy in the eyes of other people makes you feel they'll accept you more?"

"You think that about me?"

"No, I don't but I am just suggesting alternatives."

"It seems to me you have a problem with sincerity, too." She answered. *Could it be signs of disease from a social profession?*

"Why did you stop?"

"Just now . . . somehow I am realizing all the things you told me . . ."

She smiled a victorious smile and immediately turned her face continuing her journey down the corridor.

I awakened from my consciousness and analyzed the situation when she opened the door. A large room lay before us. There was a long table with fifteen chairs or so. It was brown with a white tablecloth. In fact, there were several white cloths, spread to look like. Nevertheless, there were not only two plates on the table but five. Surely I was not the only one who was surprised because she called aloud . . .

"Could somebody else be eating with us?" She pronounced it with substantial nervousness as if suspecting something that did not make her happy. I was certain when I saw how she sat – clumsily. Her elbow shifted one of the tablecloths resulting in movement on the table – her plate, fork, and knife shifted. In any case, she managed to capture it fast with her other hand and quickly aligned everything. She sat next to the head of the table – I went to sit across from her.

"Don't sit there, believe me, somebody else will want to sit there . . ."

"Who?"

"Apparently Parker."

"Parker?"

We were the only two there for the time being but I had to respect her suspicion Elvis would come with Parker and possibly P. Although the plates told the story themselves.

"Why do you think they will come?" I asked.

"Only Elvis sits at the head of the table." She said it impassively.

# 16

# Fine Dining

I noticed Elvis' photo hung approximately above each place at the table. My eyes moved across the opposing wall – there were a lot of photos. All of them were of young Elvis. None were of his fame in decline. I sat with my face turned to the wall. If I wanted to watch the already restless woman I had to turn my head slightly to the left. We were sitting without announcing us to someone who had to cook for us.

The room had two doors. One of them we used to walk in, and now an elderly lady was entering the other one. An elderly well-preserved lady. She was wearing a cook apron and a smile, worth of remuneration. I smiled while she smiled even more. A pleasant emptiness was in her face. Suddenly, I knew she didn't contemplate any sense of life. She just finished cooking – why worry? She did what she could. Certainly she perceived that she lived as she could. I would say that about her.

She came with two saucers quite close to Elvis' wife. She close she almost touched her.

Still holding plates in her hands, she was already speaking, "Boys called and stated they'd be coming. That Elvis is hungry." With the word hungry she made such a face that expressed, allegedly . . . Good Lord. She rolled her eyes. "Your husband didn't ask you to wait, may I serve you?"

Priscilla did not answer. Her face began playing another monodrama. Everything suggested Elvis would still be in a state of need; at least that is what I perceived from her grimace.

The maid filled the plates before us. She put plates on plates to do so. The soup plate landed in a shallow plate filled with bean soup. I always hated bean soup. When I saw her – I looked into her eyes and knew I could not refuse; I would offend her. Although . . . Elvis' wife didn't seem to care. Priscilla's eyes indicated her mind was absent. Her nervousness was not escaping from her, rather the opposite.

"Enjoy your meal." The cook staff departed.

We watched the steam rise from the hot soup.

"The steam is escaping as our life is . . ." Priscilla said, her voice sounding like the steam.

I'd heard that somewhere before but I didn't care at the moment. After all, whatever we see around us may define our lives in some mood of our souls . . .

"Our life is perhaps more meaningful than the bean soup . . ." I continued, "I would say it makes sense to feed us - I mean our souls. The lady would not satiate us, indeed. The steam has no meaning but the soup has." I took a deep breath wanting to act funny and make her laugh. "Life can be the steam as well as the soup . . . ee . . . depending on whether you want to suck steam or eat the soup in this session, where you can decide only and only yourself and only and only freely. Unlike steam, soup will feed you . . . so . . . somehow something is meaningful here and something is not . . ." I immediately grinned at what I said. Judge for yourself but I really thought it was funny, at least a little.

She did not react. When you desire very much to make someone laugh or at least provoke some reaction and fail to do so . . . you know it.

"Have I already said enjoy your meal? I don't know even myself."

"Yes, you have. Well, it's just me who still haven't said that, but in any case, the soup is still hot . . ."

Suddenly the door opened and Parker entered the room. He was holding Elvis around his shoulders. Elvis was dragging himself along. P. walked beside him. He wasn't holding Elvis around his shoulders nor supporting him. Elvis probably refused it, trying to give the impression he was okay.

Priscilla raised her eyes to him. I saw the look of the year. Elvis' eyes met hers.

Two very different facial expressions. Two very different kinds of madness.

Priscilla returned to reality her fear suddenly standing before her. Her lover was also standing in front of her. The love she was afraid of. It worried her obviously.

Parker looked like an employee at his workplace waiting for the end of his shift.

P. was looking at Priscilla but Priscilla did not see him.

"Are you already eating? I requested you wait for us. Elvis wished it. He said he wanted to eat with his wife." P. emphasized Elvis wanted to eat with his wife so much that Priscilla's observations of Elvis were interrupted and she moved her eyes to P. He waited for her to do so. He smiled faintly.

"We haven't eaten, we waited for you."

Elvis smiled at her.

"Sit down, I'll announce you've come . . ." she responded. She pushed her chair and almost fell backwards but managed to capture the table with her hand and steady herself. It was similar with the tablecloth earlier – she appeared nervous around the King. Without looking at anyone and with her head bowed she seemed to whisper to herself but we could not make out what was said. She exited through the same door as the cook had.

"I want to sit down . . ." Elvis stated to Parker.

"Well, sit down." Parker replied like a father with indignation and as he did he released Elvis who nearly lost his balance. He looked over at me and smiled even though I doubted he knew who he was smiling at.

Instead of taking his place at the head of the table, he sat nearest to his wife's side. He sort of hovered over his chair supporting his body against the table. I figured he was gambling with his balance for a couple of seconds. His head was deeply resting on his chest making the maneuver more difficult. He was resolved to sit down without being aware of it.

At that moment he resembled the King of a castle in a stupor who despises his own kingdom. Finally, his position shifted and he plopped down next to me. At the moment of full seat execution – he smiled heroically. He raised his head, "Home sweet home." He sounded like a stranger ridiculing the manor. He did not look at us – he just muttered into the great abyss.

P. responded with a compassionate tone, "Elvis, you are at home."

"Home . . ." he said again and then began a rancorous laugh. "Finally. They take you home even if you . . ." he trailed off finishing with laughter instead.

Without the slightest intermezzo, P. sat down next to Priscilla's place-setting. Compared with Elvis, Parker and P. appeared to be the only sober man at the table. I could see they drank as rich men drowning in the great absurdities of their lives.

P. fixed his eyes on my soup, breathed in and said, "Oh, the bean soup."

Elvis remarked, "Where is my wife?"

"She went to call the cook. Something to explain . . ." I said to her defense.

P. stood and said he was going to look after Priscilla.

Elvis didn't raise his eyes.

P. rose and left the room; in the meantime Parker looked at the empty plates in front of him. His emptiness indicated dissatisfaction. Before long, he looked at Elvis, who was looking at images of glory used to belong him.

"You've greatly organized it here . . . people want to eat and they're totally neglected . . ., Parker commented in a stark manner.

Elvis, however, did not comment on the Colonel's dissatisfaction. He focused on his images and began to talk about them . . . "Let's see, this used to be me when I believed in what I was doing." He swallowed hard adding, "Colonel, a man visited me today. He told me this is not all I have in me . . . that I have . . ."

"Yes, Elvis" Parker answered. "The man is sitting here next to you." He looked briefly at my face.

"No, that man can't be here …" Elvis again trailed off.

Parker waved his wrist and looked at me again then added, "Will you not eat?" He spoke to me more personally.

I responded, "Well, I don't like bean soup. Since I was a child …"

Parker had no desire to hear my story, "So, give it to me. Give it here!" He raised his voice. Parker had a Napoleon personality. Listening to his orders was easy, whether they were good or bad. His voice, his charisma, especially when escalated provided listeners with freedom from responsibility. Like a child I handed him my bean soup. And, Parker did not wait for the arrival of Elvis' wife nor P. He immediately set to slurping his soup.

The juxtaposition of a broken Elvis to his manager was disparaging from my vantage point. As he ate, the Colonel didn't look at anyone. He was focused on consumption. And, I realized much of Elvis' life was filled with individuals focused on consumption.

Finally, Parker stated, "Good soup." He peered at me and licked his teeth with his tongue.

Elvis chimed in, "I can't do it anymore."

Parker shook his head. He tapped Elvis' shoulder with a satisfied grin on his face. "You can do it Elvis! I'll give you what you'll want. We'll pay you what you'll want."

The King was not listening.

In the meantime, Parker winked at me.

Where is the doctor?" Elvis chimed in. "He said something about being hungry, where is he?"

"I don't know," the Colonel retorted. He belched and grinned.

The conversation returned to Elvis and his music. Elvis was staring at his immortalized image of Jerry-Lee Lewis, Carl Perkins, Johnny Cash and him with a plague reading: Christmas 1956.

He started, "Did you ever hear his music?"

"His songs!? He's not a composer."

"Aha … well … well … maybe you've heard some? He asked carefully.

I was delighted by question. "No." I answered. "Not unless you are considering Love Me Tender, which shouldn't be considered at all … should it?" Although Elvis signed as co-author of the song *Love Me Tender*, I believed it was a trade agreement.

The door opened and the cook arrived. "Did something happen I'm not aware of? All these guests. I heard raised voices … Colonel … good evening. Are you staying a while?"

He answered, "I didn't know."

"Well, I'll bring you some soup. The second course will arrive shortly. Entirely happy she turned around.

Parker looked at me as if I was his young partner. He handed me an empty plate.

"I'll get another soup – no need to tell her you don't like it."

"At least we'll make her happy," I responded. As I finished saying happy . . . the door opened and in walked Priscilla. The door was perpendicular to the table and Priscilla stood i in the doorway with bloodshot eyes. Her eyes were the first thing attracting my attention originally. Immediately, I noted P. was looking at her as a lover. Her gaze moved toward Elvis and she resembled the sentiment of a wife. She entered the room slowing. P. remained a half-step behind her heel. He looked at her without interruption.

I returned to her eyes; the closer she became the more unnatural her eyes appeared. They were large and dilated and there was a blood and milk in her whites. If she had extremely sharp features during her departure, her face was even more accented. She clench her teeth without interruption again and again. Her facial expression indicated an incredible inner turmoil. In spite of it, she smiled at me, I perceived her smile for my professionalism alone.

Parker looked at the two of them less than a second. He only noticed they were coming. Before and after this, he looked at Elvis with satisfaction.

Then, suddenly, and quite by surprise, Dr. N. arrived.

When Priscilla saw Parker sitting at the table top, corner of her mouth jerked. It was a mimicry of exertion and anger at the same time.

"Why isn't Elvis sitting here?" Her voice was demanding.

Parker raised his eyes slowly and with a certain contempt and looked at her. For a while he was looking at her and then, without any thinking about his question, "Now I can at least see why there is a doctor here . . . but why are you here Priscilla. Did you come to support your husband in sniffling?" Parker's question her surprisingly left her unaffected, if her ironic smile is not considered affection.

"Well, once more, you' a bit dim-witted." Her tone left an impression of extreme alienation. "Why are you sitting at the head of a table, which does not belong you Colonel?"

Parker grinned and, friends, it was a very similar grin to that of Priscilla.

"You know why honey."

"Don't address me as honey."

P. stood next to Priscilla. He did not want to sit down, he wanted to support the presence of his mistress at least with his "standing" presence. Because according to facial expression he was considering her his wife.

Dr. N. sat in one of the vacant seats formerly belonging to P. He had a calm, serene expression on his face. The only thing preventing him from sitting next to Parker and opposite Elvis was a plate full of soup that was gradually growing cold.

"Come on, baby," Parker pressed on harassing Priscilla.

"Stand up! And change places or I'll call the guard to march you out."

"Relax . . ." Parker melded out like a malt liquor and changed his irony to seriousness, raising his voice. "No one is going to throw me out of a house I earned money for."

I could see the cook bending an ear toward our direction and heard some murmuring in the kitchen . . .

"What? What did you say?!" Priscilla continued.

"You nipper, you know (beep)."

"Stand up and walk away."

"You'll be alone against me, honey. I am not going to leave." With a visible joy in his demeanor Parker returned to his power of a shadow king and Elvis just sat quietly. Perhaps he even heard something of what was happening around but if he did it was only an echo of his self-proposed futility.

"Elvis!?" Priscilla addressed her husband, in a voice of faith there was something left she could fight for.

Elvis was facing wall so he had to turn his head to see his wife and he didn't.

P. stood appeared damned to love a woman scorned.

"Colonel . . . maybe you should stand up." P. etched the statement out with a fearful voice.

Parker grinned. "P, you can't be serious . . ."

"He is!" Priscilla answered glad somebody intervened.

Meanwhile Parker happily and serenely put his hands on his belly. "You know what . . . Let's ask Elvis. As far as I know, Priscilla, he is still the master of the house . . . or am I wrong?!"

Priscilla narrowed her eyes and looked at her husband.

And despite the fact Elvis didn't turn toward his wife, he answered her. "Come on, Priscilla, why should we mind? Sit down . . . I want to eat . . . with you . . . That's why I came here . . . It's a long time when we ate together. I want to eat you, love . . . No I don't care at all. Please, sit down . . ."

After Elvis' words ceased to from, we all began to gaze at him. He spoke as if he was listening the entire time.

Priscilla and P. remained standing on their spots. Parker winked at Priscilla. Maybe he wanted to feel even more like a winner . . .

"You know what, Parker? I was determined to go out, let Elvis say what he wants . . . but the wink overdid it. I'll stay and I'll sit down next to you, opposite to my husband, whom you all love destroying." She peered at Dr. N. who just looked away to avoid her glaring at him.

"All of you will suffer, as I do and as my husband does. I'm saying it mainly about you, Honorable Colonel . . ." Priscilla seemed overwrought and sat opposite Elvis.

A second after Priscilla's move, P. made his way to sit near Dr. N. There was neither cutlery nor plates where he sat.

Dr. N. looked at him and quietly asked, "Did I occupy your space?"

"Just sit." P. answered unamused.

At last, Priscilla said, "Along the way you've somewhere lost my husband." She looked at Elvis as if he was a stranger. Her look comforted P.

"Does it agree with you? Who of us is destroying him more?" Parker retorted.

"Colonel, what you have done will return to you... What are you doing and what you still will do to Elvis, it will return to you as anyone else at this table."

"Doctor, I must admit that today you've mixed a very good combination for her. Next time prefer giving such a combination to Elvis, when he will go into the studio to record his new top..." Parker looked at me rather than Priscilla - his glance at me was fleeting. Then he settled his gaze on Priscilla. It was the gaze of a lost dog, who wants to attack but has already some hidden respect. He preferred to stay silent.

"Somehow you are holding your own among us." Dr. N. turned the conversation to me. "The first day at Graceland and you already eat with us." It wasn't an attack nor a provocation, he merely stated what he saw. I guessed he just did not want to continue in quiet sitting and gradually loosing appetite due to their annoying bickering.

"Yes, you can see it this way, too." I answered quietly.

"You see, you see, now you're siding with them again." Priscilla turned her head toward me. I couldn't overlook P's grin. I had a good mind to say something but I defended myself by adding, "But I'm here for Elvis, not for the Colonel."

"Well, all of us are." Dr. N. gave a faint smile and shuffled a little in his chair.

"And I've found the best person to record a new album with Elvis..." The Colonel chimed in.

I don't know, how the others understood Parker's words but I heard an underlying sarcasm. Maybe it was just my feeling. Perhaps Parker wanted to get Priscilla's anger off the table and move to something new. Perhaps it wanted a new challenge in me. It was obvious Priscilla and he had played the conversational lute a few times before our meal.

"After all, *you're all alike*." Priscilla looked at me with distrust.

I looked into her beautiful eyes. *How many times have I done so during this visit?* I thought quietly.

Parker chimed in, "Priscilla he is solely responsible for his inability to defend singing of songs that he wants to sing."

Elvis shuffled, "Shut up! Where is . . .?" His voice trailed off again. Again he started, "Where is the meal . . ?"

Parker and I were both relieved by the King's desire for a quieter atmosphere

Priscilla wasn't finished, "Dr. N. if Hippocrates saw you, he'd turn over in his grave."

Dr. N. remained quiet. Everyone knew her words were spot on and she didn't need to hear an answer. She furthered, "We should all be committed for trial and then undergo some treatment."

I was not surprised by Parker's faint smile.

The Colonel couldn't resist, "Please, God, let us once be committed for trial, for such a society and for such a fame. Hardly, sweetie. People like me and you, such people are rarely brought to trial." Parker was riding high, while Priscilla was somewhere in her mental abyss.

"I think we should be more humble," P. made himself heard.

Dr. N. added, "What would you do along with Elvis without me in this crazy world?"

Priscilla looked at Dr. N. like a murderess. Just as she was beginning to speak the kitchen double door opened and the cook pushed a trolley into the dining room. It issued an annoying squeaky sound to wit Elvis turned his head.

"Well, finally." Parker barked ahead of Elvis in his enthusiasm.

Priscilla looked bitter.

"I'm thirsty," Elvis' words were silently spoken.

The cook pulled inquired, "What would you like sir?"

"I want water," came Elvis' reply.

She poured some mineral water for him. Before she put the glass in front of him, Elvis reached for the glass.

He drank it down and requested another.

She filled the glass again and he drank it nearly as rapidly as the first time.

The cook placed the mineral water in front of him and continued her path around the table to begin service. It began to whistle again. She stopped at Parker's side and laid soup before him.

"Thank you," Parker smiled. He was happy she started with him.

Priscilla wasn't pleased, "Why the hell are you beginning with the Colonel, when the master of the house should be the first?"

The cook apologized mentioning the seating placement determines the service.

I thought to myself, *Here we go again.*

# 17
# Tet-y-Tet

The cook returned her trolley placing the next bowl of soup in front of Elvis.
"And where is my wife," he asked.
Priscilla responded, "I'm here, I'm sitting in front of you."
"No, you are not my wife. This is not my wife. Where is my wife?" He looked at his cook for an answer.
"Is this some kind of game?" Priscilla asked with a hard voice.
Parker shook his head, picked up his spoon, dipped it into his soup and stirred then shook his head again. "Enjoy your meal, friends." He chided semi-quietly.

Elvis' conversation drifted off, "I loved her . . . I loved her . . . And how I loved her . . . I'll love her forever . . ."
Priscilla looked at Elvis and he at her. It was tragic.
"I loved you, Elvis . . ." She added.
The substances that had been donated to them by Dr. N. seemed to shift the couple to such phase of expression that worked notwithstanding the number of people around.
"I never came to know your love . . ." Elvis' face indicated he was losing interest. "Where is my one true love? Where is she?" He looked at Priscilla. "What about our child, where is my baby?" Elvis' voice rose. "She is not here is she? Why isn't she here?" Elvis fell silent. He grabbed a spoon.
"The babysitter took her on a trip Elvis, to the old garden house."

"So the babysitter is the mum here?" Elvis words were not angry – only sad. "From time-to-time as a father I want to see my daughter and her mother."

Priscilla did not say a word.

"How could I love my wife!?" He furthered.

Priscilla clenched fist on her right hand, her left hand clutching the cloth and crumpling it, "And, who the hell can love you?"

Elvis remained puzzled, his forehead and his eyes were creating a symbiosis of surprise. His eyebrows lifted a bit, his eyes opened slightly and his forehead . . . well, his forehead became wrinkled.

Priscilla continued firing, "For entire days I'm here told to tolerate your moods, your supposed failures, your lack of fulfillment! And, you even don't let me feel that I'm your wife?"

"I don't want to listen to you!" Elvis fired back. "I don't need you! I don't need anybody. Get out of here!"

"Get a grip son," Parker raised his voice; immediately afterward, Elvis looked like a boy admonished by his father.

Priscilla went to stand but at the moment she did, Dr. N. grabbed her hand. "Relax." His voice was calm as he assessed the situation. "You should stay with us."

Parker's look was eloquent with a go away grimace.

Priscilla sat realizing a woman defeated in her own house by visitors is not very strong. After all, she knew she was relevant no matter what. "Enjoy your meal." She sounded as if she was saying: suffocate on it.

Parker grinned and indulged his second serving of soup.

"Colonel, sitting at the head of our table does not mean you command here. As a polite and mannered guest you'll wait until we finish." Priscilla was enjoying herself now.

Parker observed her as soup escaped her lips.

"Soup is on your chin girl."

"I can't stand it here anymore." The fun ended for a second. "I'll eat later!"

The cook was busy serving the second course to the king.

"Stop, stop all this craziness. Why are you intent on making a puppet of fate out of Elvis? Will he be more useful after his death, huh? Will you earn more!?"

"It's too much!" Parker attempted to shout her down.

Priscilla turned to the doctor and in unchanging voice that was fighting with the walls of the room, her voice raised, "Do you think he doesn't understand me? Is he not hearing what I am saying? Did you even know what are giving us, doctor? It's about wanting and can't you all see he doesn't want anymore? We are living with a man who already doesn't want to live! And, you are all parasites!"

"Eat or leave." Elvis said impassively. He was eating as if he was alone and wanting to enjoy his solitude.

She turned to leave - halfway to the door she turned and in and raised her hand, "Remember, I'll never love anyone like you again. There are so many types of love but we have already exhausted all of them! I don't believe hate will ever overcome what you have shown me!"

Elvis picked an almost gnawed bone from his plate and (apparently) without thoughts he threw it after his wife. He started to laugh but it was forced laughter. He didn't. The bone struck one of the photographs of his past glory.

Priscilla stood still and he stopped laughing. Their eyes met. The whole room stopped breathing. Priscilla opened her eyes without blinking. Elvis stood up with greasy hands.

"I, Priscilla, I . . ."

"You're disgusting!" She retorted.

"Disgusting!?" He answered questioningly as his forehead wrinkled. "Disgusting?" He began to laugh as a king of Satyricon on a funeral of the only friend who could tell him that only truth for truth exists in the world. He surprised all and changed the conversation somewhat, "Music is already in me . . . huh . . . the eternal guillotine . . . like you, Priscilla . . . Without love and without a woman men use to be disgusting . . . huh . . . You know that, don't you!? The only person I need and for which I could live is not here . . . no . . . And not thanks to me!"

Parker lifted his chin, narrowed his eyes, and furrowed his brow: "Let him be. If you were ever useful for him in anything just leave him alone now."

"Shut up!" Priscilla lost control. "This is between me and him, in this relationship he is not yours."

"You wanted to leave."

Priscilla ran wildly back to the table and grabbed a half-empty plate and threw it at Parker. It hit his chest. The soup poured about the room and Parker got the biggest hit. The others seemed spared. Just at the moment it hit, his chair was on its hind legs, it disrupted the balance and Parker fell uncontrollably. As he fell Priscilla's face tensed. The chair was heavy. The fall was swift and painful. The first thing Parker hit was his head. It just boomed in the space. The doctor became a bit shaken by the boom. He stood up quickly. As a result of an insignificant chance he stood up in the moment when the first "oh" could be sound from behind the table top.

"You. You don't know!" A half-smile of satisfaction appeared on Priscilla's face, when she looked at Elvis.

From the height of his standing he looked at Parker who was keeping his head and his continuous moaning was mixed with expressive words.

Soup flowed off the table.

Priscilla returned to her chair, her hands grabbed the backrest and she bowed her head between her shoulders and quietly began to laugh. In that laughter she proved she was still Elvis' wife.

Elvis slowly meandered of the siege of his own chair, while almost stumbling across it. He approached Parker. Still stumbling a bit. He bent to Parker like a son, who despite everything must remain clinging on his paternal chest till the very end.

"Okay?" Elvis asked seemingly suddenly sober.

Parker did not answer. He opened his eyes still lying his hands passed his dirty white shirt and cursed impressively.

In spite of Elvis' offered hand, the Colonel stood up alone straining as he did. Elvis smiled at Priscilla, ignoring Parker. "Do you know what it is like to love a person who you used to be? It's like loving a wound." Elvis returned to the table and sat down winking at the cook. Of course, in the shock of all she'd seen she didn't know what Elvis' wink meant.

"Once more?" She asked wiping the spillage.

Parker looked at Priscilla with rage in his eyes.

Priscilla, however, had her head bent on her shoulders and in the silence it appeared she was giggling.

Parker couldn't bear it. He turned and shook his head in resignation. He stretched his old shoulder. He didn't look at Elvis. He was not interested. He bent his head to see what damage was caused by Priscilla and swore loudly.

Priscilla giggling made Parker increasingly angry but he didn't say anything. He just shook his head.

I must admit I liked the feeling someone finally defeated Parker.

Parker made a step toward the door. His face was tense. He was reddened and his fists clenched. He barely swallowed the phlegm from his anger. During his exit he shook his head some more and generally appeared unhinged. "You said idiots?! But at least we're fine!"

Parker's theatrical cry made Priscilla happy.

The cook again inquired, "Once more?"

Elvis imitated her in a laughing with her manner.

Of course, everyone had lost their appetites.

Neither P. nor Dr. N. had any words.

Immediately after Parker's exit Priscilla returned to Elvis. By doing so, her face changed from rather satisfied to fully disappointed. She returned just in time to hear Elvis say,"Once more".

She raised her head slightly. "Do you wish to have seconds?" The cook seemed confused.

"Yeah. I'd like to eat finally."

P. didn't seem to be losing hope, he peered at Priscilla's face.

Elvis was attracted by the new food.

Priscilla finally looked at P. When she noticed his gaze she promptly turned her head and looked at me.

Priscilla rose to leave too - Elvis smacked his food as she began taking steps toward the door. His wife took another and another step and her steps were audible. The more distant she was, the louder Elvis smacked.

He looked up to her but she turned away exactly in the split of second when his eyes rose toward hers. She looked up to the heavens. He raised his eyes too.

Priscilla wailed like a queen who lost a king after exchanging the Kingdom for life.

Elvis bent his head and he saw gnawed bones on his plate. "So this caused everything? It's just me. How is this possible? How did this happen?"

P. observed Priscilla leaving but did not have the courage to speak or stand.

Dr. N. began to eat as if the universe had righted itself.

The cook served the second course to him. He was hungry and ate with zeal.

"Didn't you eat yet?" P. inquired.

With his full mouth Dr. N. answered, "NO, I didn't."

"Didn't you want to eat when you were leaving the old house?"

Dr. N. looked at P. in the way "Why are you asking, I am eating!" He swallowed and answered quietly. His silence gradually turned into mere talking as if he suddenly remembered he wanted to tell a story, "You know, it's strange, I was just sitting in the city in a pub. Nothing high, mainly pensioners visit it . . . but I like it. I just had to leave it. Well, I don't think the reasons of my leaving would be interesting now . . ." He trailed off again.

Elvis supported his chin with his hand and began to gaze at Dr. N. Their eyes met.

In any case, one thing was certain, when speaking, Dr. N. was often looking to Elvis, who looked like a defeated gladiator, with his hand on his chin. "I ordered every day, perhaps even about five years since I was going there, I used to see there such a hilarious pair, an old man and old woman. They were walking to their table very slowly, really slowly, they always walked so slowly . . . They were holding hands, sitting together, ordering together, they were always waiting until the food was brought to the other one so they could eat together. It was for me a model relationship. I admired them. Whenever I was sitting there, I was watching them with joy, they gave me hope. Sometimes they even stroked each other when they finished their meal. They looked at each other, they blinked . . . and sometimes they even laughed. So once . . . about two months ago, I asked them how long they were married . . . And she told me sixty-three years. You know . . . that day I enjoyed my meal really the best of all meals . . . I'll never forget them when they were holding their hands the last time. Dr. N was really emotionally excited.

With his eyes open, Elvis straightened.

The cook took his half-empty plate because he signaled to her he would not eat anymore. He was listening surprisingly attentively and with interest. The same could be said of P. Even the cook during her takeaway of the dishes kept her eyes peeled for Dr. N.

Gradually he visibly manifested he was glad to tell something that was interesting for all. "And today, when I ordered and they were just bringing me my soup, I've seen the woman coming alone. Alone and . . . in black . . . you know. I was sitting alone at my table and any other place were accidentally occupied. She approached me and asked whether I had a vacant seat. I knew she was sad and experiencing, well, crisis. I had seen her body before and I know how she used to keep it but today she appeared languished. She sat next to me and ordered. I wanted to eat, but somehow I could not concentrate on eating. I was eating but I did so like her. I do not know how to say it exactly . . . like a limp ragdoll? So I asked her whether her husband died and she said he did but immediately she lowered her gaze to her soup. It was bad.

"There was still one vacant seat at the table and so an old woman sat down that had known the widow. She expressed condolences. While she was eating I tried my best to eat but lost my appetite although I was very hungry. I felt sorry for her and yet I knew its just life. It is all so unchangeable. Just when I was there looking at the soup I had to stand up and go. It all seemed so strange. Then Priscilla called me to my medical office and it was all. And now I feel even weirder because again I have to force me to eat.

During his last sentences Dr. N. was already constantly looking to Elvis. When doctor finished, Elvis looked down.

"I'll tell you, Doctor, now I feel like that woman." Elvis' heartfelt statement rang silent. "Oh sixty-three years, how sad."

"Truly, sixty-three years. Yes Elvis, incredible." The doctor gained confidence from the fact his story was heard, he concluded, "Today I faced death and love at the same time. I don't know what should I think in this light of all this. Let's face it, we have nothing more than relations between us and anyway we are destroying just as Priscilla said," the doctor shook his head, "she was right, like idiots."

"Doctor," Elvis sighed, "Do not think of anything. Let's not think of anything. You'll forget that death tomorrow. We'll forget it."

# 18
# Enlightenment

Dr. N. furrowed his face.

"Lola, pour me a whiskey," Elvis commanded to the cook.

She gave him a glass and filled it to the brim. He even didn't look at us and immediately he drank the whole glass.

"That was not the reason why I shared my story. Elvis. I rather hoped you'd recognize you have a wife in Priscilla."

Elvis stood up and an iconic glare appeared across his face.

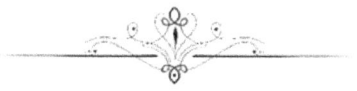

P. still didn't eat. His plate remained full. He looked at it several times. The same applied to me.

"Get out of here. All of you. Clear out. Stop eating. Lola take their food. Get out!" Elvis roared.

Dr. N. stood first, he didn't smile. He was serious. He slid his chair, nodded toward the cook and took his leave saying, "When you need me give me a ring." His comment was incidental as if he were leaving of his own will.

"Get out, everybody! Get out!" He hammered further.

We stood and moved our chairs. I looked at Elvis but he ignored that someone was looking at him. He sat back in his chair. He looked like a king whose reign just ended.

Lola collected the plates. She had the face of a woman who had been trying hard but her efforts went to waste.

I stood and made a move toward the door with P.

As I departed, Elvis cried, "Stop, you stop!"

I turned around and P. turned too.

"I didn't mean you, P., not you." Elvis looked at my eyes.

Yes despite the fact was sleeping with Elvis' wife, P. was willing to listen to Elvis' moans bit today he chose me. I was glad of it. Did not have to impose.

"Sit down, sit where you want, just sit down somewhere." He softened his voice.

P. disappeared out the door Priscilla had exited.

I didn't care whether he went after her or not. Looking into Elvis' face I could hear the sound of his future recordings. I said to myself, *in that sound may be the biggest and the best despair.*

The cook continued removing dishes and Elvis changed his command, "Let it be now, I'll clear away it later. Leave me alone. Leave us alone."

"Okay sir," she said with a slight quiver.

"Let's start where we left off earlier today," Elvis spoke in a broken voice. "Fill my glass and yours, too."

I looked around the room and didn't see a bottle of whiskey but remembered the cook pouring whiskey and returning the bottle to the trolley. I filled Elvis' glass and then my own.

"You forgot ice." Elvis declared.

I found the ice and dropped it into his glass then my own. My plate remained on the table because she had not removed it before Elvis had the cook depart. I must confess I was thinking of the plate more than Elvis because I was hungry. I eating. Elvis had been watching me – he smiled at.

"Eat." He said as he gulped another full glass of whiskey. "Just eat." He smiled this time.

I hesitated a moment but finally I pulled my old plate to me. In my imagination I felt victorious, but in reality, I suddenly started to feel like somebody who has mixed feelings of the plate before him.

Elvis refilled my whiskey, although I didn't touch it yet. I started eating, the refilling started my eating. While I was trying to eat the best I could, Elvis began to speak, "A long time ago I figured out the sense, you know the sense we talked about earlier depends on each person. Especially when we are alone." He shook his head. "You see it, you see it. I'm not looking for it. Things used to be so nice, when Priscilla you know. There was that sense of things." He leaned against the backrest and closed his eyes as if he was concentrating on the alcohol, which he drank seconds before.

"I'm lucky," he furthered. "Everything that is sweet ceases to interest me eventually. Imagine I just exist. I care for nothing. I am Elvis and that's the sense. Being Elvis. Nothing more. Do you understand?"

Despite the fact I was eating as a honest man I resolved to answer him with my mouth full, "So you completely freely accept you are an advertising machine and you see sense in it? That is nice, you can be proud of yourself." I took the term advertising machine from Bob Dylan. Irony with a full mouth, already goes somewhere toward the realm of dreams and Elvis was impressed.

"The only thing I was trying to say is that if a man can't stand with himself . . ." he trailed off. Then started back in, "If he can't stand himself, he is doing just what takes him from his essence. Sometimes I can still be Elvis when I'm alone! Advertising machine? I don't give up! I won't stop!" He defended himself.

I nodded and swallowed.

"You're right. Advertising machines need neither marriages nor children." His retort was in a completely different voice, I wondered, *could he be bipolar?*

I ate quickly in a controlled manner. My eating began gradually make me more quiet. I drank whiskey, everything I had poured. When I was finishing, our eyes met.

Elvis continued, "The man who behaves as badly as I do, is generally considered crazy. He can see everything even more painfully."

Fortunately, I was eating because Elvis was still talking about the same thing over and over. "Elvis, do not be mad at me but I'll be honest, maybe you really feel I want to help you, so listen" I swallowed again "I know you just a few hours. I you are continuously repeating the same thing and this is, what you are saying just now. We had this conversation on the original rounds of whiskey."

Elvis fell silent with surprise in his eyes.

I continued, "Do you want to spend your whole life in the same pain and nothingness?! I understand you less and less, I'll tell you." Again, no answer.

He filled his glass. "We all are so . . ."

"Well, if we were all so, there would soon be nobody remaining alive here. I already told you once that you have to survive at least better than now. Should I repeat my words, too!?" I slightly raised my voice. I felt I was being shifted into Parker's position that the man in front of me needed to be led and formed a lot more than he thought of himself.

Elvis had an unconcerned expression on his face, who spoke quite loudly, "You needn't say more."

I did not need to see more. Calmly and serenely, like a man who had finished his double whiskey just a while ago, I declared while eating, "You don't have many choices anymore. You'll find nothing new anymore here. Only your studio remained you. In my opinion you can find your old faith there. Because I'll say it, only there you can find the meaning of your life. From what I've seen today you can hardly find it elsewhere." I bent my head back to eat. I finally ate freely, as if in solitude, without the thoughts of my being with Elvis. And while inserting food in my mouth, I again poured a whiskey and noticed Elvis was missing his fluid of grain. "More whiskey?"

Elvis looked at me, his eyes said, "Teasing me?"

So I poured him.

He asked, "Couldn't you bring more ice?"

I stood up with my mouth full, and once again walked to the trolley. I took ice to an empty and clean glass and gave the glass to Elvis. He inserted two ice cubes into his glass.

He picked up his glass and declared, "Toast!"

We pushed our glasses together. I washed down my food with alcohol causing some volcanic activity in my mouth but men at work should not complain. In the state in which whiskey made me brazen I continued, "Perhaps some interest in some Eastern religions would be beneficial for you. Those that force men to work on themselves."

"I believe in God." He answered. "That should be enough." Again and again he drank what he had poured. "This is my answer."

I did not know whether he meant God or another glass of whiskey.

"Not really my answer. God is my answer. He's our answer but you knew what I meant. That's the most important answer. Do you understand!? I'm not a naive fool! I'm not, sweet chicken on a plate."

He looked at my plate that was nearly empty now. I grinned. "Well, you see, at least God cares for you."

He scowled and brushed off my statement impertinently, "When I don't care, nobody does. You'd better . . . you'd better go." He said it so resignedly, as if he didn't really want me to leave.

"I think I still have not finished my meal, it was you who told me that I should eat." I was just trying to use his uncertainty. I said this with certainty.

He looked at me. He stretched out his mental hand to me.

I bent my head again to my plate.

"Are really all of us so lonely!?" He asked while looking at his photos.

I finished my meal, I just didn't have anything to rinse it down because I was tired of the whiskey; so I got up and took my glass with my hands and went to the trolley to pour a mineral water. When I sat back, I noticed he had an empty glass. Without asking, I poured him another dose. Some ice was still in the glass, so I added no more ice. He drank so fast that even the ice had no time to melt.

"And so it's still around, you told me alcohol was harmful to me but you are pouring it for me yourself . . ."

"You're the king, you have to decide and you have to say no. If you say nothing, what can change?"

Arrogantly and with cynical grinning Elvis drank his whiskey. He grinned before and after. "I'll tell you one thing, when you try so hard," he put his cup in front of him. His eyes were asking me for more and more glasses, "Maybe I should die for all people."

"Elvis but then you'd die without being remembered as the man you want to be remembered for."

His faint smile was full of whiskey.

At that moment, I thought to myself, if I had a good mind I'd tell him, *You know what, I don't want to talk with you anymore.* But I just put my fork and knife side by side.

Elvis poured whiskey with a shaking hand because I didn't seem to be willing to do it any longer. He drank his cup – this time with the ice. "Once again, what should I do?"

I don't know if it was just his best irony or his greatest sincerity. His condition prevented me to penetrate to his soul so I continued, "You should go to the studio as soon as possible and sing in the same manner as you did today. Elvis, give into all that pain and nothingness. I tell you, after what I saw today, I'm looking forward to it . . ."

"Will you be there with me?" And again he smiled again a little a whiskey grin but now it included a restless honesty.

So I smiled too but only as a human. And thought to myself, *And you even don't know how glad I am.*

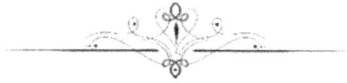

"Tell me, you saw me the first time today, I guess you'll not lie. Do you think I'm a bad person?"

I hadn't opportunity to answer him before a young woman stepped into the room, her hands bearing a sleeping baby. The woman looked like a young model who was not able to care for a child to my estimations but I wasn't a parent.

When Elvis saw his child's face, his face lit up. The baby was sleeping. Elvis stood heavily and approached the woman. When she saw Elvis' condition, her face changed for the worse. In any case, in the seconds when Elvis was approaching the child, she said nothing. He was standing there with bare soul of a fine man, but as if he feared to caress the sleeping child's face. He was standing there and did not know what to do with his love. He already seemed to touch the child's face with his palm but when the palm was now only a few inches from the face of the sleeping beauty and purity Elvis hesitated and the fingers of the hand that had attempted to touch waved in the. He did not dare. Surprisingly, he turned to me and shrugged. But he promptly turned back to his child.

"Where is your wife?" Asked the young woman.

[129]

Elvis smiled drunkenly. "I don't know … What do I know? Probably somewhere upstairs." Elvis asked the woman, "Can I hold her now?"

The young woman stared into his face with suspicion, "She's asleep, you'll wake her."

"But I need to hole my daughter."

"Well …"

"After all, I'm her father."

"Do you want to wake her up?"

"I'm her father, I want to hold my daughter."

The woman frowned but slowly placed the child into his arms. She remained close at his side. Elvis cuddled his daughter against his chest sort of clumsily as if he hadn't held her very often." But his smile was eloquent. I finally saw happiness in him in that moment. His eyes glowed. His left-hand pat her head. He longed to be a unencumbered father but he wasn't alone in his happiness or un happiness:

His daughter began to cry. Elvis appeared speechless and uncomfortable. The nanny snatched the child from her father's arms and he did not resist. The baby was crying and the woman cuddled her in her arms as a mother. She was patting her head, and the child cried less and less. And, the less the baby cried, the more it appeared Elvis housed his own tears. He bent his head. It was a painful yet ludicrous scene. Here was the King afraid to hold his daughter. It was, at the same time, another kitsch scene. A single tear ran down his face (at least I noticed a single tear). He wiped it away. At that moment the baby stopped crying too and closed her eyes once more.

"I would like to close my eyes," he muttered so we both could hear him.

The woman shook her head. "I want to return the child to your wife. What is her condition?"

"What is her condition?" Elvis had a knee-jerk reaction to the nanny's question.

I answered for him, "She'll be surely delighted. If I may, why are you arriving with the baby so late in the day?"

The woman looked in my eyes, I saw that she explored who I was and what I was. "The Mrs. called me herself, said I had to bring her daughter to the dining room. She was sleeping but I did as I was asked."

Elvis caught his opportunity in that moment, "But tell me, why are you coming so late?"–

The woman looked at him with rejection.

"Do you know what time it is sir?"

Elvis looked at me and I answered for him, "It is half past ten." Elvis swallowed.

The woman smiled again and went back to the door, through which she came.

"Where are you going with my daughter?" Elvis inquired.

"To your wife sir. She requested I come to her after the dining room to you."

"Stop!" Elvis declared.

The woman turned around.

"I am going to go with you."

The woman, of course remained quiet. She didn't appear happy but just stood and shrugged. She turned back to the door once more and stepped out. Elvis followed her.

I decided to follow them.

I said to the woman words of necessity, "I'll go with you, should anything happen with Elvis . . ."

We ascended the stairs to the second floor heading toward Priscilla's reclusion. The closer we were, the worse was my feeling. In the middle of the stairs I seemed to hear some sounds from above. But when we came up the sounds disappeared.

"Give me my daughter. I will take her to my wife alone."

The nanny reluctantly passed of the child to the loving arms of the King.

Elvis walked with his daughter toward her mother - his wife like a king of Satyricon. He walked slowly and cautiously. The woman walked with him and constantly monitored the welfare of the child.

I remained behind them by about two feet. In any case, the hallway was not built for three people walking side-by-side. Elvis issued a hoarse sound and opened the door.

From the room sounded album "Elvis is Back!" The music was just loud so the lovers were not disturbed. The two lovers were accelerated and no one noticed our entry. I don't know where Elvis' soul was going, I know only that Elvis quietly closed the door. He became stone-faced. He looked at me still holding the child in his hands. The child began to cry under the influence of the pressure. This time it was hysterical crying.

Elvis immediately gave the child to the nanny.

Suddenly, Priscilla opened the door. Her body covered in a white sheet. She said. "Give her to me." Priscilla's eyes met with Elvis' eyes.

"Where you holding her when she began crying?" Priscilla did not have the slightest remorse regarding making love with Elvis' friend.

Elvis did not answer. Suddenly he turned to me and asked, "Who is the culprit?"

I remained silent.

Elvis turned back to Priscilla, "What were you doing there, love?"

But Priscilla didn't lose her assuredness, "Elvis, I have suffered in solitude all my life." She smiled unhampered by the fact her husband suspected something. "Do you know why I had the nanny bring our daughter to you?"

Without changing his look Elvis lightly shook his head. "Go away Priscilla. You need to go today."

He did not explode!!! He did not hit her!!! I was amazed.

"Exactly, this is exactly what I want to do." She continued, "For our daughter's sake I am not leaving immediately but I will leave."

"If you are a mother then put her to bed like a mother."

Priscilla quickly hid.

Elvis stood in front of the closed door, his right hand leaned against the wall.

Finally, the nanny looked at him with compassion, which found its expression in her question, "Aaaa, are we okay?" She motioned suggesting she was moving on to other duties.

"Huh?" Elvis stammered. "Okay? Yes, of course."

The woman looked at me with misunderstanding in her eyes and I looked at Elvis, who had just bounced off the wall with his hands.

"Come on down, just come on. Let's go."

# 19
# John Casey's Lounge

We gathered in the dining room.

The table was cleared. The cook staff was finalizing the details and the cook noticed Elvis' composure.

We stopped at the table but Elvis did not sit, "Lola I forgot to say thank you for everything."

Lola smiled.

The nanny arrived once more with an inquiry, "Sir, your wife promised the payment for this month's work." She did not finish.

Elvis did not answer. He smiled in a form of self-ridicule.

I responded, "How much?"

Meanwhile Elvis shook his head. "So what amount did you and Priscilla agree on?"

"It is $400.00."

Elvis shrugged. He didn't seem to care much whether she said five hundred or a thousand, none of that would surprise him. Elvis' gaze shifted to me and he asked me, "Do you have $400.00 dollars to give her? I never carry money with me."

Fortunately, I had $500.00 in my wallet. I rummaged about and handed the money to the woman. Her eyes thanked me. Everything was over for her now.

As soon as she had money in her hands, she longed to leave. "Thank you."

"Yeah, you did your work, didn't you?" Elvis puzzled her because she could easily understand his sentence as heavy irony and Elvis perhaps even used the irony as a catalyst. He didn't look sad or bleak at all. During the sentences about money his death mask changed to a face of an ordinary man who cared nothing more than what the others were saying. This change of him made the woman even more uncertain.

"Well then, Sir, goodbye."

Elvis looked at her and smiled.

It was evident the woman hoped for a quick departure.

"Wait, where are you going?" Elvis surprised her. He said it quickly.

"Pardon? What do you mean?" She turned and appeared uneasy.

"Which way? You'll take us to the club – it doesn't matter the way you go really, you can just drop us." He ordered without a care. He turned to me. "Do you still have some cash?"

The woman clearly did not like the situation but she remained silent.

"No, you needn't pay me anything, I'll gladly take you, Sir." She force a smile. "How long will you need to prepare?" She asked.

Elvis looked at me. In his eyes I saw enthusiasm of a young boy, a boy who had neither wife nor a child. "We're done here, right?"

Willy-nilly I nodded. After all, I saw and experienced, I would expect a night club the last place where I would end my day but it sounded refreshing to be quite honest. It was hard to determine whether his plan were intending a revenge of some kind.

In the woman's face I saw so much enthusiasm an obituary could be written.

The cook asked Elvis if she could leave.

Elvis nodded.

She wished us a good night.

The woman who waited on us was probably anxious to wish us the same.

After the cook's departure, we moved off.

At the gate for departure, Elvis shared, "I don't wish anyone to protect me today. Today I want to just be a normal man." For Elvis, was this even possible? He was naturally entertaining.

The woman let us into her older Buick. Elvis took the shotgun position, I settled into the back seat.

"So where to gentlemen?" The nanny asked without enthusiasm. She watched Elvis' face, as if she wanted to gauge know how long his boyish behavior would last.

Elvis smiled at her. I think his smile disarmed her. "Do you know Graham's circus, uh, John Casey's pub is?"

The woman swallowed. Her facial expression suggested she was well aware of the type and where the club was.

"By the way, why are you going with me?" She inquired.

"Sometimes there is nothing better than to just go and be someone else. Today, or tonight, I'm beginning again and I want to ride in the style I came from."

The woman said nothing.

Elvis continued, "If you would like to you could come with us. What is your name?"

The woman smiled slightly. In the dark I couldn't see her face, but I heard it I heard the flutter of slight female smile maybe the first indication on the way of release in the proximity of the king, "My name is Elizabeth."

"Call me Elvis Elizabeth, after all it is as if you are the mother of my child – we can be on an intimate level."

The woman remained silent before asking, "Everyone calls you Elvis?"

I remained quiet feeling like a third wheel.

As time progressed, the woman appeared increasingly honored by the fact Elvis exhibited interest in her.

"Nickname?" Elvis turned to me.

"King?" I retorted and Elvis began laughing as well as the woman.

Elvis felt something that was giving him a male power:

"I sick of all of the fame but folks tell me without a talent like mine people would be less happy."

"I believe you. It must feel like a curse." The woman apparently wanted to remain agreeable.

I looked out the window into the black night.

"Are you two friends? I mean, good friends?" She asked.

"Friends?" Elvis asked himself.

For a moment, there was silence in the car.

"But . . ." the woman seemed to hesitate, "But . . . Elvis . . . just why do you plan to visit the largest mafia enterprise in the city?"

"I'll tell you. Elsewhere is not worth it. I'm glad I am going for a change of pace."

We were not travelling not five minutes further before Elvis slowly placed his hand on the right knee of the nanny. The woman did not do anything. She neither looked at him nor moved his hand away.

Elvis held his hand there a long time. He didn't go with it anywhere, his hand remained where it landed.

Suddenly she asked, "Should I stop?"

Elvis did not respond. The woman turned her head to him. Elvis was looking in front of himself. His hand and eyes did not cooperate at all.

The woman decided to stop by herself. She stopped on the side of the road. There were no street lamps on.

Elvis turned his head to her.

If I felt like a third wheel before for certain now.

The woman herself led the king's hand up her knee, I was not surprised. When her hand moved down there my hand moved towards the door handle.

In that moment the King surprised me.

"And what?" He asked with a boyish voice as if a little boy asked a big woman (whether possibly his friend could too?).

"He?" The woman smiled in the dark. "Let him get out." So, we had another ice queen here.

I got out of the car. I looked skyward and saw a lot of bright stars. I felt like a humiliated man. Although I really did not want her.

After about three minutes, the passenger door opened and Elvis' head leaned out.

"Get in." His voice was already suspiciously angry.

I hopped in the car. Atmosphere materialized nothingness was waiting for me. The woman did not say a word, her face all the time turned to the windshield so she could see the road well. Elvis looked at me. His face was stone. I didn't know what happened and by what I saw, I did not even want to know what happened. I didn't want to know it as a person but as an agent I was longing for it! And so we drove through Memphis without a word. The woman didn't seek to establish contact at all. She turned on radio and we listened to some reports, results of an unimportant baseball match. The result of those two teams interested me but I don't remember it now. The radio even mentioned something about the weather.

According to the files, I knew Elvis wasn't sufficiently manly. It was a theory at least. We traveled and then it happened, the radio began to play, "Love Me Tender."

When the woman heard introductory notes of the song, she smiled slightly or was it a grin.

"Please change the station," Elvis demanded.

In that moment there was no winner in the car?

"This is my car."

Elvis turned his face away and looked out the window. "Love Me Tender," continued and Elvis became increasingly saddened. Perhaps he perceived his situation. The journey lasted thirty minutes.

We stopped on a street full of beautiful cars. Impressively dressed women were standing outside and men were walking around everywhere.

The woman looked at Elvis. "I think we're here."

Elvis smiled a little, "Come with us I'll make it up."

The woman smiled as someone who regretted the man he saw in front of her. "Maybe you'll be more successful alone. Good luck." She gave him a final look and drove away.

I got out the way I'd gotten in the car – unnoticed.

"Come on, this pub is something you've never seen before." He smiled.

Elvis led me through the throng of people. Some women shouted at us.

I forgot to mention as soon as we stepped out of the car Elvis put on his black glasses. At night it helps. The street only made sense at night. It the daylight it was empty and pointless.

"I love the night life," he exchanged in my direction.

We walked a short distance to where a line of people waited to get inside the club. Elvis began to do his "Elvis" bit. He became somebody everyone wanted to be with. In the middle of the entertainment among hundreds of foreign young people he was King. Till now nobody knew a genuine King was coming. The guards were a different story. One of the two noticeable guards immediately disappeared in the dark of the entrance door. A smile of megalomania appeared on Elvis' face. I've never seen him more satisfied before. He was like a machine.

I continue to remain silent.

We came upon a mass of people and Elvis wanted to push forward without guards into the crowd. I pushed behind him.

"Why are you pushing?" Someone shouted who was pushed off by Elvis but he did not respond. As soon as the words *why are you pushing* sounded from the crowd, the guard started toward the masses like a wild bulldog and he was yelling.

"Let the King go." He began to thrash people who stood in front of Elvis. Moreover, in the very moment when the guard began to attack people, some tall, powerful men emerged from the underworld of the pub. They were dressed rich and sexy. They joined the bulldog facilitating Elvis' journey. Elvis looked more and more wistful. He was happy. The more more the machos got the crowd to clear the more he appeared to be the King entering his Kingdom. People created a corridor as they were forced to do so. Manifestation of strength was enough for them. In any case more and more of them began to realize who he was and the reality of their situation. I was pushing behind Elvis. One of the overly zealous security guards grabbed me and tossed me toward the masses. Elvis simply forgot me. He was intoxicated by the success and power it provided him.

I barely witnessed the events. I noticed Elvis was walking boldly onward. This was the maximum social game but what else remained to Elvis when his real world was becoming a victim of? I saw a woman jump at Elvis and start kissing him.

I had to speak up, I knew Elvis was in such a rush he would forget me. "Elvis, Elvis, they pushed me away." I screamed as loudly as I could. Elvis finished his kissing with the woman who had jumped on him. His hand said to the guard to push the woman away. He tried to turn his head to the source of my voice; in any case, he couldn't see me in the crowd. I raised my hands and I was trying to wave in the crush.

"That's my man over there with those hands," he shouted to one of the guards: By chance it was the same that had pushed me. He began to make his way to me and yelled.

Soon he was with me. People were getting out of the way in fear and I'll tell you it was enough for me to have a good feeling they did it for me. Being an unimportant person it felt interestingly good. The man grabbed my hand. He immediately pushed back pulling me as a lucky loser. I felt magnificent. In those seconds, I was suddenly on the side of Elvis. Finally, I was beyond the border where we were all equal. The man immediately stopped holding my hand as soon as we became free and quite brutally he pushed me toward Elvis where more strong men were standing.

Elvis' was embracing a smallish man who had a brilliantly maintained beard. It was everything I could see because of their hugging. They appeared to be best friends they even whispered something into one another's ears and laughed. Now I could see what it meant seeing the happy King, who was just overcoming his Satyricon. They were hugging as brothers . . . The only thing I heard was, "Whatever, Elvis, anything . . ." Then they stopped hugging.

Elvis immediately turned to me and grabbed my hand. The same hand that had been pulled by one of the guards who pulled me to him. Now I was not surprised anymore by his theatrical and exaggerated introducing me to his powerful friend, "I'll tell you, this guy gave me a lot today. More than anyone in recent years! It seems once again I will love the only thing I know to do best. He winked with his right eye but immediately laughed and said, "Salvation and music, John!"

The powerful man laughed, leapt up to me and hugged me. I felt like being in a dream, which was neither good nor bad. In fact, in the hugging I felt somehow foreign but the man was whispering to me like someone actually very, very extreme, "If Elvis tells me someone had given him a lot, the entire pub is his. I'm John Casey, baby! And John Casey isn't just anyone. Today, just like the King "you" are the King here. Just enter my pride and take what you want, drink what you want. Everything is yours." Then he winked at me. He didn't want to know my name, Elvis was my warranty because that's the way of how things go. One evening I was a great person – it was my 15 minutes of mafia fame. John Casey was not the only one who winked at me. When the hugging ended – Elvis winked at me, too. In that moment I felt like the most powerful agent anytime and anywhere.

John Casey was a very small man. He may have been only one hundred and sixty centimeters. He had mafia charisma. Think of Don Corleone from "The Godfather," played by Marlon Brando. He also had remarkable differences you cannot easily find in any mafia movie. While I mentioned his beard, I must also mention his gelled hair piled up like James Dean; however, at this time – it was no longer fashionable. I could not exactly recognize the color of his eyes but they seemed to me to be brown. His face was charismatically American, equipped with several scars denoting a survivor. And, like Parker, he had a double chin. His tummy, was equal in merit as Elvis' all-American boy façade in as far as terms of success and fame; except John Casey was an all-American boy in terms of food and drink.

I focused on his nose last. It appeared flattened, there was no doubt John Casey was a rough fighter. And yet it was out of the question he would have enough money for plastic surgeon. He probably looked at his nose as a gem I figured. Given his height, his nose said he was not just anyone. He was not Mr. Soft. He probably won his post as boss.

John Casey wore a very expensive black shirt, which I complimented. I knew who John Casey was. In Elvis' file he was present as another collaborator, as another liaison, although his business interests were not good. John Casey was important. Removing him from the local infrastructure would prove a big mistake, even if he imported tons and tons of cocaine and heroin into the States because he contributed large amounts to the state budget.

Elvis approached me. He hugged me. He tried to hug me even more than John Casey did. John was standing close to us and I think he understood it very well. He could understand, what was Elvis was attempting. In his forceful embrace I was almost certain Elvis had forgotten catching Priscilla as he had. Well, this was a survival tactic, especially at night, which was just beginning for us.

We were three altogether different men. Yet we were sentenced to create a trio that would make his way through the night.

Elvis finally stopped hugging me. I was able to breathe a bit again. It was my last inhalation before entrance into the underground. Immediately after his hug, Elvis entered the inner sanctums of the club boisterously.

John Casey walked ahead with his security far behind us. With his figure Elvis was hiding the figure of John Casey. Elvis slid through the dark entrance, which was faintly illuminated. After about one meter later, stairs emerged in front of us. They led steeply somewhere down and were made of marble. Shoes with heels generated raunchy sounds on them. Everything around us was made of quality wood. Even when touching it, the wood seemed soft and the fragrance spread by the wood was even stronger than the rising stench of cigarettes, which seared our nostrils.

I was not sure whether I felt just the smell of cigarettes and wood but everything was so new it was all combined in my mind as one single feeling. Black wood, marble stairs, intensifying music and Elvis, who walked ahead of me.

We walked about two minutes, which was too much for an entrance in my estimation. There didn't appear to be any people standing in this staircase that led us lower and lower into the underbelly of the club. With each new inhalation I perceived the pub as a guarded and perfectly controlled place.

Finally we entered. John Casey parted slightly something like a curtain, which consisted of several parts. He was parting and parting what looked like a single curtain, at last manifested as more curtains. I did not count them, but there were a lot of them. Parting of all curtains lasted very long but the look that I was given, I think that if I was speechless for a moment. First, what stunned me was the room. Never before (or after) have I have seen such a large underground space, which would serve for entertainment of people. John Casey built his club in underground parking garage. It had two floors. Each contained at least six bars. Professionals were working at each of them. Everyone in this great club could feel like something divine. The second thing that surprised me was the number of people. For such a large space there were very, very little of them.

Imagine a hundred to two hundred people in one big, even giant underground parking garage converted into an expensive crash pad.

When Elvis entered, eyes of all women landed on his person. Of course, Elvis was aware of it. He kept his black glasses on. He was walking like the King Rock n' Roll. While Elvis was walking theatrically - when I looked back - I saw the entire place was full of theatrical walking. Like anything else, in a short time what appeared odd to you – you begin doing.

I was also walking equally theatrically. I guess I would also think that every child of God was looking at me but I knew Elvis offered people a lot more than I did. So, I calmed my walking behind him and started to concentrate on my work. I was observing people. First thing I noticed was that most visitors – especially women – had already been in a particular state of mind. Someone unknown abandoned his place behind the bar. A female figure, I knew it exactly according to her walk and a smile. The woman was aiming for us. She had an irradiated charisma in herself and her smile (in spite of the fact that it expressed also her drunkenness and clearly revealed that she was stoned) was a spark.

John Casey saw the woman the first. He immediately stopped hugging Elvis, stretched out his arms to her and hugged her. The woman did not care for being hugged by John Casey, I saw it in her face. Her eyes were continuously on Elvis. Elvis looked at her but by the expression on her face he did not know her.

"Elvis, I think I needn't introduce you this lady." John said in a magnificent voice.

The woman had no make-up and therefore her face seemed to be compelling in a club where a strong make-up just swarmed. During the introduction her expression was very indifferent. She moved toward Elvis as if he were a tourist attraction while her eyes and her face seemed to express the truth who Elvis actually was.

"I think he doesn't know me," she said with a grin. And the idea crossed my mind just at that moment that the fact that the King didn't know her was making her happy. After a long time John finally looked in Elvis' face and just then he probably also realized that Elvis didn't know the woman indeed. He was surprised but his hesitation took less than two seconds – and he immediately smiled. "Well Elvis, this is one of the best blues singers in America today.

Elvis donated another irrelevant look to the singer. Obviously, he did not need any big stars except of himself. "Name?" Asked Elvis. His voice expressed his real lack of interest.

The woman began to laugh. Her laughter was honest. She honestly laughed. Delighted with the laughter of the women, John Casey also smiled a little, while he threw in during that smile, "This is Janis Joplin Elvis."

Elvis rightly assessed the laughter as a mockery, probably he was looking for support from me. I was looking at Janis and trying to assess her personality. Although I caught Elvis' eyes but I did not consider it as important. I knew something about Janis. I got the basic information but all the information had one thing in common, "Janis is not dangerous. She's an alcoholic and drug-addict who can sing. In any case, her music was not dangerous."

I looked at Elvis and asked myself whether the only difference between Janis and Elvis was only the fact Elvis had a broader scope. He sang to the masses - otherwise the same people were standing opposite each other in the moment.

Elvis looked in Janis' eyes, at least he seemed to do so, although his black glasses still indicated nothing. "Do you love music?" He asked her as a teacher.

Janis looked as if she did not relate to the question. "I sing music . . . Have you ever seen someone singing without loving it?" she asked.

From the first moment she saw him, she did not like Elvis. And I didn't know why. Maybe just the new generation did not accept him. He was visibly touched by what Janis said. Elvis looked like he had standing at Priscilla's door.

"Everyone calls you a King here today and each pussy will want you. But don't ask me any crap, I'm not your villain. Nobody here will never be your villain. No one who loves the truth about how it is going here and she made a grimace. She touched her lips with her tongue, which was accompanied by a wrinkling of her face and a showcased smile. She was clearly a woman who was dependent on nothing and nobody.

John Casey remained puzzled. In this situation, he could only defend his great customer, "Maybe you drank a little much, don't you think?"

"Oh, the force is attacking." Janis waved and left as someone who did not need a King, while she had created her own artificial kingdom.

Elvis remained standing.

"Don't worry about that - she is already so – she drinks too much. Who knows what else."

Probably. She hasn't been famous long – it wears on you at first." Elvis devised something in his defense post her attack.

Janis had clothes I hadn't seen on any of her photos. She was dressed all in red and unlike her style that was presented post-mortem, she was wearing a skirt here in the underground.

Elvis and John were certainly not appreciative of her sparkle in the moment and although I had not spoken with her, she seemed to give a hint of her true opinion. If she were sober, maybe she would explain it further.

Suddenly Elvis said in broken and depressed voice, "These people will never be interested in what I'm doing." Now everything was on John and me to bolster the King once again. John was fast.

He caught Elvis under his arm and apologized in a loud voice, "Forget it, you're the number one here, you know it. Just look how all those our small models are looking at you. I'm inviting you to the bar, be my guest." He suddenly looked at me and continued in the same voice in which he tried to highlight his obligatory enthusiasm, "You two my kings. You guys I could never hear a word against you."

I don't know, did Elvis love this pathos in the voices he was hearing? It seemed so, because he let John pull him over to the bar although his face was not exactly the freshest and most joyful. Mafioso who could help Elvis, was not yet just Mafioso?

We walked to the bar, to the largest and the most occupied one. In spite of the fact in entertainment night clubs blur differences between social groups, this pub was different even by the stratification of its clientele. When I was gradually acquainting with the guests sitting at the bar I saw only famous and important personalities. And most I didn't know. It was immediately clear he didn't sit at the first bar in error.

We sat down on black leather bar stools. John was still flying around Elvis, even when sitting. Immediately he ordered something special. It did not take long. The waiter brought us blue fluid in half-liter glass, with a strange reflection. I noticed the color of the drink only briefly because I could not get enough seeing one particular man who was sitting about three spots far from Elvis.

Elvis was sitting to the right of John and me to the left. I got the last place on the edge. The man was Jimi Hendrix. Not that I admired him, I just remembered what I read about him in our reports. He had talent. He influenced people.

Jimi had beautiful ladies next to him, who were, as I learned later, were paid by John. Jimi's rebellion could be successful – and not because he was black.

All the beautiful women here, who were beautiful without meaning anything, were paid by John.

Totally ignoring Jimi and his two girls, Elvis was staring trancelike. A smile appeared on his face as late as when he saw the blue drink before him. He put down his black glasses. His eyes lost nothing of sanguinariness that accompanied them since the injecting expeditions of Dr. N. He patted John on his shoulder and he asked in his great while sweet naivety, "Listen, John, what would you do if the cops barged here and began checking.

John Casey smiled and returned to patting Elvis' shoulder, "Come on, Elvis, I know what I will make you happy."

Elvis grabbed his cup and clinked it with John's, then began to drink. After about two swigs he realized I was there. He immediately turned and stopped drinking. He turned a little before he could be in control of the cup, which was just drifting away from his mouth, so he splashed himself a bit, but he didn't care. He shrugged, so I couldn't know whether he did so because of the splash or because he had forgotten me. He clinked with me and said, "Peter, this is the drink of truth. Really, it is. Get ready, this is no longer about where you are and what you got. This is about whether or not you can find the power in yourself to accept it, so bottoms up as they say."

At that moment I thought he would continue talking but he stopped and drank. He drank six generous swigs.

I tried to look as if wanting to imitate him but my swigs were small and short.

Elvis and John drank like masters.

While we drank I divided the people at the bar into two groups, those who really meant something did not look at us – and if so their glances were only fleeting. Those who meant something had self-control in the world of fame, competition and intellectual castration that they rarely would lose control.

John stood up and went for Jimi, with his glass in his hands. He clinked with him, then he was saying something to him, and then he clinked with him again. But the best of his little visit was he did not even once look at the women.

Meanwhile, Elvis leaned to me and was something telling me, something that I did not understand because he spoke quietly and dimmed.

At that moment, I forgot about Elvis' voice. His mouth opened again and again but I laughed at the music I heard instead. The club, which was, as we know, a retelling of the rules of the society, resonated with a song of a group that still should become a legend of any underground, which will aim for ignoring the society as much as it will be able to afford. Suddenly Jimi was standing next to me with a smile from ear to ear. I saw Jimi was sincerely fascinated by Elvis. By the way, Jim was widely far one of the few blacks I had seen there.

John put his hands simultaneously on the shoulders of both of them. He looked at Jimi and said, "Elvis Presley, this is another inimitable genius, Jimi Hendrix."

Elvis smiled. Jimi's smile had a positive influence on him. They shook hands as of businessmen. The photo would probably circle the world but in such a case unimaginable amount of pictures should fly around the world . . . I had the feeling and the feeling immediately became belief that Elvis was delighted someone of whom he had heard was a genius, was very pleased he could meet him.

"I've heard about, they were talking me in the studio that you're somebody."

Jimi did not stop smiling from ear to ear, as if he did not hear what Elvis had said. "Listen to me, man, you know what's just playing? That's really good, it's something new. Although it will always be just something that only continues in what you once started."

Elvis narrowed his eyes for a moment, he probably tried to listen to what they played. That pose of him lasted a very short time.

Jimi slowly began to undulate in the quiet atmosphere, which was induced by the song by Lou Reed (who wrote and sang it). The text was not very consumerist but who listens to lyrics in pubs.

Elvis did not know who was singing. He was listening but did not seem to be excited about what he heard. And while Elvis in his happiness couldn't answer, chance was once again caught by Jimi. "It must be clear to you, isn't it?" Jimi did not stop smiling he used the teacher-like tone. Jimi could afford it, geniuses are permitted some leeway. After all, Jimi was genuinely a friendly type.

"I don't know that song, but the guy singing it doesn't not have much of a voice, I'll tell you."

"You know, you know. But that song is composed by him. But anyway." Jimi wanted to continue in the sentence but Elvis interrupted.

"What do you mean?" Elvis' intonation gave way to his stigma as f an artist.

"What do you mean by what do I mean?" Jimi's sincere smile turned into a mischievous smile. Was Jimi already then plagued by the domination of whites in music?

Meanwhile John Casey sipped his drink. He did so sparingly. Then he curiously, with the question in his eyes, so what happens next, looked at both of his golden guests.

"Lou Reed is good, but let's be honest, we're not rookies. None of us thinks if he were black, people would listen to him." In a moment, Jimi shared his phobia acquired from experience."

"I'll tell you one thing, you black are the best and you always will be." Elvis nodded to indicate his agreement. And he continued as a true king by placing his hand on the shoulder of Jimi who was standing next to him:

"Without you I would not be here."

"What?"

"After all, it's clear, huh? If just one white would be better, he would stand here instead of you."

Jimi was speechless. He bared his eyes like fangs. He took a sip with cheesy shaking hand, forcing Elvis to sip. John sipped with them, just as I was observing them and the situation so much I didn't get to drinking.

"You're right. Only the king can say something impertinent like that and get away with it. They always say you have a black soul like us. But you're not blacker than me Elvis." Jimi sipped again. He shrugged and if jokingly. Money for the music of the 60s belong mostly to blacks but after all it was not promoted by blacks?!"

Elvis smiled at Jimi with such a fatherly smile of an older artist.

"You should appreciate the United States."

"Listen to me, I'm sick to death of whites but I'm in this club because I like white wagtails. There's nothing better than white wagtails. Have you ever had a black beauty?"

"No, I don't think but I don't remember. Strange things take place time to time. We artists know it . . ."

Jimi laughed and patted Elvis' shoulder. Elvis grabbed his hand.

"You've something good in yourself. Sadly good but don't worry, once even I thought I was doing a revolution." Jimi looked at his wagtails . . . He remarked impassively, "Shake your hand with Dylan. He also wants just to entertain. By the way, did you meet him already? He's here and he looks like you. A mastodon."

After the words Bob Dylan is here my heart began to hammer. I knew Dylan. He was a former assignment prior to Elvis. I looked around the area but didn't see him.

Elvis, however, didn't care the remark about Dylan at all, He just wanted to talk with Jimi. Waiting for Jimi at bar tables, the ladies were already beginning to fidget dangerously, they were nervous . . . probably they would also like to visit Elvis but nobody called them over.

Elvis drank up the little amount he had left in his glass.

John nodded to the bartender and he immediately understood. The beverage was on the table immediately. He clinked with us and drank. His eyes turned into werewolf's eyes. I was looking at Jimi who was having fun with the ladies. The ladies were glad he returned to them and that he wanted them.

Elvis stopped talking. He fell into darkness. The entertainment was like evenings in gulags - as described by Solzenycin.

John and I looked at each other. He picked up his cup and I picked up my cup and we toasted. John smiled bitterly when he finished, and he again beckoned to one of the bartenders. I did not even know it, I missed to recover from the finishing of my drinking and I had a new batch before me. The drink began to do miracles with me. Something happened.

I stopped thinking, everything seemed to be very funny, my work, my life. A few seconds after I finished my drink, I felt above it all. Now it was me, who caught Elvis around his shoulders, "Do you feel as I do?"

"I feel relieved."

John interrupted, "Oh is coming . . . she is coming . . ."

I immediately forgave him for his interrupting me.

He was looking toward a woman. I did not care, she was an elderly woman. I have not really thought about what she was actually doing in a pub where there were only younger people . . .

Rather I looked toward people dancing. I saw at young women and in that moment I did not need anything more.

John leaned over to us and delivered as an usher somewhere in the Baroque Hall, "Gentlemen, this is the wife of a senator who is in the hospital with a heart attack . . ."

I was not surprised at all. I did not feel it strange.

John smiled like a candidate for president. John introduced her, "Madame George of Los Angeles, wife of US Senator . . ."

Elvis slowly turned around. Their eyes met. His face remained serious. I think he was playing a scene from some of his sad films. He said as a redneck, "Elvis Presley, son of a worker from Tupelo . . ."

The woman acted like someone who just met God.

"Signature?" She approached Elvis and tried to whisper. The music played a little milder than before everything could be understood. "I've experienced many possible receptions and embarrassing situations, believe me but don't want me to feel most embarrassed now."

John was the only one whose smile from ear to ear did not disappear.

"Well, let's say, it was an attempt to joke." Said Elvis in a voice of a man who was impressed by refinement of an older woman.

"Let's say, yes." She smiled at him.

The lady was quite sober and okay, indeed. I started to focus again. My soul returned to Elvis.

"May I ask one thing?" My first question was more diplomatic useless. We are already familiar with it, in the state where you are not entirely under your self-control, you produce specific and sometimes unnecessary questions. In any case, the first unnecessary question did not harm the lady yet.

"And who are you?" She asked me.

Elvis intervened, "He is my friend. What have you studied?"

After his words, John and the lady both stared at me - I noticed the same sparkle in both of them. I had no choice. But after all, it was helpful for me, "Philosophy."

The lady smiled and her face lit up. Conversely, a sneer appeared on John's face, clearly indicating the idea so you won with it, boy.

"I used to lecture at the University of Los Angeles, UCLA." Her smile became more pronounced and nicer, as far as a smile of a woman in years it can be prettier and prettier.

"Philosophy." Her smile became just perfect. "And where did you study?"

"Peter." I quickly added.

"Peter." She repeated my name after me.

"Princeton."

"Um, so Princeton." Well, she did not tell it just like a wife of a diplomat-politician. At that moment, I did not realize at the beginning of the day I mentioned quite other university (an irrelevant university in Memphis –while even P. informed about the University Illinois. But Elvis fortunately had no knowledge of universities.

My role became someone who graduated. "What is a woman like being a senator's wife?" I asked with a smile, which was probably the only way of mitigation of the question.

She was honestly pleased with the question. Her face, her body language indicated she was glad. I was interest in her. Elvis was pleased with the question to because he amicably banged my leg under the bar. Only John Casey remained neutral.

"I'm looking for something. It's not youth. I've had enough of it all," she said meekly. I knew it was just a beginning - she paused for a moment to assess our faces . . . whether she should say something more or rather she should remain silent seemed to course through her mind in the short silence but she did not want to remain silent. I noticed she was holding a glass of white wine in her hands. That was when she stopped in words. John was apparently the only one who was not interested in speaking to the wife of the Senator because he asked her, "Where is your guard?"

But a woman who wants to speak, whether it's correct or not, must speak to avoid suffering. "Come on, let the bodyguards be."

John was quiet.

"My husband has had a heart attack. He in the hospital. He is 51." She announced.

"I told them," John smiled but his smile and his voice indicated he was delighted he could interrupt. It was a bit strange as if he did not respect her at all, as if he didn't want to listen anymore.

"John, was all she said him."

He returned his gaze toward Elvis.

At that moment, there were no other women existing in the pub, except those standing before us. She was standing and John did not offer her a place. So far it crossed minds of no one of us, probably because we wanted to hear her words.

"I'm here. I'm not saying I want to make up for my lost years. I am not naïve. Oh, you know, all the diplomacy and politics, and all those people. Eventually it kills you. It drives you crazy. It was like flaying alive, all those years in high politics. Everyone watches everyone, everyone is trying to be slick . . . and then, when you consider those people manage something you just want to get drunk or go crazy. And to love servants. But what will change as a result of that feeling, what will change because of your pain, when you can't act? I had the good fortune my husband was a senator. At least I do not want what most people of my generation want. And you see how it changes. Most people like you, Elvis want to be just like you and not like a president of the United States."

Elvis stared at her but he didn't want to tell her anything so I made myself heard because I liked what she was saying. Even though it was one-sided. I wanted Elvis to hear from her as much as possible, "You know, if you were with Elvis even a day, you would not want to be him . . ."

"It's possible. But today I don't want to be the only senator's wife here, but I know . . . I know well that I'll never get rid of it, just that I'll be it, pure and simple." She sipped her wine and then her eyes fell on our big glasses with our blue drinks.

"What's that?" She laughed at how she asked. She was really relaxed. And it was one of the small miracles because people who are forced to live most of life in self-control use to feel very insecure and awkward.

Elvis was comforted with her feminine laughter. The woman made him relaxed. He looked at her as an honest man who needed neither to inflate nor play the star. It is a minor miracle in the case of stars.

"It's a drink that will make you relaxed and let you forget who you are, in a so beautiful way that you'll not get lost . . ."

Elvis probably ran out his words, so I quickly added for him, "Well, he wants to say that you'll not lose track of the fact that you live . . . or so. Well, well . . ." Elvis nodded.

John Casey slowly turned to the counter and ordered the blue drink. Still today I can imagine his facial expression because I think George made him finally happy. Blue drink to the senator's wife." Maybe John thought that the more the senator's wife would be away from reality, the better . . .

"And aren't you afraid of the articles in newspapers?" Asked Elvis. And it was a quite right question. Although from Elvis it looked a bit artificial. He was simply only very careful to say that sentence correctly.

The woman smiled and she said a sentence that probably did not comfort John very much, because attention began to turn to him, "John has everything under control here. No journalist with a free pen will penetrate here . . . as I know John . . . After all, it's no art to have fun when your husband is not present."

Elvis looked at John as a man looks at a man when he suspects something and he indicates in this way that he suspects something. Of course, John caught the view. There was a need to develop more sentences about John and the senator's wife, and I saw it clearly . . . I suddenly knew John used what he could to obtain the right to establish his club in the old garages.

John didn't reply to the sentence of the senator's wife. After all, what he had to say?

[148]

When the bartender delivered her big drink to the bar, John finally realized the woman was not sitting - she was standing.

"Sit down, George." He said as a man who had no reason to hide.

George smiled at him as a woman who had nothing to hide, with her wine in her hand.

"But I want to sit next to Mr. Presley. So move over. So I'll sit next to you and next to Mr. Presley – and –" she smiled.

John looked at her as a husband who knew the vagaries of his own wife and he shifted.

The woman sat down and she laid her glass of wine next to the glass with blue miracle.

"What is it made of?" She asked John about her new glass.

"Let yourself be surprised, as the boys kept did."

"Is it good?" She asked Elvis.

"Even too much." Elvis smiled. His smile was became friendlier and it infected George.

She stopped drinking her wine and attacked the glass in front of her. She sipped and then she evaluated the drink, "It's good . . . They don't drink things like this at diplomatic and political parties. Hahaha."

Elvis did not stop smiling. He added some nodding toward George.

"You know, this is a great liberation from the world, where everything is checked, every word is under scrutiny, and everywhere there are some secret agents and between her words she began to stare at me. This is a great liberation, I always knew you artists were the most free because you had something we ordinary people do not have. Friends. All dimensions of spirit, everyone has some but equality?" Her eyes rested at the blue fluid.

Elvis ceased to smile. His face grew serious. Despite the blue drink and substances that spread from there to blood vessels and veins, gullibility of a woman won. She attracted him as someone who had experienced, something he would invariably never have. At once, however, his view on her changed, "When listening you I hear we experience the same frustration. Everything is under control of someone whom ordinary people never see. And it is still the same. We live like idiots. Like fools. Money and success, showing off, I have this and you have that. But otherwise, we know nothing. Do you know who you are? Well, you see, we are in error. Maybe you like my music but I'm entertaining just to prevent others from asking what is wrong with life! Managers and companies, royalties and all parties for the wives and children of the recording companies . . . I'm famous, I am, but my fame and success, no, that is not freedom as you imagine. While a common man has to go to and from work, and then he can do what he wants, I'm non-stop at work. Even when I'm alone, I know it still haunts me." Elvis was fascinated he said what he did.

The senator's wife gave power to Elvis to tell his peak truth that he probably will not remember tomorrow but he will live it – so why wouldn't she tell him her truth? Truth for truth, even in nightclubs it is mostly an illusion . . . However, here I experienced it firsthand, the woman surprised Elvis, she put her hand on his shoulder as a mother to a son because in real life there was never time for something like that, "But . . ." She swallowed in vain. "But . . . I actually suspected none of us can be free under the pressure of our lives we must live as successful and famous people, live our lives like people who are exhibited. At least we can think. Think based on what we know about life. That even though we have everything society wants and what we need, we still have nothing more than we did in the beginning. We can still search, the biggest loss is when we stop searching. As a career diplomat, and then a politician, my husband ceased to search a long time ago. He paid for his eventual inability to be independent in thought on what he had to do." She sighed but her sigh was more than sentimental, it was a sigh in which she put her truth! Then she continued; however, not as intimate as previously, "Animals need to do something to survive. They miss it when they are hungry . . . we miss it when we are fed . . ." She smiled, "That we, Elvis, me and you, our lives – it all depends on people who are around us, whom we allow to surround us. It will always be so. See, I let no-people surround me because the people from the diplomatic circles they often know nothing on the basic requirement of survival. They believe life is what they are doing. And where is the problem?"

Elvis had the pleasure of her hand on his shoulder, maybe he even did not listen to what the woman was telling him in her attack of some sort of intellectual power after her first gulp from the blue glass. However, I listened carefully. Elvis probably appreciated her hand more than all her words. Sincere touch of a woman who did not speak to him as a doll but as an adult woman. It was a rarity. He didn't need her words of truth, much more he needed her touches of truth . . .

John Casey started to smile. He knew Elvis. He knew for him it would be increasingly difficult to understand the former professor. There are boundaries, which cannot be overcome. There are boundaries of intellect in social debates. When people with higher intellect do not pay attention anymore to the fact presentation is reaching those with a limit of understanding with theirs much higher than with whom they are talking.

No, Elvis told his truth, and as a great artist he did not need to hear any more! The woman thought he was looking contentedly and happily for her words. She began to caress him with her hand, which had been previously lying on his shoulder.

Elvis had suddenly face as a young boy. He needed an older woman as a mother. Since his mother died he was probably never feeling to be devoted to a woman, while being more devoted by his soul than by his body.

Then George pronounced a sentence, which was a little off dialogue. It was pronounced as late as she sip of her blue glass. That sentence put the crown to all that she had told before, "Connecting capitalism with the freedom of beings, it's like talking about the freedom of an animal when it must hunt to survive . . . And it is not freedom, it is only predestination to the animal cannot change, because it has no means to do so. Half-mafia – half-bourgeois club!"

John began laughing after her words. Even I smiled, too but only because John did. And in his laughter John moved to touch her shoulder and to the words, "The drink is somehow heating you up!"

Oh, yes . . ."John's laughter startled her - she realized she had gone too far that she began to say things nobody understands and no one had an interest in.

Hearing John's sincere laugh, Elvis laughed too, but the caressing reined his laughter. It was the laugh of a man who was too afraid to laugh too much.

John's laughter was loud but after a while of relaxation he stopped. He had, however, another major change - he stopped George in her philosophical flight and brought Jimi Hendrix back to his thoughts.

He heard the song of laughter and in the connection with seeing Elvis beside a woman who did not look too young at all, he decided (also under the influence of the new spirit and pharmaceutical information in his body), Jimi came back to refresh a bit his experiences from the underground pub. It was a surprise, given that his women had already started to fondle him live in open view. The direction of Jimi's evening was immediately apparent. He returned to us with the same drink, which we drank. Jimi was an experimenter. "You interest me." He said toward the older woman in a manner which hit exactly to the enterprise and the music.

In that salutation, a kind of disgust appeared in the woman, "John, today this man had already behaved disrespectfully towards me. I do not know who he is but saw he was talking with you . . .?"

Jimi smiled like a drunkard.

"She is a senator's wife, Jimi." Said John - I was not quite clear whether he warned Jimi in this way or wanted to provoke him more.

George was still caressing Elvis, which, of course, caught Jimi's attention.

"Are you here together?" Jimi looked at Elvis and he did not answer. By the tone of Jimi's voice there was no mockery in the question, probably he was not quite indifferent to the love without the generation code.

"No." Replied George hardly for Elvis.

"But I thought there was good fun here. You politicians live in your sand castles I could tell you something real; they'll never tell you something like that."

"And you are living somewhere else? According to your behavior . . ." George probably did not realize she began to behave as an offended politician's wife.

"He's a brilliant guitarist." Added John but George did not change the view given to Jimi. He understood he was not welcome.

"It will not change . . . John, it will not change." A slightly disgusted Jimi looked at John and soon after he looked at two white women who had again to wait for their original vagabond.

"Or did it already change?" He returned back to his two white women.

"I want to get out of here, now" Elvis said surprisingly while looking at George. I saw a big surprise in her face. She did not expect such an offer by somebody like Elvis. But Elvis said it to her as to a mother and what was most strange, he said as if he saw a kind of protection in her. It was a fact I could not believe for a second.

I had to open my eyes once again – Elvis' head was still staring at George.

John chimed in, "Elvis! If you wish, my driver will drive you anywhere."

I did not even breathe when George said, "It will not be necessary, I have my driver here . . ."

John grinned, but he said nothing.

Elvis interjected, "Yes, I want to go . . . with you . . . You'll take us home."

Was George still under the influence of the drink? "I never had children." She said sadly. The only thing her sentence had in common with the words said before it was the sad voice resembling Elvis'.

George had everything a woman needed in order to be able to think that she somehow miraculously attracted Elvis. But she said a sentence that just did not fit . . . was it a sentence that had no logic?

"Elvis . . . be my son tonight."

I almost fell off my chair. Secret Service nurtured such paranoia in me that I immediately saw in the senator's wife someone who was deployed to Elvis to restore all the filial values in him in one night, which every son of a mother has, who died without their relationship somehow peaked! Was it really just a paranoid construct? Elvis looked up as a prisoner, who was exempted a second before carrying out of his execution. He did not believe that someone could say something like that. And John Casey was looking at George similarly dumbfounded as I did. None of us was able to say a word.

George had to be scared but it was too late to try to take her words back or to try to somehow to steer the conversation in another direction.

Elvis returned to the blue drink once more, he caught it – and lifted his glass toward George and he clinked with her! Given his condition, it was almost another miracle of the moment.

She was liberated by his gesture. They took their sips concurrently, which was also a challenge for me and John to return to your glasses once again.

"Let's finish our drinks and go away. I cannot be here anymore. Sorry John, but I can't be here anymore." Elvis addressed John as if George had said nothing as if he was ignoring her crazy offer. Even his facial expression indicated he was focused only on himself.

In any case, George was not radiating disappointment, which in turn slightly could appear she was pleased her emotional challenge was not laughed at it ended at least ignored. She took a little sip but she laid her glass back still almost full.

"I want to go with you." Elvis said devotedly.

George was pleased. Her face, her body, her breasts, her everything immediately stood up from her barstool. "Let's go." She motioned to Elvis. She said it as a woman who was expecting victory an entire lifetime and now felt she was close to it: She felt it with her soul!

"Yes . . ."

John didn't care for George or me anymore.

"Come on," Elvis turned to me, "come on. You started it." He repeated in a voice of a boy for whom one certainty named George was not enough. He turned with eyes of a stray dog, which I did not expect. I needn't understand his look, it was enough I could understand his come on. I wanted to go with them but I was once again feeling like a third wheel. I felt an awkwardness in myself when my eyes met George's.

"Do you wish only to drive when he is going with you?" George and her question perfected the awkwardness in me. Thank God she did not ask as an intellectual. She inspired me after a while and I decided to endure another mission.

I looked at Elvis. He silently said over his shoulder, "Come with me."

George took us in direction we had come but her face expressed her disappointment.

John immediately stopped her, "You should not leave that way there will be crowds. Don't go that way, indeed."

George stopped.

"I've a back door here."

"But John my driver and my car is out there somewhere."

"You need to go by your own car?"

Elvis took her under her arms and led her, following John, to the rear exit. I was walking behind them.

I heard Elvis saying to George in his boyish voice, "I want you to come with us. I know you feel alone and abandoned. Let's help each other, for what have we left."

As I was walking, I suddenly perceived everything too unrealistic and ridiculous. I would not have expected Elvis leaving the club an older woman. And then the strength and depth fell on me, of the music that was just beginning to play, Bob Dylan, *Rainy Day Women* 12 & 35, 1966.

As I was walking, what I saw in front of me coincided with the text of the song that played loud and penetrated to me, everybody must be stoned but that's only because the unrealistic feeling was continuously merging with grotesqueness in me. I experienced a miracle, when I saw the king, I was deployed to by the Government, as well as the senator's wife, that surely used to be object of deployment of somebody minor by the Government, within the following meaning: after all, at each workplace you experience small social control of your behavior and labor passion. After all, does the Government judge everybody according to his merits – and skills – and luck – and character? No.

Seeing two people who were only too different and yet kept themselves around their shoulders because throughout the ages their souls could not find anybody more like and more necessary in the society. She was educated, he was an ignorant, but both were rich in terms of social perception of wealth, ho, ho.

He was disappointed, tired of life she did the same but each from a totally different aspect. She began hold him as a woman holds her last chance, too convulsively, but he just needed such kind of holding to combine in him whom he became . . . with whom he wanted to be? Maybe she saw and felt what his soul had become, which was suppressed. Maybe she felt in him whom he was and whom he became during his life, when nobody asked nothing him. A child who did not manage to mature in the devastating solitude and tragedy of his adult life, which no one of us has solved the sense in the big and adult society.

Did she want to save him for one night, did she want to love his soul? That was the reason why she was holding him so devotedly? She knew what she needed. She and he? Had this woman returned hope to his life? They were walking and I would swear they found themselves together.

# 20
# Post-Dylan Era

The song that played approached to its finish when someone jumped madly around my neck. It scared me, and in self-defense I knocked the striker down. And I saw a familiar face of someone whom I respected and regarded him as one of the few geniuses in music for the masses. Bob Dylan was laying on the ground and his eyes were red, even in the gloom of the pub. I perceived him similarly as his song *Rainy Day Women # 12 & 35*, he looked as one of the first video-clips of the song. I saw remnant of another man on the ground. Even on the ground he was trying to hug me laughing. None of the people with whom I was in the pub noticed that Bob had jumped at my neck.

"How are you, you reactionary?"

I liked Dylan, although it was not the real Dylan, contemplative and thoughtful. But every great man who suspects he is under control (and Bob Dylan was one of the few who suspected the truth) just as it was, sometimes had to turn off differently than all the other great artists. He turned off otherwise as Elvis. He did so to suffer as a performer should suffer – and not to be turned off to avoid suffering?

"So what is your level of paranoia today?" I asked him the sentence that he himself liked to ask Brian Jones (Rolling Stones member, death in 1969).

He winked at me. With both eyes, as if I startled him with a question. But then he replied like a man who was ahead of us in the blue drink 12 to 35, "It's bad . . . bad . . . worse than it was, cannot you see?" (In fact, Dylan lived family life in isolation in 1967, with his wife Sarah. He was also being treated for serious injuries after his motorcycle accident in 1966 in which he nearly died.)

I could become a friend with Dylan but my work like my real life hates friends for life and death. And after all, he had always suspicion who I was but never said anything that would reveal his suspicion. I knew and he did, too. And that was why we sometimes could be closer than we were with other people – he in the art industry, and I, well, with our people. Closer, because for a while we thought that even though none of us knew why, we know the best of all how. And he called accordingly his own genius, or the genius of anything and anybody.

"You needn't know why, but you know how, you know exactly how." He passed his period, when he hated ordinary people as I did. I knew that I hadn't much time to stay with Dylan, even though I liked him. You know, I already got paid for him but that's another story.

"Bob, who you are with?" No other, more personal question, crossed my mind.

Bob looked at me like Elvis used to look at men when he was sober. And he said, while I was sure he was looking elsewhere than at me, "I'm here. It's irrelevant. I don't even know but she's so artistic. A woman who can run with the wolves, what more do you need to hear?!"

I patted him on the shoulder, and extended my hand. "Bob, I have to go. Sorry."

"You're here with Elvis aren't you?"

I had time neither to lie nor to mislead, I just winked with my right eye like an old friend. (I cannot wink with my left eye – just by the way.) I wanted leave without hugging but he wanted to hug. He hugged me as a friend, with whom he had experienced something. And I hugged him as a man who didn't care at all for the hug in the moment, while just wanting to finish it as soon as possible. At that time I did not regret it, it was later when I did. He remained standing there, a little trembling. Maybe he was afraid to move in any direction.

I left him at the mercy of ladies who wanted to be fucked by someone famous.

I ran behind people who meanwhile disappeared in the darkness of the back exit. A big bouncer unblocked my way at that speed the idea crossed my mind I've already seen you somewhere (today I guess he had finished one training together with me). I think he greeted me. As a professional, he certainly had not greet me. I ran out just in time, John was standing in the warm of one of those nights when you immediately get sweaty, so high was the American air humidity. He was standing and just closing the door of the limousine, which had ordered for his darlings.

I will not forget the proud rotation of his head wondering who was seeing him when he was leading Elvis and George to the back exit. I saw it in the introduction of his accompanying, before I became a wrestling competitor of Bob Dylan. (Anyone who can be used by us, will be caught on something. He was caught on his own importance.)

When he saw me as I ran out, he smiled, and as someone who knows at least something, he said roughly, "You almost missed it." His smile immediately enriched with a touch of irony. He opened wide the door that was already half-closed and while doing it he said so the passengers could easily hear, "Elvis asked where were you. I told him that maybe you wanted to stay in the bar with some of my playmates. He smiled again and showed me with his hand "Go ahead."

It was a big limousine. An extended Lincoln. There were two rows of seats at the back, facing each other. I sat on the empty seat, although I did not like to travel in the direction opposite to the direction of the drive but I had no choice.

Elvis was glad that I entered the car, he even said, "I've thought already you preferred some young woman to me."

George was caressing Elvis' shoulders once again. Her gaze remained unchanged as well as that of Elvis' face. If she was sitting in her own car, she would probably instruct the driver not to stop.

But there was even one more thing, I was glad that we did not drive her car each agent feels more confident when he is certain he is alone in his own action. Elvis had no reason to suspect her and my eyes were waging silent war. I was in a position where I could quietly enjoy it. For a moment, I was really enjoying it: I was just looking at her without words. It was rude, it was, well, maybe even stupid because my age and her age. But excuse me, till today I don't think it was a matter of age. Fortunately, I soon remembered in she was useful in the gentle destruction of Elvis' personality.

"Elvis, I have a feeling that I should not be here. Am I wrong?" What more could I do to support a bit of conciliation with George? In any case, I did not intend to get off and leave as a loser. But George did not change her view and after my sentence she rather again focused on Elvis.

Corners of Elvis' mouth were twitching, but he didn't say anything. That question made him happy and he did not want to destroy the moment with his answer, George seemed to understand because she smiled at him.

George chose the tactic of ignoring me. She simply decided to ignore me as much as possible. I could understand her, she longed to have Elvis to herself. And after all, Elvis did not look so sad and childish he would strictly need me. In those seconds, I started to feel redundant. I had yet ignored Elvis as George ignored me. But my disregard ended when I realized it was exactly what George wanted to achieve – to make me nervous about her so that I would forget Elvis. And in that moment, I felt my strength.

"Elvis, where are we going?" I asked naively.

"Where are we going?" He contemplated once again he looked at George as a child. His view relaxed her, perhaps so much so she disregarded the fact I was with them.

I thought that she thought something like this, *Well, let him be here, fool, in any case, I don't care for sex . . .* Senator's wife, as late as now I could see her face without fluctuations caused by the shadows because the driver left shining lights in the back part, above our heads. She had a lot of wrinkles, especially around her eyes but surprisingly, although I increased her estimated age by about five to ten years, she still looked quite well. I would not call her directly a well-kept woman but a woman with a spark of fascination in her, for all educated men by her side. She was a woman with whom I'd like to talk about life but in these moments I would have preferred not to see her. There was a big difference between us, I needed her (for my work on Elvis) – she just did not know it. She certainly did not need me:

She was still caressing Elvis' shoulder.

Elvis gave her the look of whipped servant of God.

If I did not sit in the car in front of them but in a cinema I would consider the scene impossible. She finally passed over his chin with her hand. Elvis closed his eyes. I didn't know whether I should laugh or cry. I had heard a similar sentence today.

I decided to interrupt the unreal crashing of barriers between two people who were so destroyed by the society that with their respective morbidities each one hit the exact center of the soul of the other one.

"Are we going to Graceland, Elvis?"

Elvis looked at me and there was something in his eyes. I was a little afraid of, but I also wanted very much. "Be quiet for now Peter. Don't disturb the vibe." Elvis caressed her chin. She remained silent. "May I call you mom just for the night?"

Her look I would gave an Oscar. Love of a woman was in it who found her dream motherhood at least for minutes.

"Mom," she quietly repeated. In her whispering I was sure I ceased to exist. "May I hug you?"

"Don't act like a woman in that hug."

For a woman who had never had a son she was suddenly hugging a man as a son. Maybe she never hugged any man in such an asexual way. She allowed him to hug her but she herself was hugging him too. Like a real mother she kissed Elvis on his cheek but it was a kiss of a of a mother to a son.

Elvis caressed her hair.

I was looking ahead and thought of an Alfred Hitchcock film.

What I saw before me was so unreal I felt the need to hug somebody. And the best thing about it all was that any sparkles of sexuality occurred neither from the Elvis' side nor from the George's side. In what I have seen there was no way for the idea to cross my mind whether George had to control herself as much as she could to prevent development of her pretend son's hugs to touching a man with whom she wanted and desired to make love. George was hugging an adult male as an adult woman. I saw the happiness that simply could not come from reality.

The car plowed through streets of the empty city, where most people slept without thinking of their children, to their mistresses, lovers, husbands, wives. None of us in the car cared for the outside world. No one from the outside could be interested in our world because there was nobody outside.

When Elvis and George hugged I forgot for a moment who my mother and my father; I desired to be the son of Elvis and George. I did not want to disturb them. I did not want to breathe.

Elvis kissed George's forehead.

Her gaze fell on me. I felt she suddenly didn't want me to leave, she seemed to need my presence.

I didn't smile, my face was serious. I nodded.

Elvis had the mother he so desperately needed and he did not care for more.

"Mom, touch Mom." Elvis seemed to be in a trance. He something he needed and he absolutely did not care if were real or not.

"Please stop Elvis, this cannot lead anywhere – we'll feel even worse."

"Worse?! I feel worse after sex. This is something else. In any case, you wanted it yourself."

"Elvis, Elvis. I'm sorry." George recoiled.

Elvis wanted to feel good and he did until George raised her voice.

I said nothing. I was still silent.

"Elvis, you do not understand." George passed smoothly from addressing a son to addressing a lover during dissolution.

"At least caress me once more. Don't say anything." He was insistent.

I wondered if I should support either of them.

"Elvis, where do you want to go, where should you be driven?" George was presenting an altogether voice,

That non-motherly voice woke Elvis up. In a second his eyes passed from enthusiasm to disinterest. "I don't want to go anywhere, I'm sad. I am very sad." He turned his face away from George and me, and he began to stare out the window.

"I don't want to go home." Resignation was in his words.

"So, where should I drive you?"

"I don't care, they say I'm loved by all and I am not loved by anyone." He was still behaving like a spoiled child whom his mother refused something he wanted very much.

George looked at him this time there was no motherly feeling in her eyes.

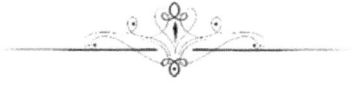

I needed destroy Elvis, but not completely liquidate him. Therefore, I showed George to be silent by putting my finger to my lips.

Elvis, saw my reaction, perhaps in the glass of the car. "What are you doing? Why do you want her to be silent?"

"Elvis you should go to Graceland. We are already turning around." I breathed in - I was not sure whether what I was saying was right, "Obviously, you are living every day in the same way."

He interrupted me, "Tomorrow I will feel even lonelier."

George smiled the first time as a dominant woman.

"Elvis Presley." She shook her head. I believe everyone's blue drink was wearing off.

Elvis shot a quick glance, "Let me be. I do not want to talk to you any longer."

"You're really like a child, Mr. Presley. It seems that you did not manage to mature." She smiled looking at Elvis.

He turned his face back to the window.

"Tell the driver to drive and let him go where he wants." Elvis was still looking into the window - it was clear that he was addressing me.

"Well, wait, when you don't want to go anywhere, let him drive me home first. My driver will manage my car or let's go back and I'll get my car."

"Let it be. You, after all, you'll be my mother today."

"Elvis Presley, I will not be your mother because I am not your mother and I have no reason to be, do you understand? I did something I should not have done, it was a moment of weakness. I cannot any longer."

"It is only a game. I know you're not my mother. But, at least for a few hours, caress me." Elvis turned to her.

"Jesus, Elvis, what are you trying to do? Do not ask me to do this again." She touched him with her hand, which was shaking maybe with a last resistance.

He touched her too, his hand also shaking rather of the joy he still reached what he desired.

Both were suddenly happy again. Each of them in their separate realm of thought.

"Mom, you see it works."

"I'm touching but feeling pain Elvis."

"That's my pain, mom."

If I could not breathe.

Elvis kissed George on her lips, he wanted to kiss her, and he wanted her as a son cannot have his mother. Did he violate the rules of the game? The rules in his own world, which thus became more George's world? So it goes among people.

George indulged him. She passionately replied to his kiss. I think in that kiss she did not care at all whether she was kissing Elvis or son or anyone. She let herself be seduced in the moment.

I began to feel uncomfortably again and wondered about her husband.

The kiss made Elvis recoil and he pushed George away. It was obvious he was confused with his feelings. "What are you doing?" He asked.

"If you suffer so much, I thought we could take a moment together and suffer together."

"I want to be your son! Don't kiss me!"

"This is madness Elvis, it was you who kissed me."

"I need a woman as a mother." Elvis repeated as a command!

The window opened between driver and passengers. The driver asked, "Where should I actually drive to?"

They were two candidates for the first word, George and Elvis and he won, "Drive out of the city, somewhere where we'll be alone."

The driver did not say a word, he slipped the window back.

"Well, I'll be your mother." George said but there wasn't joy in her voice despite the fact Elvis had told the driver, "Where we'll be alone."

She accepted the game . . . without any necessity of her special adherence, without wanting anything personal of it. She became an intellectual worker. She could play with Elvis that was it. For a moment she looked out the window. And she shook her head. Elvis did not notice.

"Do you still have parents?" Elvis asked me in a voice, which marked a kind of shift. He was asking as an adult male who did drink quite a lot but was aware of what he was asking.

"Yes, I do."

"Do you love them?"

"At a certain age only a donkey cannot love his parents, no matter how they used to be. Even when he matures, even after losing illusions about them, this is my opinion."

George laughed out loud.

"Why are you laughing?" Elvis inquired, his voice altered. He asked as children ask their mother.

The car become silent.

"I love my mom." Elvis stated. He turned back to the window again and decided not to respond more. He thought he had the right not to respond.

A few seconds passed.

"Be my mother, be it at least tonight, I do not want anymore. If you want, if you'll caress me, if you'll hear me and you'll pass your hands through my hair then together we can . . ." He trailed off and buried his head in his hands. For a moment he looked like a thinker whose forehead supports the weight of the world. "Then you can do with me what you want. Just be my mom for a while. Tell her – tell her she must do this for me. If she only knew." His endeavor, however, was short-lived.

George repeatedly shook her head. "What did I believe?" She asked, but why?

Elvis turned to us again, his face finally looked like a face of an adult male, and his voice was innovative, too. He was looking at her as a grown man who wanted more – much more than an insignificant sex. In these seconds, George had a "new man" before her. George had to reconsider her behavior again. She faltered a bit. She had good reason. "I must smoke," she said quietly.

Elvis was looking straight, somewhere in the black glass that separated passengers from the driver. His eyes neither asked nor demanded.

"Elvis, when I saw you at the bar I wanted you." George added.

Elvis did not respond. He neither smiled nor puckered his face. He did not look at her. When George noticed Elvis was not looking at her - he was still looking in front of him as a man who saw an execution of a loved one - she looked at me. She addressed me but her words belonged to Elvis.

"I'm sorry. Being insincere in my age I don't know is it stupid? I didn't know. I still don't know what I want. A woman my age should know but no one knows. There is a mystery here and we are not delving into it I'm convinced of that."

Elvis shook his head, he wasn't a man who would so often shake his head outside, "There is the mystery here but at the moment you have to make money the mystery ends. For a short glimpse it Mephisto! Blue drink hauled off but it immediately returns the soul back: Elvis went back to the child faster than any of us managed to respond, "Do you want to tell me what you wanted from me? I'll give you it if you give me mine. Please, please."

"Actually," apparently she first wanted say something other than what she finally said, "Yes, I'm accepting your offer." George drew on her cigarette, and she exhaled immediately, as if she was thinking about what Elvis said but there was nothing to think about. George finished her cigarette. She reached her goal. A man was next to her with whom she could speak more frankly rather than insincerely.

Elvis grinned.

George maintained her diplomatic decorum. But what could she do? Just admit before she would be enforced by me to do so, "Actually, you have a bit of truth Elvis."

Elvis was obviously glad that he could play, "Face it, Mom."

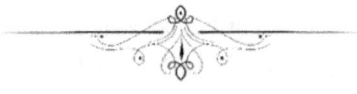

We were travelling and every street looked the same from the car.

I was hoping the driver drove us somewhere where Elvis wanted to be, somewhere, where we can be alone. Because we were alone among millions of sleeping people.

I also wanted to be alone. Alone with two people. It would not be a problem if they wanted to be alone with me.

I knew that I had to focus on something other than them. I did not feel in their presence as a free man who needn't overcome his hunger for some sort of purpose, which is still just the same game.

While Elvis was very close, I could hear his words to George in my ears as if from a distance, "What are you talking about? I experienced a lot of ordinariness. I don't want to speak with you anymore."

"Why?"

"Why!?"

"Because I am saying what I want and not what you want?"

Elvis remained silent. "It's bad air here. I'll open the window."

"Do what you want. Opening it, when you need it, my God."

Ten seconds of silence.

"I'm not well. I want to be quiet for a moment."

"I'm not well, too. That is why I have to talk. I want to tell you."

Three seconds of silence.

"Yes." He inhaled fresh air, after all, I am accustomed to be with people whom I must tolerate."

"You wanted me to be your mother and now you are tolerating me? What kind of nonsense is it?"

"So, let's make it clear once and for all. Will you be, uh, you, uh, please, uh, so are you my mom or not?"

I had to be silent, and I was

"Are you my mom or not?" Elvis' boyish voice had an undertone of expectations and drugs in trembling vocal cords. With a bit of awe, Elvis embraced George. He was hugging her, as if he did not care for her response. He was taking her motherhood, notwithstanding her agreement or disagreement. It was the hug of a child that was not completely released in the embrace, but nevertheless it was obvious that he wanted to hug.

George did not do anything – she did not have to.

The moment when Elvis timidly snuggled against her, for the third time, she looked at me. Her eyes did not express surprise – rather, there was a mockery, real ridicule, whom was she actually dealing with in my wanderings through the creation. I'm still sure with that message of her eyes. She was not afraid of his madness, she allowed him to embrace hugs as a harmless lunatic, who is satisfied with the hug . . .

"That's how it is with you?"

"Mom, I know everything, I know about everything, but I cannot avoid this. I would like to, but what would remained me, if I really prevented it.

I have nothing else, Mom. Nothing else," his right hand began to wander around her face.

George did not push him off during his touching. She still held her body close to Elvis. Her hand was shaking but she did not abandon the head of the king. At this stage her urge would be noticed by everyone except for Elvis.

"Mummy, my mom. I have always loved you, but now I know what it is about. And since then I love you even more. Terribly, terribly, because no one ever comes and tells which way is the right one, but you're the only one who didn't judge any on my ways. None of my songs of life! I never told you. Only you know. We, men, sometimes don't say such things."

For a second, George looked up to me. No new despair, no complaining. She had what she had wanted at the beginning.

"Tell me, mom . . . why don't I love my daughter as you love me? Oh yes, I love her, I love her too but when she is not with me I do not think of her when she is not with me. I cannot do it like you, mom. I'm a bad father. I cannot think of her as you always used to think of me, I would give for all on this earth for it. Mom, I cannot do it. Please tell me, mummy, please tell me how to change it. Mom, why are you silent? I know you love me, even when you are silent. But why are you silent?"

George could not remain silent anymore, she had been silent as long as she could. And perhaps she also felt a little sorry for the "little child" who, despite everything before, was suddenly sincere. He was wounded and bled as only the soul can bleed . . .

"Son, not every father who loves can be a good father. Maybe we somewhere made a mistake." Her face was no longer the materialization of coercion, it was a face of a woman who was trying to be as honest as a woman can be honest in a game.

"Where mom. Where did the mistake happen?" Elvis finally got it.

"The mistake, perhaps I loved you too much. The greatest love never gives maximum freedom. Have you been ever loved so that you were bounded by it?"

"Yes." Elvis answered as a boy defending his mother even though he did not know why. He just felt that he ought to defend her.

"I don't think so, my husband loved me just because of himself. And a woman sometimes comes too late to a man's world"

"Surely it was me, who was loving you in this way, mom!" He would probably never open in this way before his real mother – the game helped him to be more and more honest.

Were we overcoming the remaining blue drink in ourselves or were we supporting it? After all, who cared?!

# 21

# A Game in the Night

Elvis was immersed in his game. It was enabling him to feel freedom. It was a confidence booster suggesting he had his pain under control.

Under pressure, in the atmosphere of the space and surrounding people, George was beginning to become a mother with a taste for love.

"Mom, I no longer want to live in such a misery, where nobody loves me." His words were serene. "Mom, I know why – it is because I am afraid to love."

"What are you telling me - you can love – you've got your wife and child - you gave birth to love."

Their dialogue was becoming more and more denomination of life in its beauty, in its variability, in his human sincerity – to admissions that rarely surface.

"Mom, I don't know whether I gave birth of love. I don't know." He was expressing his sense of loss as a child freeing himself from the clutches of deception. Too bad that it was only in the game to son and mother.

"How do you mean . . . you don't know?" George was actually using the voice of a mother who was able to empathize with the pain of the son, as only a mothers can.

"I don't know."

"Do you love your wife?"

"I loved her, but . . ."

"But what?" She was actually sounding like a mom.

Again, I did not even breathe. They got me again.

"With the world, with a failure and loss of motivation to try something original, I am being deprived of love.

"What are you talking about? There is nothing more beautiful than to love your wife and have a baby with her."

"Why are you yelling?" Elvis was suddenly Elvis. His game was impeded by the fact George's roleplaying became realistic and with it came criticism.

Was it a pity?

"You are telling me something I cannot understand. I feel it sick! She ceased to love you?! Women with children who they decide to have a child with rarely cease to love them by themselves. Do you understand?"

"I know, mom. It doesn't work anymore. Something broke. I'm not that guy anymore, I used to be when you were alive."

Silence arose. George swallowed.

Elvis looked out the window for a while.

We were just leaving the city and there were hardly any cars. We'd gotten rid of millions of people who slept in their homes, hotels and other establishments.

"So where did I go wrong? Am I losing it?" Elvis' appeared to carry a cross of burden on his back. "Do you understand me, mom? What if I didn't exist anymore?"

"Stop it, it's disgusting. Never say such things to your mom. Just look, what you have done in life. You had to be born. You reached the highest success a son can reach. Never say such things ever again." George became heated. But Elvis led there.

Either he had no force to tell her anything or he felt humiliated in his confession or he was satisfied. "I made a mistake then, mom? Where we went wrong, mom?" He asked her.

She returned a response to her boy, "Was it a protection – to protect yourself?"

"The mistake, I don't know, surely God knows. Mom, God is my nearest . . ." Elvis changed the subject immediately afterword George finished her words.

"He is close to all who let him be close." Said the mother in George.

So far, I hadn't ascertained whether the senator's wife was Christian or not. But in high politics you need to be what the nation wants of you, the majority of the nation.

"Mom, I think I'm dying. I am still think I am something a Son of God in spite of all."

George put her right arm into Elvis' hair. Her hand was not shaking anymore. She looked like a happy woman. She realized it was actually her who was dictating the rules of their game. "Elvis, tell me whether your marriage is wrecked?"

"Mom, today I caught my wife making love with my employee – a supposed friend." George fell silent. She was viewing Elvis' face. Even as if she did not believe him for a moment.

I knew half of the truth, and I knew that Elvis wanted to tell the whole truth. And: he did. He suffered much when telling it, very much.

"Mom, I am paying him to fuck her. Because I cannot make love with her anymore." He caught her hand and squeezed. I cannot guess what the force of his squeezing was but once the son tells his mother about his impotence, he must be feeling the worst he can feel.

"How could I love her? When I cannot make love to her, mom?" Some tears emerged in Elvis' eyes. A man must bear his impotence but not with crying in front of his mother.

George opened her eyes differently than she had opened them so far in our journey.

"Tell me what should I do? Nothing, Mom, nothing. Just listen to me."

"Well . . ." George looked like a mother now.

"I," Elvis inhaled and choked on the words he was pronouncing. He shivered struggling with the words.

George squeezed his hand constantly staring at him. And then she looked at me as an actor in her role but I know that she was as honest as she could be, "Tell me, why young children have to suffer this way?"

I had nothing to say, her question reached my vanishing point. Today, I would probably answer what most of you would answer, who experience September of their lives but have survived several winters too.

"We just have to live and watch before us and enjoy everything possible. Suffering? Okay. Also we can find beauty of shed leaves or sprouting of new and beautiful flowers. I experienced it and I survived it. I have learned of it as a tree that sheds leaves after a week of unfortunate winter weather in the middle of summer." George's words seemed spatial. Older people get that way.

I said nothing. Just my eyes replied, *I don't know internally.*

In the meantime, Elvis was preparing words of great pain but George stopped him when she answered her own question. "Oh, there are already too many human worlds to endure it in your own world. All worlds that preceded us and you are enough. Our consciousness is like a small child, which we describe as brilliant." She was philosophical.

But Elvis did not understand her, "I don't understand you mom, are you listening to me?"

In her thoughtfulness of a mother she was confronted with pain that her son – another human being – could not endure. She did so in such a way he could find something more in his life. Fortunately, she caressed him with her voice.

Elvis slipped from the grip of her palm. Elvis grinned

George's genuine deep feeling was gone. She decided she would control and speak only what she would think Elvis would have wanted to hear.

"Mom, maybe I know what is wrong."

George caressed his shoulder.

"I need to ask you something. You live and you know that I will live after you, I will live, even when you have already died because that's how things go. Right?" He conjured a grimace. "You see yourself in me. I know it. You are proud of me. When I look at your granddaughter, I don't see my continuation. I do not see anything. I like her. You know I love her. You know, I'm good. I know it too. But I do not take my daughter as my great continuation even when I am holding her in my hands. It is the most beautiful thing I know. But it isn't me mom. I don't think it is me."

"When I was young I often felt that way son. It happens." For a moment she paused, her eyes narrowed, as if thinking, as if trying to feel what a mother would say. "I believe in you son. As a mother, I cannot do more than this." Her voice was not bearing dramatic pathos and exaggeration. She said what she did with some pain and abruptly but it did Elvis a world of good.

Elvis shook his head up and down, which was a sign he digested what George the Mom had said. He went on, he had still much to say to his mother:

"I would like to change it, mom. But I don't know how. I am striving to look at people as someone who lives with me in this world. It says nothing to me. I feel as if I am striving as an idiot. I am striving to say to myself look . . . look . . . for example when I look at small children, at my beautiful daughter that will live after me it says nothing to me." He looked at me and said, "You know yourself best. You saw it all."

When he addressed me I decided to put the opportunity to good use, "Elvis, use this chance. Put all this into your singing. You have many good works in your hands."

Willingly or unwillingly, George played my note. Her voice, her facial expression was the most severe since she adopted the mother game as the game that can teach her something, to accept something and throw away something, "Elvis, you're my son. Now listen to me! You seem as if you want to suffer. Everything you said, everything was best answered by our fellow traveler here."

Elvis just shook his head. He inhaled, a kind of force was in his inhalation, which he probably hid up to this great moment. He was preparing to say something more. "Now listen to me. I've had so many dreams until I became famous, so many dreams. One thing I know, it's not a coincidence I am who I am. It was predestined. And, the proof is, in understanding there must be some deeper meaning to all of this. I often feel if I wanted to be different, something would not let me."

No, no, Elvis was not predestined to tell it. The greatest things are to be carried out rather than told. The biggest things only rarely need to know words in advance.

The moment in which Elvis was prepared to speak again, the window between us and the driver opened, the driver turned to us and in a hoarsely heavy voice of a smoker he slowly, wearily and impassively said, "This is where I used to catch fish. Nobody is going to be here. It's clean and quiet."

When the window was rising back, I distinctly heard him philosophizing for himself, "Every man needs nature, especially when he wants to be with a woman after a hard night with a friend."

In my concentration I didn't realize we'd stopped.

[168]

George opened the door on the side where she was sitting. She didn't give a single view to Elvis. She got out quickly.

Elvis was looking at her with eyes of a son being abandoned by his mother in the most important moment.

"She is not interested in my thoughts Peter."

"She's a stranger, Elvis." I thought he knew what to do. It was enough to listen a little longer. "Come out of the car Elvis." I told him almost as a father. I got out through the door left open by George. There was no dawning outside yet. Night and darkness were reaching their peak. At least for us the people of the city stopped and nature started. Elvis remained sitting in the car. Meanwhile George pulled out another cigarette.

"What would one do without this?" She meant cigarettes. It is strange how the human thinking and interest of the society are changing. Today we live in an age when all intelligent people are striving to quit smoking but in 1968 everybody strived to smoke.

She turned to me. Her face looked differently than it did in the city. She did not belong here but with a cigarette in her mouth she was looking like a sincere creature. I started to miss Elvis. I didn't come here to chat with to George. "Elvis, get out of the car, otherwise we'll begin to think you are afraid of nature."

"Let him be, now he must settle it himself." Quietly twittered George. Here I saw her age.

Darkness, night, and pleasant coolness covered our differences. In the large area, which was somewhat marred by cigarette smoke, I finally considered her my peer.

"I don't think you're his great friend. A friend is more or less an insult. Rather, you are a person who has his hours in his hands," George said it calmly. She exhausted cigarette smoke from her mouth when she finished.

I could only smile and remain silent.

"His manager pays me. Elvis' career declines. We want to change it."

She smiled as a woman who knew the truth but remained silent.

"What's his chances?"

"He must do it," I said so confidently.

She drew on her cigarette. And again she moved into new waters, "I do not like his suffering. It's so unrealistic. That suffering of him is leading him nowhere. I always thought true artists suffer Elvis is heralding weak men. I see an axiom in him."

"He does not compose his own music and he does not sing his own texts. He doesn't feel he relates with the whole generation."

"I know. Sinatra didn't sing his own songs and what a great performer he was."

"This is a new generation."

"What do you mean? Are you listening yourself at least a bit?"

"By the way, Sinatra was controlled by the mafia."

He had to sing as for his life, the best he could. When I listened to Sinatra's albums, he sang as if someone had held a gun to his temples. Every second of singing he was close to collapse."

"People with Elvis use to know a lot about music." I smiled again.

She looked at me with dubious respect.

"Does that make sense I mean, what do you do?"

Fortunately I did not have to answer because Elvis climbed out of the car. He was getting out of a large spacious limousine as if he was getting out of a FIAT 500.

He did approach us but he headed off to the forest line where he took a leak.

We stayed silent with George. In any case, the silence did not last long because she approached me and in a whisper she asked, "Do you think I helped him today or I hurt him?"

"I don't know, what do you think?"

She slowly shook her head, for a few seconds when retreating from me, she bowed her head to the ground.

Even after Elvis finished, he still left us alone. He walked alone.

When we noticed Elvis did not acknowledge us, George wondered, "Shouldn't you follow him?"

"You said yourself he needed to be alone. So let him be alone."

She smiled at me and returned her gaze to Elvis.

In my new view on him he appeared to be a man who wanders without soul through dark night without knowing why.

"Elvis, come over here, why be so alone?"

He didn't answer.

"Solitude is calming. Such solitude I haven't experienced in a long time. Unfortunately, you're here." He chuckled under another grimace.

Neither George nor I have not responded to his statement, we just looked at each other. We stood on a small natural plateau where two trees grew. One was on the Elvis' side, it was smaller. The other was on our side. I did not care what species it was for me it was just a tree. The plateau was surrounded by a landscape that could be called "micro-valley". We were standing on green grass that was not burned with sun because there was a small river flowing around that was big enough for fishing. In its flowing, the river was making a very soothing sound.

The driver's door opened and the driver got out. He lit a cigarette in his mouth. He did not approach us. He walked in the opposite direction toward the road – it was the last possible direction if he wanted to be alone.

He did not say a word. I figured he was looking in the mirror and saw nothing to prevent him from getting out. Probably he thought it was the usual case when he drives couples home from John Casey's club. He stood about fifty meters from us. I saw only his silhouette. I saw him looking at the sky and observing the stars. So I looked up too. George followed me. She lifted her head, too. We were imitating the driver but it was satisfying.

I suddenly smiled. I used to observe stars many times in life but the last time I did so I was perhaps twenty. Since then, it never even occurred to me anymore.

"Why are you smiling?" George inquired. She asked quietly, she did not want to disturb the atmosphere of silence, which occurred after the driver got out and opted for solitude.

I didn't answer but I still said something, "Let's sit down under the tree."

Now it was George who smiled. She immediately added to her silence a charming smile, "Last time I sat under a tree I was about twenty, I was with my first lover."

I said nothing to her short nostalgia, I led some space in her soul, so that she could remember and love life as well as she can.

We sat down. And I think that we suddenly felt well.

I was glad that my inside turned this way. I was feeling the tree when I rested against it. And I felt also George's warmth and breathes, because I was also touching her arm: Shoulder on shoulder.

This was a new life. We did saw neither glory nor destruction, we did not feel the loss of human nature in someone else, and we saw Elvis when he – also – sat to his tree. Did he imitate us? Or he just wanted to naively feel a living organism in the contact of the "insignificant" tree?

Could he forget in the nature that just a while ago he was trying to fool himself with a mother, whom he was trying to cover all his wounds?

Hard to say whether he imitated us or not, when he sat down, but he reached what he wanted (explanation of this certainty this will come soon):

He found his purpose without any forcible seeking. It was enough to sit under a tree in a pleasantly cold night, when he did not feel forced to breathe, sing, live.

He began to sing on his own accord, as a free man, he began to sing for himself!.

Of course, we did not hear his heartbeat, but by singing his heart was beating just for singing, in which he was becoming who they wanted. He was becoming an artist. A few minutes the most sincere minutes of his life was enough – and listen to his singing between the lines.

*Even Sinatra would take off his hat and join us under the tree.*

*Alone as we sometimes all are alone*

*All of us seem to be here, even I can't see your faces*

*I lit candles for myself*

**The Stars We Wrecked**

*You can be silent*
*In the darkness, the silence is best*
*I love you thus anonymous*

*This way you're only my best friends as I am yours*
*Should I open the window?*
*But light would enter. Let the night be the night*

*I love this room*
*I like its darkness*

*A lady came, I can't see her face*
*She is saying something about her beauty*
*But it's meaningless*

*I've seen nothing for years:*
*I had not why. Life is already so?*
*Finally, you just have to seek only what only you want to seek – in*
*the dark or in the light*

*I loved a girl and she loved me*
*There was so much love in the world that one would only cry*
*So many beautiful destinies and unheard ones*

*I saw you but it was only a small glimpse of your faces*
*And I got tired*
*I want to be alone with my misery and incompetence*

*But you want to share everything in the dark. So let's sharing*

*Although . . . I will not lie to you: I needn't share my pain*

*Nobody says anything, so I guess you think*

*your suffering and your pain are the same as the mine ones?*

*You hope the good luck but what if it's only that earthworm that loosens the earth?*

*Hope*

*Bless you*


*Everything is perception. And everything is happiness*

*Live*

*That's is the only purpose I found*


*I loved her and she loved me as you have loved*

*And I still love her but we'll never gave birth to children*

*I loved her and we did give birth to children*

*She loved me but one day she asked me*

*with a child on her hands:*

*How many mistresses could love only one lover?*


*I'm sad but I insist*

*You know I would want to be happy*

*honestly singing in my life "Only God knows"*

*how to be free in the "Only God knows"*

*But being happy violently, no, no one can be*


*If I cry then I cry alone*

*Crying with others is no pleasure for me*

*Bad luck that one rarely cries for something*

*None of us does cries for something*

*So much I would like to cry for something*

*I would like to cry for something*

*I would like to cry for understanding*

*But I'm not naive anymore*

*I cannot stand this life but what more can I do than to live?*


*And maybe he was even singing for the nature that once gave birth to his ancestors.*


His song was not cheerful. He finished his song and I was happy. I had a desire to applaud but knew it would disrupt the peace and serenity and solitude. Despite the fact he used the words best friends in his singing, I felt the confession included a lament for sincere friendship. He sang so loud that even the driver heard him. He had no reason to keep quiet, he did not feel Elvis wanted to be alone and that he did not need to hear anything.

That was great! He shouted from afar. I do not want to give an unsolicited opinion but you should sing that in Vegas. Nobody answered him. So he remained silent, he was not happy no one answered I figured.

Elvis stood up. I thought he would yet stay sitting but leaned his right hand on the tree and spoke loudly in my direction, "I think I did it!"

I was sure that he was telling it to me, but after that scream that interrupted the peace of nature (because his singing did not interrupt the peace of nature, he was the nature, he was a natural expression of a man . . . and he just complemented the atmosphere of singing of the brook – river!), he continued with even louder acclamation, thereby somewhat disrupting everything beautiful, what I heard:

I think I broke it . . . mom!

He disappointed me just because of my faulty expectation.

George just twitched, I felt the twitch as if I was twitched myself. George did not know what to say, so far she decided to remain silent.

Was he speaking still with her or already just with stars?

"Mom this was it, what I wanted for so long, mom!" He declared excitedly. "All my life . . . I wanted to sing something like . . . this! It was a gift! I sang it . . . only God knows how! I sang it! I can sing it!" In that moment Elvis did not care who heard it, he did it. He was suddenly free, suddenly he was able to talk like never before.

I knew it, George knew it and the driver knew it.

George stood up from the ground. I remained sitting. Why Elvis needed to play the mother-and-son game even after such a lovely performance I didn't know; of course, unless it was no longer a game. I did not know the answer. At that moment I did not understand it. He said he was freed. But in his question, Mom . . . his life along with his tragedy remained still the same. When I heard him in this way, I felt that with the song and some cries of joy his new enlightenment ended.

"So many people . . . so many people I would like to see here to hear this . . . I want it again . . . A long time has lapsed since I wanted everyone to hear what I sing. I know I can do it again.

There is nothing better than when an artist begins to believe in themselves again. It does not matter where it happens, whether at a small river or in a studio.

Suddenly it came even to me, *I completed my mission. I have heard Elvis saying half-madness, half-reality, and half-naivety.* I felt – then I did not know whether it was a correct feeling – but I felt that everything was combining in Elvis for a moment. His goodness, his perversion, his artificiality, his love and hatred of the world.

"Mom, I'll survive! Mom, tell me that I'll survive." He was exuberant.

George remained silent.

The driver was silent. He wasn't certain what was happening and probably felt it was an emotional train wreck best to avoid. After all – as a driver he wasn't paid to converse with us unless we asked.

"Well, hell say something my mom would say." Elvis was loud – he wanted the immediate gratification he had become accustomed to.

When a human being becomes only confrontation of emotions and loss of emotions, loss of personality and definition of personality, among other people . . .

"Elvis, live and sing the best you know. Survive in singing." Her words seemed compulsory, tired and uncertain.

# 22

# The Fall Before the Rise

This was the beginning of the peak of the decline of Elvis and his best control mechanism, which was going to culminate in recording of his masterpiece. I was invited to dinner with Elvis and while talking with P. he told me Elvis intended to start recording. He needed to complete two Hollywood films first though.

Priscilla left Graceland with their child. P. shared Priscilla's final commentary while leaving, "I tell you, I do not know where Elvis was day before yesterday but since then he hasn't spoken to anyone. He did tell me he found something and that he wants to live again. Imagine he was telling me this while I was packing to leave. He didn't even look at me. He didn't even look at his daughter."

"I really don't understand how he could have ignored Priscilla and his daughter." P. furthered. "Priscilla wanted to visit him but when I told her what state he was in – she quietly said it had already begun. She suggested I ask you and Parker. Then she told me you are programming him somehow, but . . . I know what I know, we know.

"He was not sad when she left. Really, not sad at all. You should have seen his face. I don't believe he loves her any longer. Priscilla said to wave between his daughter and him but he went to his office instead. As she left, he turned on Sinatra. He's never listened to Sinatra as far as I know. He always to just complain about him. And suddenly he turned on Sinatra. Something had really to happen him . . . Priscilla seemed sad. She said she still loved him but she wasn't going to raise their daughter in his proximity given the state of things. She said, "I've had enough of it."

"On that day she left, Elvis did not drink at all. He told me he was going to live past his suffering and that he is able to be true to his art again."

When P. finished I patted his shoulder – I was satisfied with his information. I was happy my invitation to dinner from Elvis was conveyed directly by Parker. He complimented me in the phone, "Listen, something you are doing is going really well. My boy called me and told me he wanted two people for dinner and nobody more. He said your name and my name, nobody more. He said he wanted to talk to us about the future."

My work achieved, I was content. There was no reason for operations to worry about Elvis – he was back on track. I had to share why I should stay a little longer with Elvis and why I should continue spending taxpayer money. I flew straight to Washington, DC that afternoon. In-flight I outlined relevant points for my presentation, "How to influence an asset."

My work was not to prevent Elvis from creating something antisocial; rather, just the opposite – to control him to create something pro-social. This was intended to aid society, I wrote, "Elvis – an ordinary man with natural talent distinguishes his psyche and intellect as God-like – nothing gained from consumers necessarily. He doesn't need to destroy more than he is being destroyed himself. He needs help. Help according to approval. He is addicted to prescribed medication. He has to discontinue this and consume less alcohol. He can perform again his own works and aid society. Initial stabilization steps have been undertaken by me already."

"There are positive and negative reasons for this action. Positive: Elvis has a reputation and will attract and entertain resulting in a productive social paradigm for generations to come. He can shape the future through his art. He can create works from lyricists initially because he is currently not self-confident. This provides an opportunity for us to completely predetermine his artistic direction in agreement with Parker.

Negative reasons: I know no such reasons excepting cost."

When I got off the plane in Washington, D.C. a taxi was waiting at the airport and drove me to a suburb of the capital. I got out on a dilapidated street – it reminded me of the emptiness of the street in Memphis where John Casey's nightclub resided. I felt satisfied. Despite the emptiness of the street, I wanted to fight for my idea to influence Elvis even though there was no reason to fear his activities as potentially anti-social.

I met with two no name men – that is what I used to call them. They were important people, my bosses and bosses of my direct boss. They had money in their hands to move the world so no one could see. They were above the mafia and sometimes above the government. Their names were unknown to ordinary people. They did not evoke panic in me – I'd met with them before.

The psychology of manipulation applies equally anywhere, except for the top positions in terms of management of the world – they can be as honest as possible, when he wants to meet someone as insignificant as me?

I had no fear, just respect.

The only thing I thought was Elvis was very important to them and they required first-hand information. I appreciated to occasion to speak with them because only very few such mental agents were able to speak with them. They chose an ordinary house for the meeting, with ordinary cars standing in front of it. The house had two floors. It appeared it could have been built in the 1800's. Its coat was ripe for paint and updating.

I knocked at the door.

"Who is it?" A common man's voice answered.

I'm expected from Memphis.

The door opened. Upon entering it was shared, "We are very happy with the work you've completed." He said it as if they already received as much information as they needed. We walked up the stairs and it reminded me of walking up the stairs at Graceland with Elvis for no logic-driven reason. He continued talking up the stairs, "We have some news for you. We feel that you will like it." This man who had not yet introduced himself, was taller than me and gray headed. His hair was to his neck and well kempt. His eyes indicated he knew a lot, which were reminiscent of George's eyes. His face was riddled with experience. Something like Parker's face. His chin reminded me of my own. His cheeks were sunken. Reminding me of Elvis'. Without looking at me, he opened the door to a room penetrated with sunbeams – just the opposite of life with Elvis.

The room was furnished very purposefully. There were white walls, a large black table in the middle of the room and two chairs. I already knew where I'll be sitting.

There was a green carpet and a Petrof piano.

The second man stepped up and did not look as friendly at first. He was the first to extend his a hand and introduced himself though, "Call me Peter." I knew they need not introduce themselves – they knew who I was and I wouldn't know who they were truly. But the social mores was extended.

"I'm also Peter." I smiled but Peter only exhibited an abortive smile - I did not feel comfortable, I quickly added my real name, "I'm Isaac." Peter had military polish; if I had to gauge intelligence and intellect my first impression would land on the companion on the stairwell. Neither of them lit a cigarette.

The second man had moved through the room avoiding the sunbeams. When he moved toward me, his face was irradiated with them and I could see his face was more strained than the face of the first man. He also appeared older. He was worthy of respect.

Peter mentioned militarily, "This is Leonard – shake hands." I extended my hand.

He continued, "We can start them. Sit down, please." It was more of a command than request.

I sat and Leonard walked to the piano. Peter sat on the single chair across from me. He immediately turned to Leonard who had sat at the piano and without the slightest readjustment or modification of the small swivel-chair he opened the keyboard. It felt like theater – a well-rehearsed performance. To my surprise, Leonard began to play the song I heard for when I was with Elvis playing billiards.

> *And when also the dreamless sleep disappears,*
>
> *And I'll stay here next to you, you'll be my last disappearance . . .*

Leonard was playing the melody only – no one sang. He did not play more than a quarter of a minute and stopped. He turned to me and said (to my surprise), "Such songs are as original paintings of the greatest masters . . . there are no copies."

I didn't know what to say or how to react. I didn't expect these men to be so aware of Elvis' daily activities. He paused for a moment and without concealment, he nodded, "You were not the first man and you'll not be the last, sent to Elvis. You are the first man to achieve the best results."

"Quite clearly, quite clearly." Leonard added to Peter's words.

I waited for what would they tell me next. In that moment, I hadn't the slightest thought to mention my big news. For several years we looked for someone to get close to Elvis. You achieved this in a surprisingly short amount of time. Hard to say how you got to his heart. We have gone through many agents in the past. We are collaborating with many people in his proximity in varied forms. Most of them, of course, are not aware of it. We need someone inside to fulfill requirements for us. Due to security risks we cannot on-board anyone processed in his immediate proximity. We told you that Elvis might try to record some anti-social album. You have probably figured out we were misleading you." He continued.

"You performed your task without knowing you should. Our operations are not always fruitful – but you have triumphed." Leonard focused intently.

"We need to continue what you have started. Some time ago we came to the conclusion it is better to prevent songs and albums of an anti-social nature. Today, we want to ensure Elvis is lead to record more work. Rather than prevent him from issuing something for hippies and anarchy, which you can see – he won't do anyhow even if he wanted to due to the issues with drugs. You should know his publicists and even his drugs are under our control. This is our control to prevent him from creating works we don't want the masses to be fueled from. His drug use has gone adrift a bit. After all, we are constantly learning too. Unfortunately, he is currently beginning to approach an issue harmful in the eyes of his audience and we don't want that either. We wish to hold him as a form where women from the middle-class can identify. They are the driving force of many families and many ideas.

"Elvis is an American export. A good album with little dramatic plot and slightly advanced topics would not hurt our objectives."

They told me the same thing I wanted to propose them myself. I was not able to say a word.

"So, how do we manage it . . ." Peter immediately started.

Leonard cut in, "Wait a minute, I think we caught him off guard."

I still had nothing to say. Not that I doubted my own innovativeness. I dropped my head for a moment but I did not want them to see their touched me – I added, "Everything I had to strive for was only a test?!" with a bit of resignation in my voice.

"Exactly." Peter answered smiling. "Elvis is an ordinary man who . . ." he stopped momentarily and his appearance.

Leonard picked up, "is looking for the same thing we all look for but you have probably realized this already."

Peter caught his military voice and cut in, "You'll help Elvis in his searching. Be careful though. You know what he is looking for and you know how to deliver it to him." There was certainty in Peter's questioning statement.

I breathed in an attempt to answer - Peter intervened, "Do not answer. You don't need to. For the first time he smiled.

Leonard began to speak, his face changed and now he was speaking as Peter did before without a smile and like a soldier. "Remember Isaac, the longer a man has only one life purpose the more he is closer to losing him once. And Elvis will be glad he has at least that one. None of us doubts he'll eventually lose it, Isaac. Music, Isaac, that's freedom." He and returned to the piano. He began to play the old familiar song, "God Only Knows" by Beach Boys.

"You can go, Isaac. You have our blessing. Continue what you started." Leonard stated like a commander.

Peter said nothing more. He was still sitting on the spot where he sat still when Leonard started to play the first song.

I said "good-bye" and left. I did not wait for their good-bye.

With each step downstairs, the impact on me, of their behavior and what they demonstrated, was stronger and stronger. It was surprising and the swap of behavior at the close of our meeting impressed me even though I did not know why.

I do not know why but each second walking away my pace quickened. Did my existential fear come a minute later than it should have? I opened the door to the street outside knowing I'd spoken with two men involved in control of the world.

# 23

# George

The taxi was standing by. Nobody was standing on the street. No one passed from side-to-side. I opened the taxi door and an elderly man with bald spot asked, "Do you want to read newspaper." It was lying next to me on the backseat. No, I didn't want to read any newspaper, I was still thinking about the two men I'd just met with but he said it that as a person who would not accept my rejection.

I did not think, I simply took the paper into my hands. I was under the influence of the meeting, when I opened the paper my eyes fell on a small article in a black square. It read, "US Senator Robert Patrick Goebbel died of a heart attack he suffered two weeks ago. He left behind his grieving wife George." The article appealed to me when I saw the name George's name. I was not sorry of her. Rather, I felt after seeing her in the car with Elvis, her husband's death was a certain deliverance for her. As soon as I noticed the article, I put down the newspaper. The driver smiled a little.

I noticed in the rearview mirror he appeared to have set it up for me to see.

"I think you dropped something from the newspaper." He said this cheerfully, as if he enjoyed it.

I lifted the newspaper and found nothing beneath it. Then my eyes saw under the driver's seat a white envelope protruding. I pulled it out. It was an airplane ticket back to Memphis.

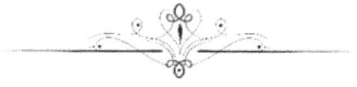

When I got off the plane in Memphis it was raining. I traveled coach and when I arrived I used my real name for transport. I still had all night to get ready for dinner with Elvis and

Parker. I was looking forward, perhaps even more than when I was flying for the meeting in Washington.

In Memphis, I bought Sinatra's *Only The Lonely* and *September Of My Years*. I was under the influence of George and Elvis, there was no doubt about it. I was pleased with the two Sinatra albums.

I met P. an hour before dinner. P. was disappointed when I told him he had not been invited to dinner. He asked me, "Am I losing him?"

I replied, "Only you know that man."

P. did not say anything further. Not a word.

I arrived well in advance of the schedule. I had an older canvas bag with me, and two recordings of Sinatra in it. Despite the fact I had learned about the relationship of Sinatra and Elvis from P., I was firmly convinced I couldn't carry more correct items with me for our visit.

"Yesterday we hired someone new at the gate – he's proud to work for Elvis," P. stated.

I smiled.

"Did Elvis baptize him in the study?" I asked in a calm voice.

"That . . . not really . . . It seems . . . probably the departure of Priscilla changed him a bit . . . he had absolutely no time for him."

Suddenly I knew (according to the way P. was speaking and looking) he was still hiding something! He touched his nose with a finger of his left hand.

I remained silent. I was sure eventually I would discover it without unnecessary questions.

We entered the gate, a guard stopped us and he immediately looked at P., "I'm sorry to stop you but according to your instructions I have to stop every car and check who's in it . . ."

P. he quickly interrupted him, "I'm satisfied, don't apologize."

The guard smiled in satisfaction and waved us through the gates.

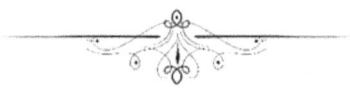

With each moment nearing Graceland P.'s behavior was telling me something was in store that would surprise me. We stopped and he asked me, without turning off the engine, "Didn't you say dinner is an hour later?" He looked at my canvas bag. "Elvis is probably still sleeping. Lola will tell you. Today, he only wanted only Lola. According to him, the one who cooks, should also give . . ."

Before I could respond, Lola approached the car. She was dressed socially.

"Oh, good day." Her eyes fell on me but she immediately focused on P.

Elvis asked me to tell you that you should not leave. The lady remains for dinner.

P. turned off the engine and said, "Come on."

I got out with my canvas bag and waited on P. As I was looking at him the idea came to mind P. was closer to Elvis than I originally thought.

He did not say anything. He was looking at me and his face changed somewhat, "Well, ask."

But I was silent.

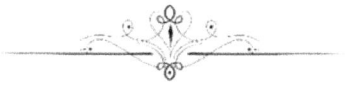

When we were walking to meet Elvis, I speculated what happened when George and Elvis demonstrated something unexpected in the car on our last night together. I recollected when we were boarding the car, he had said, "I would like to sing forever in this way. Now it's just a fight."

George had replied, "As if I heard some song Only the Lonely . . ."

Elvis had replied, "Thank you, mom. You helped me, indeed." Then he simply felt asleep.

The driver had driven us to Graceland where P. waited for us with some men. We could not wake Elvis, neither George nor I could lift him. P. said, "It's okay." A few Mafiosos had caught the king's body and carried him to the residence.

George had wanted to go back to her limousine but P. offered her lodging.

I's asked the driver whether he could drive me to a nearby hotel. He agreed. Perhaps the driver was waiting, too for P. to offer me lodging but he didn't until I was in the car. I'd needed to be alone – to contemplate everything in my head. That very contemplation helped me on my way to Washington D.C.

When I'd left I was so tired I almost forgot to say goodbye to George.

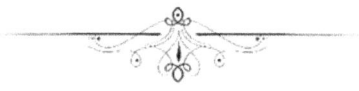

P. stated, "The lady you drove here, is still here. She and Elvis are together continuously since you drove her here. I never thought Elvis liked older women but he probably needs to be heard and to get back to feeling . . ." P. did not finish.

It pleased me a little, but it was so insignificant.

"She was here, then, even when Priscilla was leaving?" I asked with interest, even though I knew the answer.

"Well, she actually was . . . And I'll tell you, all this surprised me the most . . ."

"Is she getting what she came for?" I inquired.

P. turned away his eyes, "Elvis asked me not to say unnecessarily to anyone she is here. Actually, only Lola and I know about it. With George he is hardly leaving his bedroom."

"His bedroom?"

"Well, that is what I was trying to tell you."

"So that was what surprised you? This is what you wanted to say?"

Yes but that's not all. Well, you know, all that happened here. Priscilla was leaving and he had another woman in his bedroom maybe twice his age. To be frank, he always used to prefer very young women. When I saw his attitude regarding Priscilla's departure it seemed to me, and I think it quite seriously, he cared about the old woman more than Priscilla. And, Priscilla was a bit offended. He can see only his mother in that woman, nothing more." P. shared. "Till now, when I had a bad feeling with Elvis, I was always right . . ."

I did not have much to say – I sent P. a compelled look of misunderstanding, "Let's go." I moved toward the door, I was more and more curious to meet with Elvis and George. I was not as happy I was bringing Sinatra's recordings with George still around. I was beginning to suspect George may have really affected him.

I knocked on the door to Elvis' office and a female voice answered, "Come in." Her voice was not silent. I opened and yielded to P. who glanced at me when passing me whispering, "Now you'll see."

I entered and greeted George. She was sitting on a chair near the pool table. George had on a white dress. Compared with two days earlier, George was much happier. Now I saw a fully happy woman in front of me. She greeted me with a smile.

"So, we are seeing you again."

I greeted her seriously.

P. immediately asked, "Where is Elvis?"

"In the toilet," she replied calmly.

P. nodded. P. did not close the door completely, so I shut it calmly. Then I went back to the old well-known billiard table and leaned against it. This reminded me of the moment when I was talking with Elvis for the first time.

"Are you happier or is it just me?" I asked.

"Maybe the white color. Elvis ordered me a dress." She smiled.

I pulled out two recordings of Sinatra from my canvas bag.

"So you, too? Elvis ordered the same recordings." And immediately she added, "Actually, I think he already had one. He lied a bit about knowing Sinatra but it was kind of him. We listened it to over and over again, especially *Only the Lonely.*"

"Drinking wine while listening it is nice." I added.

"Even better was talking about disappointments, of which one is was always afraid to say. These songs pull it out of him." She smiled again.

Elvis walked in. When he saw me a smile appeared on his face. He was sober (at least at first glance) and happy. Elvis approached and hugged me warmly.

"You are so happy, what happened?" I asked Elvis suddenly.

He breathed in, "Look, you told me what to do. Now, I want to do it myself. I want to sing like Sinatra. I want to talk to adult people. I want to sing about their lives. I want to be real."

"P. mentioned that you had listened Sinatra."

"Yes, I did."

"I smiled."

"I am not worse than he," Elvis added firmly.

During the last words of Elvis I slowly moved back to Georgia, I wanted it to look casually, so that she could find my admiration in my eyes, of her achievements with Elvis. And I immediately decided to dishonor the thanks in my eyes and "I finally remembered" the newspaper article.

I said the way as if it just came to my mind:

"Your happiness surprises George, do you know your husband died?"

She replied confidently, "I know that."

Elvis looked at George, "Your husband died?"

"Yes." Her response was a materialization of a marriage that went wrong. He was silent for a moment and George smiled reassuringly. He went on . . . "Peter, you brought change here." Elvis smiled. Elvis looked at George, seemingly thanking her with his eyes.

Here is a short transcript of the conversations I heard between George and Elvis while they were together at Graceland over the next days . . .

"I would like to thank you. I've never been in that mindset so long. I believe Mom is speaking through you."

"It's okay."

"I had forgotten what it means to talk to someone and not to continuously think about who I am and who I have become."

"You will not believe me but my husband told me the same thing once."

"Did you . . . marry for love?"

"Yes. It was the happiest day in my life. And you?"

"Me? I was married. I don't even know. I got married. The love though. I felt it was impossible to stop. My marriage ended on the day I got married."

"Would you like to say that it was a wedding with which you were trying to give something back?"

"It is not easy to speak about it."

"You're right it is too difficult to speak about."

"When my wife was leaving, I heard you playing something from Sinatra. It was loud."

"It played already when you were leaving when P. called you that she is leaving . . ."

"Yes? Um . . . that's . . . quite possible . . . but it does not matter. That's not what I wanted. Look, it and when I heard his singing in the distance it helped me. He was overcoming the sadness with his singing. And he was overcoming my sadness when I was standing there. It helped me when I was looked at her. It helped me! And you know what? I desire my songs helped somebody, too."

"Surely they did."

"Do you think so?!"

"I'm convinced of that!"

"I know I should go to the studio now as soon as possible . . ."

"Elvis, when I saw you for the first time there in the pub, so you looked like a man who always does what he wants. I think you still have it in yourself you just somehow don't know how to use it.

"Oh, George, that's what I think of my audience, when examining the faces . . . that applaud. They give me energy. They paid. So I accept. I know I will miss her (the daughter) very much."

"So why then you was silent when she left? Why didn't you say her farewell at least?!"

"I would not bear it. I would not let her . . . Farewell? Don't be cruel."

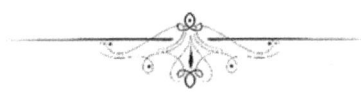

There were actually many similar conversations but in spite of Elvis' great sincerity, we would not have learned anything new about what we "did not talk" in the preceding pages. After the sincere cannonade of George, where she outlined her marriage, I still had something to ask her. Something that would be advantageous for me, "But what about the funeral? Who is handling it?"

"It's already being taken care of by his team on my behalf he arranged this prior to his death. They will not admit embarrassment in him, even if he is already dead. They think it could affect votes. They need loving and devoted wives. Surely now they are saying I am so broken I had somewhere to hide. I know them."

All my questions resulted in my satisfaction with George's replies. Her job was done, other peaks had to come today including happiness with a women for Elvis.

Elvis was looking at her. He said the words I wanted to say, "No, but it seems to me that it nevertheless hurt you"

George looked up at him and said, "I thought when I no longer loved him . . . but this is something more. I don't know why. I now have to think about the life we shared, it came like thunder and that I did not expect." Then she highlighted, "Probably I should go." She looked at Elvis and furthered, "Surely, I should."

"After dinner," Elvis reassured her questioning – was it okay to wait to face the music of her husband's death? "How much time actually remains before dinner? It was to be six o'clock, what time is it Peter?"

"It is 5:30 thereabouts – we have about a half hour."

He sat down at the piano and said, "Let's have some fun." He started to play the piano for George merrily – to perk her up. .

She was silent and in spite of the fact that she was listening to Elvis' music, her sparkle of happiness vanished.

I added, "Half an hour in sadness passes so slowly, doesn't it, George?"

She answered, "For the fact Elvis is playing – it will pass very quickly for me – for sure."

The half an hour was marked by the mental absence of George in the room. Elvis occasionally looked at her but when he found that he did not perceive him, he began to play for himself, inventing, changing tonality, having fun. A smile appeared on his face, he made laugh himself. George noticed his smile and when their eyes met she smiled too.

Elvis stopped playing and asked me again, "Time?" His voice did not change much since his first question on the subject; it was only five minutes before six.

I answered, "Time."

Elvis straightened up. He looked at George and proffered, "Come on, I am offering deliverance here."

It was hard to say whether George wanted to eat or not but she stood as soon as Elvis said, deliverance. She did not smarten up, she did not align her white dress, now she was commanded by her inside and not how she would impress the people she would meet.

Elvis closed the piano and looked at me, "I am already carrying it in me and it is fine."

I didn't answer.

George was impassively silent.

Elvis opened the door to the dining room. The table had been already set for five people.

Lola was just finishing setting of the last place and it was just the right place at the head of the table. Looking at Elvis, I had no doubt at all where he would sit today. In peace, in equilibrium, in sobriety, Elvis was strong and undisputed ruler of Graceland. Was it enough to live for something? He pushed his chair, but he waited until we settled down. We chose our places – actually, George chose her place at the right hand of Elvis, I adjusted my choice and I sat to his left. Lola asked us whether we would wait for Parker.

Elvis promptly replied, "Of course." Elvis asked her, "Where is P.?"

She replied, "I'll call him for you, he will feel better."

After Lola went to the kitchen, P. appeared in the room. His glance was foreseeable, "Priscilla's absence is still fresh to me and I'm a little somber . . . and Parker?" Asked P.

Elvis responded, "He's not usually late, I don't know where he is."

# 24

# Philistine

Just as he was pronouncing, I don't know a strong double bang on the door was heard. The young man who had checked us at the entrance to Graceland opened the door and with his hard-professional face he led Parker to the dining room.

Parker entered and nodded to the servant who immediately closed the door. Elvis stood up, Parker approached him and hugged him. Actually, it was hard to tell who hugged whom the first, they hugged each other.

"I apologize to you for the stupid things that happened here. It was bad here when Priscilla left." Elvis shared.

"I know, I know. I heard it all myself. Finally, you behave like a grown man. Well, it seems you're somewhat better."

"I had to do it already. She had to leave." Parker patted Elvis' shoulder.

He added, "Yes, Elvis. It is over now. A man should be able to establish order in his own home. I wanted to establish order for you but even the best father cannot do so."

Elvis' face indicated that despite he finally found something and neither needed to drink nor call on Dr. N. when Parker was present – he respected the Colonel to the length of kind of losing himself.

When someone enters the room who is like your boss, behaves like your boss, talks to you as a father, advises and influences you as a father – what can be done.

George noticed the hug of the two men but did not say anything.

Without realizing George didn't know Parker and Parker didn't know her - Elvis sat Parker next to George. He even pushed his chair for him. Parker was already looking at the woman next to him. She was a woman closer to his age. His face manifested surprise. At the same time, he seemed to pick up on on the fact this woman had too polished face for Graceland.

Elvis sat at the head of the table. He realized he forgot to introduce George. Immediately he stood up, "Colonel, this is George, wife of Senator . . .," he realized he didn't know her last name and held a guilt-ridden look while his eyes fell on George's face.

Of course, Parker was interested in the information after hearing the words wife of a senator . . . he responded quickly, as soon as Elvis finished, "Oh, I know, I remember I have seen you before at a diplomatic dinner party in New York. It was a political-management meeting of some sort. Your husband, Senator Goebbel?" The Colonel stopped and gave the impression he just now fully realized a senator's wife was sitting next to him. He immediately finished with what he began. "Hmmm. . . Elvis, do you know Senator Goebbel?"

But before Elvis could reply, George interrupted, "My husband died, Colonel."

"I'm sorry, my condolences." Parker was finding it difficult to speak.

George retorted, "I remember you, somebody told me you Elvis Presley's manager. I do not know, perhaps it was my husband who told me. Yes, yes, it's quite possible we spoke at the gathering." George smiled tightly. "So you're the man of whom Elvis said owns his head as a TV set? He told me you manipulate him and robbed him of the joy of singing?"

Elvis looked on in horror but it only lasted a moment.

George returned to the game and Elvis smiled.

Parker immediately turned to Elvis without missing a beat, "Guy, you're always surprising me. You have the connections. I'll tell you . . ." his words trailed off.

"We met in John Casey's pub Colonel." He smiled.

Parker became animated, "Well, at John Casey's you know. But, wait, if I'm not wrong, the late Senator told me that evening he had some music business connections. He even mentioned he was funding a classy music club in Memphis – a pub where insiders could meet."

"I doubt very much, my husband would never say something like that without good reason, I should know something about it if he had Mr. Parker." George's voice resonated.

Elvis returned to George and saw something happened, "Yes, I doubt an experienced politician would say something like that to someone." Elvis seemed just as surprised as George. "Colonel," Elvis tried to say something liberating.

"Yes?"

"Colonel . . . my friend's husband just died and honor belongs to him right now."

"I heard about the death of your husband, I read about it today. Forgive me."

In the meantime, Lola stood with the trolley at the wall waiting for the master of the house to nod for service to ensue.

George spoke again, "You can say what you want, Colonel. Maybe you're right maybe not but I'm here because of Elvis. I am insistent regarding the fact I need neither quarrels nor squabbling. I simply don't want to go from notation to notation Colonel Parker."

"Okay. I don't want to quarrel with you either, I came here to eat as we all did." The Colonel looked at Lola and moved his eyes to Elvis.

"Sir, can serve dinner?" Lola asked Elvis.

Looking at George Elvis stated, "Yes."

George bowed her head for a moment. When Lola approached her to put her plate down their eyes met.

Lola smiled at her dutifully.

Elvis spoke to Parker in the meantime, "I have to tell you something."

Parker answered Elvis just by looking . . . "Come on, talk" was his silent statement.

Elvis spoke calmly, "Colonel, I have to go to the studio as soon as possible. No movies – cancel it somehow."

"Elvis . . . Elvis . . . you will never change . . ."

"What do you mean?"

"You will sing because it is the goal of a vocalist after all to have you singing your best. However, contracts are contracts. You are a trademark now. We've worked at this for too long. It is not possible to cancel the movie. We would lose a lot. Too much in fact. You have a great artistic soul and that is great but the business is business Elvis."

George stepped in, "You are not even trying to hide it?!" She looked at Parker as if she never cared about money.

He caught her eye and answered, "Come on, madam. We live from it. If Elvis didn't splash money about . . . I mean I understand him – it's hard to stay normal when we have achieved so much! He could sing what he wants but he is a product now – he sings for people. And moreover, we are fed by films. It's true." He returning his gaze to Elvis. "I have nothing against your singing what you want as long as it will meet the standards." Parker spoke like a father leading a family business. "You know on the 27$^{th}$ and 29$^{th}$ of June we are scheduled to film your show for NBC TV. There you'll sing. We have your comeback! The factory is coming back!"

"But what about my songs?" Elvis narrowed his eyes suspiciously while exhaling.

I had to speak up, because I felt that when I (we.) worked so hard to wake up Elvis' forgotten sense, he should get what he wanted, he should get a chance to sing his own songs in the studio. "Colonel I'm here to make Elvis sing and to - I'll tell it straight, to make his soul speak through his music once again. After all, you wanted it too. So why are you saying something else now? He wants to sing. He must sing. Why are you suddenly changing your mind?"

Elvis picked up on my statement about the Colonel wanting it too, "What are you talking about Peter?" He asked.

I looked at him as his friend. I'd never looked at him so devotedly.

"You two know each other," he asked in a voice of a consternation as if cheated on once more.

Parker knew he won, "Yes, Elvis. We know each other."

Elvis' face began to lose the beauty of certainty. He looked at me hard and then at Parker and then me again. I could not say anything on Parker's words, they brought me to cold sweat. P. had nothing to say as well. Parker was behaving as a manipulator once more.

George was looking at me hard too.

"I hired him to help you, Elvis. I hired him so you would sing again like you used to. I care for you. I wanted to get you aroused for singing again." Parker lied and he knew I could not tell the truth.

Elvis scanned me from head to toe. At that moment I thought he would explode soon. Elvis was looking at me in a manner of resignation. He soon moved on to P. "You told me you knew him that you guaranteed him."

Parker's face demonstrated surprise, he lifted his chin and looked at P. as murderous as the man who knew what was happening. He understood P. was another agent. I was a little relieved - now it was P. in an unenviable position.

Lightning radiated from Elvis' eyes.

"I do know Peter. He had a relationship with my sister. We know each other longer and he looked at me and said in a voice I would not expect from him, "My God, listen you asshole: You're just another one of the poor Colonel's psychologists. Do you mean seriously, what the hell?!" He seemed earnest – I even believed the story of his sister.

Elvis laughed. And, still laughing he asked, "When?"

"I shook my head, "What do you mean when?"

George was quietly looking into my eyes.

Parker shook his head with restless grinning.

He felt to be so strong but I could not withstand it any longer, "Colonel, I wanted to help Elvis, not you. I don't give a damn about you. Look at him. He is an artist. You should let his soul sing out. If you cannot see it then don't be surprised Elvis is where he is. Take your chance. Let him sing in the show something what he performed just for George and me." I was a little bit of control – they'd gotten me.

Thanks to a few sentences and what he heard, Elvis' face was returning back into nothingness, where there was nothing, for what he could live happily.

Elvis was silent still.

George watched everything with a solemn face. "They expelled the death of my husband from me again, fantastic!"

In the meantime Parker exploded, he had no other choice, "What do you understand. You are nobody. What do you know? The only one who loves this boy beyond the grave, is me."

"You don't love me," Elvis murmured quietly.

"All of you want him to sing, but I want to help him to live! OK, let him sing! The whole Hollywood is one mafia. You cannot take the risk. We have a contract due to the fact there will be a next film. Do you understand this Elvis? You still sing like no one else. It's why you were born. But you're in the program. Accept it. Everybody in the program is based on merit."

George ironically smiled at the Colonel.

Parker shook his head. He at us all and continued, "If I want Elvis to be Elvis again that must be done . . ."

"Actually, I have no desire to eat now," Elvis said. "Lola, please pour me. . ." He asked seemingly pleading for escape.

George lost her pathos of observation and indifference. She looked at Elvis. Her look bore fruit in the form of words, "Why do not you fight to sing, why do you not fight for your art and your purpose. What is it Elvis?" She asked as a mother, a lover and girlfriend? "After all, we are talking about it all the time aren't we?

Parker looked at George with compassion. "Really!"

"I have nothing to fight for," he retorted in that voice of Elvis we'd all heard somewhere.

Parker was not in the least alarmed by the words of his charge, on the contrary, "Lola, once you've poured Elvis' glass, pour me on too. Only Elvis and I understand drinking." Lola looked at him desperately.

She inquired, "A lot of ice sir?"

"My real value?" Elvis dipped his voice into the air aimed at Parker.

"Boy, you still haven't learned anything." Parker returned him his words like a boomerang.

George and P. found each other without knowing – their expressions were the same and I was not in the room any longer in my mind. I waited for Parker's response.

"Without me they would kill and destroy you Elvis. They would tear you apart out there in the hatchery of bloodthirsty dogs. It's me, who is protecting you, boy, so pull it together."

I think now, my daughter I need only hear the voice of my daughter. Leave me alone. I want my daughter. Leave me alone. Please. Her voice." Elvis was annoyed

P. grimaced as a person who was trying to understand his friend, as a friend who knew anger and disappointment in the years spent in the proximity of a loved person. If this had to be an effort to help Elvis and participate with him, then it was very strange and unsuccessful. The grimace of P. had to bear the message Elvis, you are again losing everything you did not want to lose. But P. didn't dare to speak up. He had to remain silent.

Elvis was overtaken by his own feelings and irretrievably lost in the void of his private American Vesuvius. Did he believe me? Probably yes. Did he believe what I told him? Yes. Did he want to reach what I told him? Yes. Did he believe George? Yes. But now he was standing symbolically naked, bereft of hope.

Parker threw the clincher into the air, "Elvis, after the movies you'll record an album of your own songs and play it to your daughter. I promise you."

Elvis exploded, "We are all traitors. We all eventually betrayed ourselves and what we desire. To what can I trust now?" Elvis was yelling. His soup began to move quickly under the blows of his hands on the table. It was like a sea in the universe pouring out disappointment as much as the man it belonged to. "I was so happy I was going to tell you I found something in me that would allow me to sing like Sinatra. May I at least do that?"

"As who?" Parker was really surprised.

"No, this is not you. This is not someone who wants to fight for something." George said markedly but Elvis did not look at her.

Elvis did not stop. The question of Parker, the sight of P. nor George's truthful statement stopped him, "Once I'll record the album "He touched me" but then my soul will not belong me anymore." . . .

"Elvis, don't tease me." Shouted Parker.

Elvis managed a sober smirk, "I'm not teasing you. I'm nothing. I'm just a musician."

Lola resolved to wipe up the spilled soup since Elvis calmed down a bit and Elvis continued as she wiped, "Well, now you should slap me, shouldn't you, Mom?"

George looked at him and in a voice that was perfectly harmonized with her face she said in perhaps a too diplomatic manner, "Say what you like - you're the King." Elvis looked at George and emboldened her to catch her breath and continue, "It was unique under the trees and starlight, you gave me a diamond that cannot be emulated, didn't you? No, it cannot be emulated." George did it, she smiled at Elvis' face as a woman who had nothing to lose.

It was Elvis who was just losing everything we were giving him honesty all the days. He was on the edge of losing of his volition to become more than just an entertainer. Did Parker destroy our house of cards in Elvis? Within a few seconds he found the old purpose in his great and legendary suffering.

I did not understand it. How this lack of will could happen again so fast perplexed me. Why had I tried?

"I'm crucified for the people. Where is Dr. N?" Elvis stopped and suddenly I knew he did not care who was listened to him.

"You're just ridiculous and embarrassing – like the first time I saw you." George allowed him to provoke her as a naive girl in love that still does not know anything about men.

"In your case freedom may only redeemed only by pain boy." Parker nodded and Elvis laughed at himself. "You always understood this Elvis – if you want to sing like Sinatra or even much better you have first to suffer through it as he did. You know why he suffered. You know why he sang so well. All of us are redeeming our freedom by our pain. The greatest ones of us by the greatest pain. And, you, boy, you're the greatest of the greatest." The Colonel smiled again like a father but this time as the father happy because his son still bent to his will.

Elvis continued, "P., where is my doctor?" Elvis was a materialization of mourning and repeated cyclic assault into himself. He could not fight the giant, who swallowed him up. And when the giant offered him helping hand in my person, so sing what the giant needed once again, Elvis was already so lost in the illusion that he could not discern what was good, what was going somewhere, and what was bad, what was just killing him. Elvis looked at Lola but there was no human contact in his eyes. His behavior finished the work of self-destruction. He stopped believing.

I had no appetite to eat. George shook her head in disappointment, "People so often deny their happiness just when they need it most –"

Elvis smiled painfully. "There is nothing more. The only thing to do is to get pills and pray." His facial expression was fixed, "because it is at least the only honest purpose I've found here among you. And if you want to know why, play My Way by Frank Sinatra."

George stood up and for a moment she was motionless. George's standing up from her chair reminded me a bit the situation when Priscilla was leaving.

Elvis restated the previously spoken words, "For he who suffers most, is entitled to be something the masses admire."

I was seeing death of a human soul in front of me. The death, which I did not understand. P. was sitting in the meantime, without saying a single word. He was just looking at Elvis.

"I knew the departure of Priscilla would break you Elvis." Parker barked – hitting Elvis below the belt. Parker was Elvis' devil and Elvis was possessed by his sentiments.

George addressed P., "Could you drive me to the airport?"

And at the moment, in which he already wanted to stand up, Elvis surprisingly yelled, "Eat and drink like a bunch of Judas! When I have found you and actually included into my own life, you'll remain! Only a fool would abandon his role of Judas in my drama. It is a good role." He looked like believing what he was saying.

George, however, had no longer any reason to tolerate Elvis. "I want to leave, so I will go. I am not under the ownership of anybody Elvis."

Elvis was in a frenzy. Without a word he caught his half-empty plate and threw it to George as his wife had thrown a plate of the same collection at Parker only earlier in my recollections. He did not realize George had done a lot for him and she had been striving to give him purpose.

The plate flew, but did not hit George, who managed to avoid it. Rather, by big coincidence, it hit the photo where Elvis was captured along with Jerry Lee Lewis, Carl Perkins and Johnny Cash. It hit the photo where he was sitting at the piano with composers . . . glass fell to the ground emitting sound.

Lola took fight, one of the fragments landed right next to her.

When I looked at Parker, I could not believe my eyes, he was looking at Elvis and smiling. Parker was also Elvis' advocate of the signature . . . before God?

P. stood up seeing Elvis was not present in Graceland and I decided to leave and use the moment as P. did. I stood up I had nothing to tell Elvis. I was disappointed, disgusted. I did not want to say goodbye.

# 25

# American Studios

We didn't become even work friends but I understood him. I learned to understand him. My march away from Elvis lasted briefly, just months after I realized I was attempting to deliver purpose to it, which he himself was unable to deliver. I left as a defeated agent who failed to fulfill what he had to do. I did not anticipate I would come to see the purpose in Elvis' death a few years later. I was leaving and for a second look I looked at Parker, who remained sitting alone with Elvis.

Elvis ceased to perceive him. It was absolutely no problem for Parker - rather the contrary. He smiled at me as the winner and said as I departed, "Well, what? I told you you had no chance. You got room though . . ."

I didn't look at him. I knew he was smiling happily. It could be heard in his voice.

"Goodbye," he said quietly.

I did not answer him. In the distance, when I was closing the door, I heard him continuing his winning streak because he ordered Lola as if she belonged only to him, "You can call the doctor."

"We are above the right." IT seemed to me Elvis rang farewell with these words.

Those were the last words I received from Elvis.

I was walking down the corridor, the same corridor, through which I had been walking when I was entering Graceland for the first time. I started to reproach I had failed. Again and again. The same statues, the same images. There is as much unnecessary hell in the world. I blamed myself simply because I was also deceived. And again I saw the same in images as the first time. Nothing has changed, Elvis remained the same, if not even more destroyed by lying and deceiving. Only when I walked away forever, I felt regret that I had not felt for Elvis while in his house. And a kind of imbalance attacked me, *So this is the world, so this is what we are striving for . . . as paranoid kings, who missed the fact that life can be beautiful and loveable by any, even the smallest sense in us, let even in the largest ordinariness of anything we live?*

Elvis was saying the same thing over and over again. He wanted to get ahead as a unique and irreplaceable man. He wanted to be king but only because every day he was afraid of more and more desperate senses in living that he found himself in.

I was walking out of the main building of the legendary Graceland. And after a while I again noticed Odyssey depicted in Elvis' front door at the entrance to his world. I shook my head.

George was just getting into a white Cadillac. Her white dress was being caressed by wind but the wind could not touch her soul even if it was a hurricane. She saw me and she left the door open. She looked at me as at a younger brother. I got in but getting in a car next to someone who was older and belonged to such social elite increased my feeling of a scared and trampled human. We closed the door. P. slowly started up the car.

"You are coming and you are leaving with me, so it had to be." said P. to me. His words bore neither much happiness nor unhappiness. These were words of a non-participating commentator.

I said nothing.

"Finally, we failed . . ." Was stated sadly but not in a resignation by George.

For the first time after I got into the car, I looked at her eyes. "I failed . . . When I think what could he still reach, it's really sad."

"Yes, you are right . . ." She responded quietly.

We were silent for a long time. George looked in different direction than I did. Each of us was looking out to the world through our own window.

We traveled as three defeated people who knew where they belonged in society. We didn't need worry about our positions. Although, I admit the more I felt my failure and my fiasco, which came so quickly and suddenly I had a growing fear, *What would I tell my friends when I did not fulfill their social order agenda?* Everyone is replaceable. I knew it.

George added, "I told him . . . I told it him. I told him those who were around him wanted him to be a statue without purpose and without love. In such heights it is not always useful. I experienced it in politics . . ." She pronounced her words in a whisper.

I joined George, "Today we saw it. The devil in us doesn't allow us to help ourselves." It was the last words in the car. P. just quietly sighed at the wheel. George looked out the window.

I never met with Elvis again; however, George did. By chance I accessed her reports and information she had been supplying. I knew she was not an ordinary woman. A good friend of mine provided her reports, "Now you can know the truth when Elvis is long after death." He relied I would keep the secret trust. "You'll see that what looked like your biggest failure till today, it was actually your biggest success."

I got the access to the files as late as in 1979. Here are her reports without adjustments, "Elvis approached me 25 December 1968. I don't know how he got my number. Probably it was provided by his bodyguard (P.).

He called me home.

His voice was very sad but he didn't cry on the phone. He said he couldn't continue. He told me he needed me.

I listened for a long while. He was drunk or under the influence of drugs. Over and over he spoke about his suffering. I asked him what he wanted. Then he fell silent. He asked if I could come to him to Graceland. First, I replied it would not be possible. Then I agreed after he continue to urge me to.

27 December 1968 I arrived in Memphis. Previously, I contacted Colonel Parker. He confirmed Elvis was ripe for studio. He was close to self-destruction. Elvis was waiting for me at the airport. He did not hug me. He extended his hand. He told me he was glad someone came. He mentioned he was suffering very much. He repeated his words he told me over the telephone.

He drove me right into Graceland, accompanied by P. The only new information was he was not aware how had he shot the most part of the first film, which he shot in Hollywood. The he had been continuously drunken and on pills. He didn't care about anything. He was thinking of death. Later he mentioned he was already in such bad condition he only wanted to sing, regardless of the song, he needed to see only a microphone before him.

I met the schedule: I convinced him to call Parker and give him an ultimatum he wanted to go into the studio. I also met what Parker had asked me to do, when I had talked with him.

Elvis let me persuade him. He called Parker. He gave him the ultimatum. Parker called within an hour and he told him that everything was agreed, and he had to start at Chip Moman in American Studies (Chelsea Ave., Danny Thomas Blvd.).

Elvis was very happy. He asked me whether he could call me mom. He told me he had not recorded in Memphis since 1955. Then he said he would give as much suffering and solitude to his singing as possible.

Days remained before the recording, I was behaving according to our pre-agreed scenario. I was talking to Elvis about the great Sinatra's albums and what led him to record them. I started in the wee hours of the day and spoke to him about Eve Gartner and about how desperate her relationship was with Sinatra.

Again he asked me whether I was a fan of Sinatra. I replied no greater singer had walked on the Earth.

31 December 1968 I met Parker in Graceland. Elvis was preparing New Year's party for his closest friends. He especially wanted Brian Wilson to come. Parker wanted Elvis to sing as a priest who suffered. He confirmed Elvis performed the best was when he suffers on the edge of bearability. He wished he would go into the studio with him provoked into a fierce pain. He advised me what I should do, "Mention Sinatra again and say he was better than Elvis, the King."

At the party there was no new information. Brian Wilson did not come. He apologized. And, this left Elvis very disappointed. Elvis did not sleep for New Year's night. He was longing for the studio and said he would show them how to sing for life.

1 January 1969 - we came to the studio. Elvis wanted me there. He insisted he had to have me there - I was his memory of singing under the tree (Report 1 – G). I could not get the same performance as under the tree. He never called me mom in front of people in the studio.

He insisted he would only sing his own song. Chris Moman did not say a word. Parker didn't want to hear about it. He said they were only wasting time. In the recording booth Parker admitted he had been expecting more. The atmosphere in the recording booth was everyone knew in advance the song would be written off.

The song was called "Men Who Built All The Bridges." Elvis' singing could not overcome the bad atmosphere.

*Men who built all the bridges,*

*the bridges survived them,*

*their loves survived them, maybe even kids,*

*survived their lovings, maybe even hatred.*


*Men who built all the bridges,*

*the bridges, some of them,*

*fell, were destroyed,*

*and the builders didn't cope with it anymore.*


*If they did not build the new bridges for the faith that they would last,*

*then they crucified their souls alive,*

*because they were born to build all the bridges and to believe.*

Refrain:

*They built all the bridges and we are crossing over them,*

*they never asked for anymore, they believed that they had built them as well as they could,*

*and we sometimes filled their faith and sometimes we buried it.*

Elvis was striving to sing heartfelt but he sang out of tune now and again. Parker commented, "Elvis, don't be embarrassed." According to the files, it was the last Elvis song he tried to sing in a studio. When Elvis finished, Parker commanded we would use this failure to further excite Elvis so he would finally start to sing like crazy.

He said verbatim: we must humiliate him. Parker commanded to Moman to tell Elvis he should go to sleep. That he would pay everything. Elvis was accompanied to Graceland just by me and P. He was very sad. He wept. He slept barely six hours from three to eight o'clock in the evening.

I was working all night, to provoke him. I played the introductory A-page *In the Wee Small Hours*. Elvis was in a very bad psychological condition. I was afraid he would hit me. He did not call me mom anymore. Five minutes to midnight, 1 January 1969 he shouted he hated Sinatra and all who sang as they were told. He broke the gramophone. P. tried to calm the situation. A minute after midnight he shouted he can stand no music and no singing anymore.

Dr. N. had to help him. Elvis fantasized about Priscilla and his daughter for a while. When the drugs became effective he confirmed he wanted nothing to record. He even said he did not want to go into the studio anymore. He begged me to love him as a mother. He was at rock bottom. I had to perform my role again from the beginning.

Another ten days followed, in which he only drank and did not care about the world.

4 January 1969 - when being asked who the President of the United States was he replied that he did not care.

5 January 1969 - he began to call me mom even before his personnel.

8 January 1969 - we went on a trip to Las Vegas.

9 January 1969 - Parker found us. I informed him about everything. He asked me in phone whether we did make a mistake when he hired me. He thought Elvis had to be left alone and he would sing. I answered him I had been thinking about it too.

Parker indicated he had to implement expensive countermeasures. That he asked Priscilla to meet Elvis, even with their daughter. He also mentioned he had bought one song, *In the Ghetto* from the young and talented Mac Davis. That it was a risky song, slightly political.

He said it was exactly the song they needed. That it would start his comeback.

His exact words were as follows, "He sang *In The Ghetto Of Love* when he was young, and now, surrounded by all the luxuries he will sing about the ghetto. He will sing about where he came from. This is a good move.

Parker met with Elvis at 2:25 P.M. 9 January 1969 at lunch in the hotel New Frontier in Las Vegas.

He pretended to be happy he had found him. He immediately submitted the lyrics of *In The Ghetto* to Elvis, with the words, "This is what you expected."

Elvis slowly read the text. His first reaction after reading was, "Are you serious?"

Parker smiled, he was happy.

Elvis immediately got enthused about the text. But he asked, "And won't I make people angry with it?"

Parker replied that was exactly what the time and art needed. Among others, he used also the following words, "Elvis it's time to finally sing also an art for adults."

Elvis was enthused. He wanted to return to the studio immediately.

10 January 1969: we flew to Memphis. Parker traveled with us. He had prepared a surprise for Elvis. As soon as we unpacked, Priscilla came to visit him, with their daughter. Elvis was striving to behave to his daughter like a father but he did not have a lot of confidence in Priscilla and it eventually passed on to the daughter.

Priscilla informed Elvis she wanted to divorce. Elvis was unable to control himself and got into a fit of rage. He shouted at Priscilla it had been she had wanted all the time and that she never loved him. In the words of Parker, this happened before his daughter for the first time.

The daughter began to cry. Priscilla decided to leave.

Parker was happy. As I later learned, he had convinced Priscilla to tell Elvis about the divorce sooner than she wanted to herself.

Presumably considerable amount was being paid Priscilla to keep her marriage with Elvis official union as soon as since 1969.

Elvis then collapsed and Dr. N. had to be called.

11 January he wanted to be alone all day but eventually he told P. he needed only his mom. 11:20 A.M.: Elvis told me I had to be his mother till the end. That God definitely wanted it. He behaved to me as if I were his property.

Elvis had depression from the loss of the woman he once loved. Then, the depression transformed to loss of any feelings to life. The rest of the day he was drinking depressed. After lunch he commanded Dr. N. to give him more pills than usual. When Dr. N. protested, Elvis told him that there were a lot of doctors all around. Ten minutes later Dr. N. had to pump his stomach off, but before, when giving Elvis double doses, he had warned him that this might happen. Elvis then replied that he did not care.

As P. said, it was not the first time he was pumping out Elvis' stomach.

11 January - otherwise, the most time I spent with Parker. He was satisfied. He told me now finally Elvis would perform greatly. And he was sure now he would want to sing some other song than *In the Ghetto*, some song of great disappointment.

After the pumping off Elvis' stomach, Parker visited Elvis first. I stood in the room and Elvis called me mom even before Parker.

Being persuaded by Parker such a condition can be overcome only by a song that would reflect the state of his inside, Elvis did not say anything. Parker asked him if whether he knew any such song. Elvis did not answer him.

He called him as late as in the evening after my accentuation finally he could sing whatever he wanted.

Elvis apologized to Parker for his bad days, he had remorse. He said it himself.

He informed him in the phone he knew a song he would like to sing, its name was *Wearin' That Loved On Look*. That it was about what he felt.

Parker assured him he would ensure he could sing it as soon as possible had to go into the studio but soon in the morning started drinking in his bedroom and again refused to come out of it. P. called the study and explained the situation. Parker came immediately. In his words, all were waiting for Elvis in the studio.

5:30 P.M.: Elvis admitted he was afraid of people and he did not want to see anybody. Dr. N. examined him a he said his psyche was marked with yesterday's overdose. He had anxiety attacks which were mixed with manifestations of addiction to the pills. The doctor had to give him more pills. Then Elvis was drinking all the day.

During the whole day he ate only hamburgers, he ate eight of them. He vomited three times.

Vernon (Elvis' father) wanted to see him but Elvis did not want him to see him.

After he saw Elvis in the evening already for the third time in the day, Parker got angry at doctor and he threatened him, "I'll cancel the agreement for reimbursement of all debts in the casino over the black cash of the object . . . even if he has to sing without a brain, you'll put him on his feet."

Doctor could not resist. He immediately gave Elvis a large dose of sleeping medication. The medication needed half an hour to be effective.

13 January: Elvis slept until 12:30 P.M. Doctor, P., and I were with him throughout the night and morning. Doctor with P. helped him out of bed. Elvis did not know what day it was. As soon as he opened his eyes, he called me a mother, for the first time I felt it was not just a game.

3:15 P.M. - we drove him to study. The object was striving to hide his problems but when he stood before the microphone he asked where his mother was. Parker had to intervene, "She is standing here beside me, Elvis."

He objected, "Then send her to me, here with me."

At the behest of Parker I went down to the recording room, where Elvis was singing alone without contact with musicians. They were playing in another room. I grabbed his hand and he sang *Wearin´ That Loved On Look*.

Parker was happy.

Bob Dylan may have said it best, "When Elvis sang the song "That's All right Mama," in 1955, and there was feeling and strength in it. In 1969, there was already only utter strength there. There was nothing in it but violence. I fell into the same trap, too … if you want to stay in touch with what you yourself once created, you have to walk on a very thin edge. And either it holds you or it does not."

And so it may happen to anyone who reaches the top of his or her life.

Yes, we can say Elvis started as a singer and musician. He was a professional. Notwithstanding his personal qualities, his contribution to music and modern culture is undeniable. He was one of the people who were too often looking for answers and had problems coping with an inability to find them.

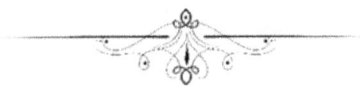

And Elvis was perhaps often asking on behalf of you, too, "Who was I actually?"

The End.

# About The Author

Author Milan Kalis love for Elvis Presley, a central character in his novel The Stars We Wrecked, began with a love of music set in motion as a child. At the age of 5, Kalis was introduced to the Beatles and their A Hard Day's Night album. His love of music began amid the backdrop of a floundering Communist Czechoslovakia, modern day Dubnica nad Váhom and Nová Dubnica, Slovakia.

Milan Kalis was born in 1979 (August 22) in Ilava, former Czechoslovakia, Slovakia now. In 1996 and 1998, Kalis received twice the Mayor of the City Trencin's prize for poetry in Jozef Branecky's literary contest. Following 1996's success, publisher Ludoprint published his first book of poetry "Shards of 20th century," in 1997. The short story "Apuesta" won the prize in Slovak literary contest Literarny Kezmarok in 1998. Kalis graduated from Comenius University in Bratislava with a Master of Science in environmental science in 2005. In March 2011, he successfully defended his dissertation in the postgraduate study program in environmental geochemistry at the Comenius University in Bratislava, Faculty of Natural Science.

# Visit the Author

On Social Media:
Facebook – https://www.facebook.com/AuthorMilanKalis
LinkedIn - https://sk.linkedin.com/in/milan-kalis-640b0b65
Twitter – http://www.twitter.com/authormkalis
WordPress – http://authormilankalis.wordpress.com

At the Publisher Website:
http://www.donnaink.com

At the Author's Website:
http://donnaink.wix.com/authormilankalis

Donnalnk Publications, L.L.C.

Publisher
www.donnaink.com

**For bulk orders, special or**
Special Markets Division
dpInk: Donnalnk Publications, L.L.C.
129 Daisy Hill Road
Carthage, North Carolina 28327
Email: special_markets@donnaink.com

**For Promotions:**
Promotions Division
dpInk: Donnalnk Publications, L.L.C.
129 Daisy Hill Road
Carthage, North Carolina 28327
Email: promotions@donnaink.com

ZENCON ART OF
ZEN CONSULTANCY
PR & Marketing

www.ingramcontent.com/pod-product-compliance
Lightning Source LLC
Chambersburg PA
CBHW060432180626
46817CB00007B/2779